Also By Cathryn Grant

Cathryn Grant

THE WOMAN
IN THE PAINTING

An Alexandra Mallory Novel

D2C

D2C Perspectives

Visit Cathryn online at CathrynGrant.com

Cover design by Lydia Mullins Copyright © 2016

ISBN: 978-1-943142-29-3

1

Tess had become elusive.

Her appearance naturally gave her a standoffish look. Five-seven, slim, favoring dark, simple but expensive clothes, and high heels. She stood out in a crowd with her inky black hair and dark, heavy makeup that drew attention to her piercing eyes. It's difficult to explain why those features made her unapproachable, but they did. Maybe she looked as if she didn't need anything from anyone, and it's the sense of vulnerability that connects people with each other.

When your boss becomes elusive, it makes your position seem less secure, even if her scarcity has nothing to do with you. Your mind begins to form meaning around it, even without concrete facts. It's the not-knowing. Not knowing is a powerful fear inducer.

Technology companies are known for abrupt changes in direction. Riding high today, shifting focus and reformulating strategy, which results in *restructuring* the workforce tomorrow. People who aren't cutting edge are shown out the door, replaced by new, cooler peeps.

Management is suddenly sequestered, ranking employees — deciding who will stay and who will go.

Now that I lived in one of CoastalCreative's subsidized apartments in San Francisco, I was more beholden to my employer than ever. I couldn't pass up the opportunity for a year without paying rent, and the chance to have my own place, but the sense that they'd handcuffed me made me jumpy despite my good fortune. It felt good to move away from my growing body count in Santa Clara and Santa Cruz counties, but as a result, Tess was more critical than ever to my survival. I prefer to keep my survival solely in my own hands.

During the five months I'd worked for Tess, she'd become an almost oppressive presence, stopping by my office several times a day, filling the hours in between with emails and text messages. Within a month of me starting at CoastalCreative, she'd instituted Monday morning coffee meetings for the two of us. Every few weeks we met on Friday evening for a drink, toasting the end of the day, the end of the week.

Blurring the boundaries of manager and employee, she'd invited me to join her gym, covering the monthly dues herself, and then asked me to go running with her, helping her train for a 10k. But gashing her leg when she ran from an imagined threat had temporarily sidelined her workout entirely. Eight stitches were required to close the wound and she was instructed not to exert herself for several weeks.

I'd thought I'd see even more of her after my move to San Francisco. She owned a condo in Russian Hill and was also working out of the new satellite office where I'd relocated. Because of the office move, she'd canceled her gym membership in Santa Cruz and put up the annual fee and dues for me to join her at a new gym on the first two floors of the building next to the one where CoastalCreative occupied a floor of its own.

Tess was a woman who made me think of the black and

blue, and gold and white dress that drove the internet to madness a few years ago. You looked at her and she was one person, blinked, and she was someone else entirely.

Over drinks, she'd confessed she had doubts about her career, doubts about whether she should jump into the motherhood pool that she'd carefully avoided. One moment she acted as if she longed to have a man take care of her, wiggling around until she burrowed herself into a cozy nest of home decorating and meal planning geared to someone else's tastes and schedule, the next, as if she'd never considered such a thing.

I was starting to wonder which woman was the genuine Tess. I was starting to wonder whether she was a bit like me, modifying who she was to fit a situation in a way that provided her the most benefit.

Now, I hadn't see or heard from her in three days. Her admin said she was busy with a lot of offsite meetings. These were meetings I hadn't been invited to. That wasn't unusual, a project manager attends a fraction of the meetings required of a Senior Vice President. In fact, that's pretty much the only thing VPs do all day long, sit in conference rooms, analyzing the past, arguing about the future, and coming up with new projects for the teams of people beneath them.

The lower level employees sit in their offices and cubicles, waiting for a truck to back up to their virtual desks and let a thick stream of wet cement slide down into their virtual in-box.

I was responsible for putting together Tess's PowerPoints for her various meetings. It was unusual that I wasn't busily gathering and copying and pasting information onto electronic slides for her.

The last three text messages I'd sent received simple, cryptic replies.

Tess Turner: *Busy.*

Tess Turner: *Talk to you later.*

And then, nothing.

Knowing a corporate entity had such control over every facet of my life, and most of that control rested in the hands of Tess Turner, was unnerving. They could move me out of the apartment at a moment's notice, moving in a more valuable person. They could sublet and recoup the company costs. They could do whatever the hell they wanted. Maybe this situation, so glamorous on the surface, was worse than the house I'd shared with a demented roommate.

Finally, I decided I could linger around my new cubicle, walking to the windows to gaze out at the San Francisco Bay Bridge, trying to guess what she was thinking based on absolutely no information, or I could slip out of the office and get settled in my new apartment. She knew how to reach me.

2

My new home was in an apartment building on Howard Street, three blocks from the CoastalCreative offices. The building consisted of a center section, six stories tall. The second floor of which opened an additional four stories to an arched glass ceiling. The center section was flanked by two towers filled with apartments ranging in size from studio to three-bedroom, with rent that went from the barely manageable to outrageous.

I considered myself lucky to be living there.

One of the features of my new home was a security guard, sitting behind a desk in the lobby between the two towers. Residents were required to check in and there was a feeling of moderate safety knowing someone couldn't wander in and take the elevator to any floor they chose.

I lived in a studio on the tenth floor of the west tower.

The studio featured a balcony large enough to hold three chairs and a small table. It offered another high-rise and a tiny sliver of the bay for a view. In exchange for the larger than average balcony, I'd given up interior square footage. If I'd thought my previous home in a seven-hundred square foot cabin was small, I had no idea what small was. Now, I had a magnificent three-hundred square feet of living space. A living-dining area, which meant I would sleep, socialize, cook, and eat in the same space. There was a small bathroom and a good-sized closet.

To some, three-hundred square feet might seem like a

closet itself. And it was definitely compact, but it was all mine. The dishes were washed and polished dry, not left soaking in a pan of scummy water like my former roommates sometimes opted for. The air was cool and if my feet grew icy, I covered them with a soft cotton blanket rather than blasting dry heat into my face.

It was a tiny piece of paradise.

The place came furnished with sleek, modern furniture. It looked great but was of the quality guaranteed to look shabby and out of style in three years. It didn't matter, I'd be long gone before three years. Although I did hope to hang out in San Francisco for the entire year of free rent. I'd never lived in a big city, and LA doesn't count. Sorry.

A handcart provided by the apartment management made it easier to move my boxes into the elevator, up to the tenth floor, and down the hallway to my place. It still took me several hours to get them all situated, boxes stacked somewhat haphazardly. I spent the rest of the afternoon unpacking and sorting.

The closet that looked large when it was empty, wasn't as large as I'd thought. My clothes were crushed together, hangers overlapping on the pole. There was no room in the closet for my flattened boxes. I piled them on the handcart and left the apartment, headed toward the elevator. My car would have to serve as a temporary storage shed.

Going down, the elevator stopped at the eighth floor. The doors opened. A guy wearing sunglasses, dressed in jeans, canvas shoes without socks, and a faded black t-shirt stood waiting. There were no lights in the hallway or the elevator that even came close to something bright enough to require the subduing effect of sunglasses. Maybe he was hung over. It was Friday, and weekend partying often starts on Thursday nights. He looked more Santa Cruz than San Francisco. He gave me a tiny smile and stepped into the steel box, positioning himself beside the handcart. Before I could ask his destination, he reached across me and punched the button for the street level, two floors above the garage where I was headed.

The doors closed and we began a smooth slide down through the center of the building.

There's nothing like a steel box and automatically sealed doors to bring your spidey sense to the surface, creeping along your skin, gently brushing against the nearly invisible hairs on your arms. I held onto the handcart and shifted my position so he was in my line of sight.

"You're new," he said.

"Yes," I said. A large city was going to offer a lot more anonymity than I'd had in the last few places I lived, and yet apartment living can strip that away in sudden, shocking ways. There's no moving into a home without being observed. There's no returning from a doctor's appointment, coughing with the flu, slinking into your private space without encountering others. There's no running out at night in sleep clothes to grab a bottle of vodka or a pack of cigarettes without risking a chance meeting. It's both more private and more exposed.

"I'm David. Eighth floor."

"So I figured."

He grimaced. "Where are you going with all those boxes?"

"There's no room to store them in my place."

"Studio?"

I nodded.

The elevator dinged and a moment later, the doors opened. He put his forearm in front of the rubber bumper to prevent them from closing. "I'm in a two-bedroom. I can store them for you."

My spidey feelers prickled along the back of my neck, up across my scalp. I like my boxes close at hand. It might seem a little neurotic, but it solidifies my self-reliance. If I need to move quickly, everything is immediately accessible. The trunk of my car was perfectly adequate. With all of the boxes pressed flat, there was still room for my gym bag. "I have it taken care of," I said.

"Recycling?" he said.

I smiled.

"They look well-used, so I'm guessing you're more of a hoarder than a recycler."

I waited for him to let go of the door.

"So do you need me to store them?"

"No thank you."

He shrugged. "Welcome to the building. I'll see you around. I hope." He smiled more broadly this time. There was a slightly vacant appearance to his smile due to the dark glasses. Or something else, it was hard to say.

3

I couldn't wait to dive into big city life in one of the world's most beautiful cities. The hills and cable cars, the Golden Gate and Bay bridges crossing the glistening bay were iconic features I'd known in movies and TV shows all my life. Living in the midst of them was like walking onto a movie set. Simply stepping out the lobby doors made my blood pump faster, the energy of so many people walking, climbing in and out of cabs and Uber rides and limos, legs snapping with a keyed-up pace as they forged ahead to nearby offices and restaurants.

The only disappointment was that the best places for running weren't within walking distance. Otherwise I could easily have become one of those people who rarely gets into a car. It was appealing.

When the pace and simmering energy of all those people got too much, I could retreat to my tiny, but very well-insulated home. It was silent inside my four small walls. Even the balcony was somewhat protected from noise, situated so far above the pavement it was risky to lean too far over the concrete barrier, topped by an iron bar to increase the height in an effort to prevent an ugly accident.

My first instinct was to mix a martini and enjoy the view from my balcony. I'd given up a lot of living space for that balcony, but I wasn't going to experience city life standing alone inside a concrete box, hanging precariously over the street, gazing at the view. There would be plenty of time for that in the months ahead.

I put on a clean pair of jeans, a black camisole with a pink cropped sweater over it, and black ankle boots. I was still at that stage with my new haircut that when I ran my fingers through my hair, they burst out of the ends, shocked that something was missing. I ran my fingers through several more times to get them used to the length — just above my shoulders — and to fluff out the waves I'd had added at the same time as the blonde highlights.

A cocktail lounge occupied the mid section between the towers with its soaring glass ceiling. There was a semi-circular bar in one corner that served coffee drinks and beer and wine. The space was filled with trees planted in enormous ceramic pots, large enough to allow some of the trees to reach a height of fifteen feet or more. Comfortable chairs and sofas arranged around low tables made intimate areas for talking with neighbors or friends. Something had been done acoustically so that the ridiculously high ceiling and the glass didn't cause conversations to explode into an ear-shattering din.

A grand piano sat in the corner opposite from the bar, a folded piece of tagboard on the bench announcing that various pianists provided music from five to seven every evening.

Now, it was seven-fifteen. I could only imagine the music pouring through the open space, rising up to the glass and falling down again like delicate raindrops of sound. Piano music has captivated me since I was a toddler. I longed for the magic of my fingers pressing on all of those bone white keys, moving over them as if directed by another force. I never had lessons, and never asked for them. All five of the

Mallory children were treated with utter fairness and we were very young when we recognized that it wasn't a good idea to ask for something that the family couldn't afford to provide for all five children.

Small desires were best.

I bought a glass of white wine. I turned my back to the bar and took a sip while I studied the room.

Most of the seating areas were occupied. I saw two vacant arm chairs facing each other in front of a plant with wide, thick leaves, juicy and tropical looking. I crossed the room and settled into one of the chairs. I flipped open my tablet. I entered my last name in the password box and connected to the wifi.

My glass of wine was half empty, my brain numbed by scrolling through Twitter, clicking on links that bled outrage at the condition of the world. Everything from the petty to the apocalyptic.

I'm certainly familiar with the thrill of outrage, and I know the way it gets your blood flowing faster, closer to the surface, makes your brain feel as if its synapses are firing with greater intelligence, with a flow of important things to say. But every so often, you just don't care. It really does not matter whether a football player stands, sits, or kneels during the national anthem.

I put my tablet on my lap and looked up, feeling something prickle the hairs at the base of my skull.

4

A woman stood beside the chair across from me. "Is anyone sitting here?"

I shook my head.

"Thanks."

"No need to thank me, it's not my chair." I smiled.

She put her bottle of Corona on the table and settled into the chair.

Her dark hair was pulled into a stubby ponytail. Thick bangs covered her eyebrows. She had beautiful blue eyes, made brighter beneath dark, almost black eyeshadow. The shape of her mouth, and her hair and eye color made her look eerily similar to Tess. She wore black leggings and knee-high boots, and a navy blue top that looked a bit off with the black. She carried a very large brown leather purse. She pulled out her phone and tapped the screen.

I finished my wine and stood.

Without looking up from her phone, she said, "I didn't mean to chase you away."

"You're not. I'm getting another glass of wine. Will you save my seat?"

She looked up and smiled. "No worries."

When I returned, she was still bent over her phone. The beer looked to be at the same level as before, sweat easing its way down the sides and pooling on the table.

I settled into the armchair and crossed my legs, propping my knees on the arms. "How long have you lived here?"

She looked up, her lips partially opened, her phone tipped forward in her hand, ready to fall on her lap, as if she'd forgotten it was there. She glanced to the side and back at me. She seemed to find the question difficult, somewhat disturbing. Or too invasive?

"Not that long," she said.

After her lengthy hesitation, I decided not to ask for more details. "Do you work nearby?"

"Sort of." A few strands of hair had come loose from her ponytail. She tucked them behind her ear. As she did, her phone wobbled in her other hand and she clenched it to keep it from falling. The hair slipped out from behind her ear and across her cheek. She blew a light puff of air to get it out of the way, which was completely ineffective.

"I just moved in," I said.

"It's a nice place. Very classy."

"It is. I work for a software company. A few blocks away."

She smiled. "That's nice."

Maybe I'd misread her. Maybe she didn't want to talk. But then why settle yourself in an intimate arrangement of chairs in a room designed for socializing? "Are you waiting for someone?"

She shook her head.

"What are the best places to eat around here?"

"Everything's pretty good."

"Everything?"

"Well all the places I've tried. I don't eat out very much. Mostly Pho. Or the deli."

"Okay."

"It's crazy expensive to live in this building."

"I'm in a studio. It's very cozy. I hope it doesn't turn out to be too cozy."

"Me too, but even those cost a lot."

Telling her it wasn't costing me anything was more than I wanted to say. It seemed odd that she was talking about the cost, suggesting she couldn't really afford it. They ran credit checks on tenants so obviously she'd passed as someone who could manage the rent. I waited for her to say more, but she picked up her beer and took a delicate sip. She kept the top of the bottle between her lips for a moment.

"I'm Alexandra. Alex."

"Jen."

There was another long silence.

"This wine is pretty good, for by the glass," I said.

"It is." She took another sip of her beer.

She stared at me as if she expected me to say more, but it was becoming tiresome. If she didn't want to talk, we didn't need to talk.

She tipped the bottle back and took several long gulps of beer. She put the bottle down and glanced around the room. She turned back and stood. "I have to pee. Can I trust you to watch my beer?"

"Sure."

She grabbed her purse and walked quickly across the room, moving her head side to side every few steps as if she thought she was being followed.

I took a sip of wine and let my gaze drift over the talking, laughing, gesturing people occupying the sofas and chairs around me. For a moment, I thought about leaving. It wasn't as if someone would take a half-empty bottle of beer and start drinking it. But considering leaving while she was gone wasn't very neighborly and I'd come into the lounge to be neighborly, so I took another sip of wine and waited.

I thought about how she'd asked the question — could she *trust* me? It was just a Corona.

5

It was fifteen minutes before Jen returned from the restroom. My wine was gone, I was hungry, and her beer was probably warm. That didn't stop her from guzzling it down the moment she flopped into her chair.

I smiled. "I'm going to go look for a place to grab dinner. You're sure you don't have any suggestions besides Pho?"

"Not really."

Okay. I slid forward, ready to stand.

"Don't leave."

"I'm hungry."

"You could have another glass of wine."

"That will make me hungrier."

"They have nuts and pretzels at the bar. You have to ask for a bowl, but if you order a drink, they give it to you for free."

I stood.

"Are you leaving?" She shoved her hand into her purse and pulled out two twenties. "I'll buy you a glass of wine."

"I can pay for it myself. But thanks."

She held out the bills, smiling, eyes wide. A tiny shiver erupted between her eyebrows. "We hardly talked at all."

It was true, she'd hardly talked. Maybe she'd come up with all kinds of things to say while she was in the restroom. It looked as if she'd spent the time washing her face. The shadow was gone, a faint smudge of black below her eyes showing the paper towel didn't quite cut it when it came to easily removing mascara.

"Do you want to get dinner together?"

She shook her head. "I can't."

"Okay."

"Please let me buy you a glass of wine. I'll have another beer and we can eat some munchies and then you can get dinner."

"I'm glad you have my evening all mapped out for me," I said.

"Are you mad?"

"Of course not. Just a little confused."

"Sorry." She waved the bills. "Please."

If nothing else, my curiosity was starting to override my hunger. Nuts would keep my stomach happy for a while. And a glass of water. I took the bills.

"Will you get me a beer?"

"Corona again?"

She smiled and nodded, her head bobbing as if having a beer with me was the best thing that had happened to her all week.

I returned with a small tray holding a glass of wine, a Corona, a glass of water, and a small bowl of nuts and pretzels that I now realized was not going to do a very good job settling the churning in my stomach. She jumped up and took the tray from me.

"I didn't mean to make you feel like a waitress," she said.

"I don't feel like a waitress. And if I did, what difference does that make?"

"I just meant I didn't want to be disrespectful, to make you feel like you had to wait on me."

"It's not a problem." I settled back in the chair and drank half the glass of water. Immediately my stomach stopped complaining. I grabbed a handful of nuts and several pretzel rings and popped them into my mouth.

She lifted her beer bottle. "Cheers."

"Cheers." I took a sip of wine. I put down my glass and drank the rest of the water. I'd gotten nowhere with food or work, so I launched the most innocuous conversational ball I could think of. "Is it always this crowded in the evenings?"

"Pretty much. It's a nice place to hang out."

"But limited drink choices. And even more limited food." I took another handful of nuts.

"It's relaxing. And not as pressured as a restaurant, having to order and all that."

I'd never thought of restaurants as pressured. "There's always bars."

"They can be pressured in a different way."

She was very pretty. I could picture her in a bar — her nervous, unpredictable, and somewhat subservient demeanor attracting the wrong kind of man. I could see her being a target for men who wanted an easy pickup, and I could see her failing to manage that with any skill.

I guessed she was in her mid twenties. She ought to have some level of sophistication, living in San Francisco. She seemed both closed off and as vulnerable and uncertain as a sixteen-year-old raised with a social life built around a church youth group, by parents who rigidly controlled her television and internet access.

Maybe she was new to the city. Maybe she'd come from a small town where things didn't cost so much and restaurants and bars weren't so full of pressure.

She turned her head, surveying the room, clutching her beer bottle in both hands. Her fingernails were unpainted, cut short, the pinky fingers bitten to tiny stubs. She took a sip of beer, glanced at me, then turned her attention back to the room. It was filled with people mostly in our age bracket, dressed as if they'd just walked a few blocks over from the financial district, all of them possessing jobs that didn't require, but fostered a uniform dress code. Suits and three hundred dollar leather shoes. Expensive haircuts and makeup. I fit in with the others, she did not.

"Who are you looking for?" I said.

She turned back. "No one."

The game was getting old. Pleading for my attention then immediately shoving it away was exhausting in a way that was becoming uninteresting.

I looked across the room again, trying to figure out who was gripping her attention.

A tall, slim man standing near the bar appeared to be staring at us. It was difficult to tell from a distance, but his focus appeared to be on Jen, hardly noticing I was there. Not my usual experience. And especially when my companion was a woman dressed in a rather waif-ish style, disheveled hair and smudged makeup and a furtive way of moving.

I tried to remember whether he'd been standing there when she went to the restroom. He certainly wasn't there when I'd bought the drinks and picked up the snack bowl.

"Do you know that guy?"

"No. What guy?"

I took a sip of wine.

She stared at me. She glanced quickly at the bar, as if she thought I wouldn't notice. The guy nodded his head.

"Do you know him?"

"I don't. But I don't want to talk to him."

"How do you know he's planning to talk to you?"

"I just think he is."

"Okay. Then why don't you go with me to find a place to eat?"

"I can't. I really can't. I shouldn't."

I put my glass on the table. The remaining wine glowed in the dim light, the effect made stronger by the dark sky above the glass ceiling. "Well I'm hungry. And the wine is going to my head. If you stay, he'll come talk to you, if that's what you think he's doing."

She turned slightly and shook her head. It seemed like it was for him, not me.

I stood and slipped my arms into my jacket. "I'll see you around," I said.

"Sure. Maybe another time we can get Pho."

"Sure. Don't let him bother you."

"It's okay. I can handle him."

I didn't think she could. And for some reason I couldn't understand, or explain, I wanted to protect her. I had no idea from what.

6

Tess continued to behave as if she was on an assignment for the CIA.

For all I knew, she was. CoastalCreative, despite its beachy, carefree name, had a fair number of government customers. And not just public school districts and state agencies. They had dark customers whose names were obscured on sales reports, identified only by numbers. Our third largest customer was one of the no-names. It made promoting our value to new customers a difficult task when you couldn't provide testimonials from some of your most satisfied customers.

Our no-name customers might have been the CIA, the Department of Defense, the NSA, the FBI, and non-US-government entities as well. For a tiny company based in Santa Cruz, offering organic granola bars in the snack machines, they ran with a rough, powerful crowd.

The computer software we developed allowed companies to take all kinds of data — about their customers, their citizens, their products, their support services, their competitors and allies and enemies, their employees, anything, really — and transform it into graphical images to help them better understand the *big picture*.

I really needed to talk to Tess, although I hadn't yet decided what I would say.

My so-called better than average rating — a *four*, with *five* being the best you can get — had generated a whopping one percent pay increase. Theoretically, that increase was the last raise any of us would receive until performance reviews rolled around again in another year.

Tess had said she would personally notify me about the amount of my raise. She'd dodged that task because she was too embarrassed to act as if one percent was a reward for doing good work. The pay increase had simply revealed itself in the slightly different deposit into my bank.

I was sitting in my cubicle, looking at my bank account on my phone. Confined to the low walls of a cubicle, using my desktop computer for personal tasks was no longer an option. Anyone passing by could see what I was working on.

It wasn't clear if the new satellite office favored cubicles so everyone had some sort of bay or city view, or if it was just that employees in Santa Cruz were a bit spoiled with non-standard privacy, and here the plan was to go along with the rest of the industry — cubicle nation. It was probably the latter, since the views were only available when you stood up from your desk. Otherwise you stared at fabric covered walls and tried to concentrate as voices hummed and phones rang and computers bleeped around you.

Cubicles are supposed to make for a more collaborative work environment.

The problem with collaboration is that not everyone is worth collaborating with. And often, your cubicle is situated near people who aren't even working on the same project. It's not like they can shuffle the deck every time someone changes jobs. So the four people closest to your cube might be people you loved collaborating with in the past, making for great lunches out, but current collaboration is non-existent.

Half the people I needed to collaborate with were

located in an office in Atlanta.

The low walls and lack of privacy drove me to my phone more and more. They forced me to start learning how to tune out the voices of other people. The room vibrated constantly with discussions about arranging meeting times and conference rooms, product launch events and all the details that were utterly unimportant to anyone not working on the event. There were conversations about market analysis and web design, raises in gym membership fees and scheduling hair appointments, analyst relations meetings and press release development, childcare crises and medical appointments, product updates and customer complaint escalations.

It was a cacophony of human life, the personal and the corporate in one enormous stew, the fallout of working too many hours so that the personal bled into the corporate and vice versa. The noise and distraction had so far, prevented me from collaborating effectively with my co-workers on the other end of the phone line, driving us to communicate through the internal chat tool.

I hated the cubicle, but I did love seeing the impressive Bay Bridge and the lovely late nineteenth century architecture of the Ferry Building when I walked to the restroom or the coffee room, which I did more frequently now that I had these luscious three-hundred-sixty-degree views.

I stared at my computer screen, tweaking my spreadsheet with useless changes in font and color, trying to think about what my next move should be. The one percent slap in the face demanded I fight back. Turning the other cheek is only a temporary response. I was raised with the directive to turn the other cheek. It was made out to be something admirable, a response that proved you were a better person. But better than whom? The person slapping you, obviously. Turning away from a slap demonstrated inner strength. To me, it seemed a bit like an ego trip. Turning the other cheek meant you were to take abuse and accept it as an indication of the other's failure. And yet, I never thought my body, my spirit and desires were there to accept abuse.

Withholding a reaction is good, in the moment it happens. But never responding? Allowing the same person to slap you repeatedly, because that's what happens, it becomes habitual...that's an assault on my own spirit.

7

My best leverage with Tess for more money was another job offer. But after Steve Montgomery's eager suggestion that we discuss opportunities for me in sales, and his assurance that his admin would be in touch to set up a meeting, I'd heard nothing. I didn't know if the admin had dropped the ball, or he'd changed his mind. Or simply forgotten. After feeling as if I had multiple options, believing I had to make a pro and con list to determine which was better, I now felt as if I stood with my nose touching a concrete wall — impossible to penetrate and impossible to scale.

I plugged my ear bud cord into the phone jack and stuffed the hard knobs into my ears. I pulled up Chopin on my playlist. I clicked around the spreadsheet, trying to think. Ringing phones wormed their way past the too-soft piano notes. I increased the volume, but trying to look busy with a spreadsheet and trying not to hear sudden bursts of conversation was splitting my brain in two.

I shoved the phone and earbuds into my pocket, grabbed my jacket and purse, and left my cubicle. I kept my head down, determined to avoid any conversation. I took the long way around, past Tess's office. Directors and VPs were not consigned to cubicles like the rest of us. Their peace of mind and private conversations were critical, unlike ours, apparently. Her door was closed but the glass walls that allowed the lower level employees to enjoy the view, if not the tranquility, showed a darkened room and empty chair.

The problem with earbuds is they block out things you should hear, as well as things you're trying to avoid.

I was two blocks from the office, walking along Market Street headed away from the bay. The music was crashing into my skull, helping to wipe out the nagging thought that Tess suddenly and dramatically found me less useful, that Steve regretted his impulsive suggestion I had the right temperament for a more lucrative job in sales. The underlying, niggling fear that my housing was dependent on continuing to be viewed as an employee worthy of the perk. I hadn't signed a lease or agreement of any kind.

The rush to get away from the banks of Soquel Creek had made me impetuous. I'd failed to really consider the tenuous nature of my new situation.

I paused at the corner of Market and Main and sent a text message to Tess. I waited through a change of the lights, but there was no response.

The light changed and I stepped off the curb. The seven or eight people clustered around me did the same. As I started walking, someone bumped my shoulder. I turned. A man about my height turned suddenly and strode quickly away. He had longish brown hair and wore a baseball cap, a brown leather jacket that strained against broad shoulders, and khaki pants.

Except for the baseball cap, it wasn't an unusual choice of clothing. And the cap wasn't odd in itself, but something I didn't normally see when I was walking around the financial district on a weekday.

The problem was, I'd seen a man dressed in the same clothing, right up to the 49ers hat, when I left my office building. It strained credibility that he'd randomly followed the same route as me. Especially since I'd had the impression he was waiting for someone, and now, he was walking alone.

It was mid-afternoon. Despite the gray sky, daylight filled the spaces between the buildings. The sidewalks were crowded with pedestrians. And yet, a chill ran down my spine.

8

Portland, Oregon

When I was fifteen years old, there was a shift in the balance of power between my mother and me.

Until then, I'd considered her my greatest ally. Not that most children grow up believing they need allies, but in my father's household, it was a requirement I seemed to know instinctively.

She didn't stand up to him, or help me dodge his rules and punishments, but she was there with a sympathetic smile, and a fierce, soft urging for me to choose my battles. Not everything required a Napoleonic stand.

My mother, Hannah Mallory, was a godly woman. Even my father, who had very narrow guidelines regarding what constituted a godly woman, praised my mother's godliness. To me, godliness suggested spineless and rather dull, a horrifying acquiescence to the fact that she was rarely allowed to speak her mind. It was proven in the way she demonstrated having my back — her protection involved sneaking around behind my father's to get me what I needed or wanted, striving to keep him believing he was in charge, his rules precisely followed.

My breasts had started to develop when I was twelve.

One evening, she looked at me as she sat on my bed to listen to my prayers. She told me to sit beside her before getting down on my knees. Her leg was warm against mine.

She took my hand. That in itself was unusual enough for my heart to start racing, curious about possible pitfalls in the momentous conversation I might have to navigate.

"Alexandra, it looks as if you might need a bra soon."

"I guess so."

"Your father doesn't believe in girls wearing adult lingerie. He believes you're a child still, and…"

"He can believe I'm a child all he wants, but it doesn't make it true. He can believe he has the ability to walk on water, but he'll probably drown."

"Please don't."

I pressed my lips together and waited.

"I've found an undershirt that has some support. We'll go shopping on Saturday. After, we can have a nice lunch out. It's something to celebrate, this first step toward becoming a woman, but it has to remain just between us. You understand?"

"No."

"Please." She took my hand.

"He must know that all of us are growing up. Unless he's blind."

"Of course he does. But give him this for a while longer. He cherishes his little girls, and he…"

"Cherish means to protect and care for," I said.

"He does protect you."

"From things he imagines are threatening me. Not from real threats."

"What real threats are you concerned about?" Her grip tightened, bone against bone.

"I wasn't thinking about real threats. I was thinking about the things he imagines."

"He's been given responsibility for you, for all of us."

I shrugged. I tried to wriggle my fingers out from the clasp of her hand, but she didn't budge and I didn't want to throw her off violently, hurting her feelings. She was working hard to explain the inexplicable. For years, it had been clear to her that I had a well-defined mind of my own, but she was afraid. The conflicts between my father and I filled her with increasing terror.

"I don't think he cares for me. Not the real me. He cares for the person he wishes I were."

"Please don't say that. It's very unkind, and not true. "

"Yes it is. He doesn't care what I think. He's only interested in people who think exactly like he does. Anyone who views things differently doesn't exist. The person he cares about is a figment of his imagination."

She let go of my hand and stood. She walked to the window and yanked the cord to close the drapes. Without turning, she said, "You need to respect your father."

I didn't respond.

"He provides a nice home for us, he…"

I held my breath, wondering what else she'd be able to come up with.

She turned. "He's your father."

Apparently, his only redeeming quality in her mind was paying for our house and the food on the table. "Anyway, it's important to respect his wishes. And even though he doesn't want you dressing like an adult woman at your age, I also think it's important to get you some supportive undergarments."

She returned to the bed to listen silently to my prayers, a series of innocuous aspects of my life for which I felt grateful, a few mundane infractions to confess, followed by blessings upon my siblings and friends and parents. And animals.

My mother had complained repeatedly over the years that animals weren't appropriate subjects for prayer, but I persisted. As far as I was concerned, animals made the world a more interesting place. I appreciated their presence and wanted to do anything possible, even if I didn't believe it did any good, to keep them from suffering at the hands of human beings.

When my knees reached the breaking point, I sat down on my heels and opened my eyes.

"Where would you like to go for lunch? After our shopping trip."

"Pizza."

She smiled and left the room, closing the door behind her.

I pulled the cord and opened the drapes. I pushed up the window as far as it would go. I popped out the screen and angled it to pull it into the bedroom. I did this every night unless there was a downpour.

Climbing onto the windowsill, I stuck my legs through the opening and scrunched down so the evening air brushed my face. Crickets chirped, their racket suggesting an invading army, relentlessly moving closer. The images on the TV in the house next door flickered and jumped like something trapped behind the too-thin curtains.

I thought about the candy-colored bras I'd seen in department stores, the lace and ribbon and satin. Two of my friends, and several other girls in my class had bras. Those bras were not undershirts posing as something else.

It shouldn't have been a surprise that my father would twist a significant milestone into something ridiculous, shrouding natural growth and development, something to marvel at, with a suggestion of shame. It was also a little weird that he preferred the risk of boys noticing my blossoming flesh right through a t-shirt rather than wanting to keep my body more discreetly covered. It was typical of his distorted viewpoint. He didn't think things through.

My mother saw the problem and was going to dress me like a five-year-old to make sure modesty wasn't compromised and my father's fantasy world wasn't perturbed. She'd thought of everything but me.

9

Tess stepped off the elevator and walked down the hall to her office. She put her bag on the floor, sat down, spun her chair to the right, and looked out at the bay. There was a temptation not to respond to Alex's last two text messages, sent twenty minutes apart. But she didn't want to play games. Acting busy and otherwise engaged when you weren't was the same as lying.

She unbuckled the outside pocket on her bag and took out her phone. She skimmed through her in-box and then opened the text message app.

Tess Turner: *I can meet any time between now and one-thirty. LMK.*

The phone was silent.

She woke the desktop computer and looked at her calendar for the sixth time that day. The current empty space of three hours was something she hadn't experienced in months. It left her feeling disoriented, unsure how to use the time. As the phone screen remained dark, there was a growing irritation with Alexandra.

She shoved the calendar window to the side and opened her slides for upcoming quarterly sales review. She modified bullet points and re-titled some of the charts. It was Alex's responsibility to gather the content and develop the slides, but Tess was compelled to make her own adjustments. She liked to fiddle and tweak, letting the material seep into her subconscious, turning it into her own rather than the result of pasted together updates from ten or twelve other people.

The phone buzzed with a message.

Alexandra Mallory: *In fifteen minutes?*

Tess Turner: *Sure. I'm in my office.*

She went to the restroom, grabbed a bottle of lemon-flavored carbonated water from the break room, and strolled to the end of the floor where a few armchairs invited people to collaborate in a comfortable, relaxed environment, unconfined by cubes and desk chairs. A ribbon of cars moved across the Bay Bridge, impossible to tell from this distance if traffic was flowing at a reasonable pace.

Fifteen minutes into Alexandra's first job interview, Tess had known that Alex had a lot of potential to be difficult. She'd also known Alex had a lot of potential to run circles around the rest of the team. She was smart and poised. She had the confidence to fight for her point of view and a drive for perfection. In a company where constant improvement and excruciatingly high standards were core values, fighting for the absolute best wasn't an attribute that could be dismissed easily.

Once Alex was hired, she'd proven herself as Tess's best employee in terms of delivering superb work and being there when she was needed, and the worst in terms of Tess's ability to exert any kind of authority over her. Alexandra showed respect when she got her way, otherwise she was curt and dismissive. It almost seemed as if Alex didn't care whether or not she remained employed.

The other problem was, Tess liked Alexandra. A lot.

Blunt people had always attracted Tess. She liked the fact

that you always knew where you stood with someone like Alex. No hidden agendas. She liked that she could get honest feedback when she sought guidance. And she liked that people like Alex cared more about expressing their views than a false belief they could make other people feel good with lies.

Lying disgusted her.

But no matter what Tess did, Alex took it and wanted more. The gym membership had been a risk, definitely crossing a line between manager and employee, but by then it was too late. They'd already had all those coffee meetings and drinks after work and conversations about life, smudging that line so it was barely visible.

The apartment where Alex now lived was company-leased, but even that very rare perk was sucked into Alexandra's maw. She continued to drop un-subtle hints about her disappointment with her performance rating. A *four* was an excellent rating, and not given out casually.

Alex wasn't happy unless she was number one. Alex's appetite for rewards had turned Tess into a coward. She hadn't shown professional courtesy, sitting down with Alex to inform her of the pay increase. She let the automated system do it for her.

She turned away from the window and went back to her office.

Alexandra was seated facing the desk.

Tess didn't think she'd been gone that long. She shivered, troubled by the feeling Alexandra had watched her leave and slipped in while Tess was in the break room.

She closed the door and walked around to her desk. "Hi. How are things?" She twisted the cap off the lemon water.

"Fine."

"Good job on the slides for Thursday."

"Thanks."

"How are you liking the new gym?"

"It's nice. More crowded than Santa Cruz, obviously."

Tess sipped her water and waited for Alex to thank her. Maybe she attached too many strings to the things she offered. If she really wanted Alex to enjoy the gym, she should offer it freely. Expecting an expression of gratitude seemed to indicate it was more about feeling important and generous than about actually wanting to do something for another person. She tried to shove the desire for a *thank you* out of her mind, but it clung stubbornly to the back of her skull.

What was wrong with her? Alex had thanked her when she'd first offered. Was she really the sort of person who needed her employees and friends bowing at her feet, telling her how great she was? Maybe she did. It was a shocking and disappointing thought. She took another sip of water.

"I saw my raise," Alex said.

"I'm sorry I didn't…"

"I know you've been busy. Swamped, I imagine."

"That's no excuse. I should have met with you to tell you about it. I'm sorry."

"It was much smaller than I expected."

Tess studied Alex, her intense eyes, as if they could burn through you, drilling smooth holes into your brain and extracting your thoughts. Her hair, once again making Tess feel she was sitting across from a stranger. The constant need for a new hairstyle baffled her. Now, it was shorter, light brown with blonde highlights and natural-looking waves. "No one got much this year."

"But one percent? For a *four* rating?"

"You just received an increase, remember?"

"I thought that was a separate thing."

She put down the water, pushed back her chair, and crossed her arms. She didn't care if it looked defensive. She felt as if she was being attacked. They were supposed to be a team. "At the time, that's what I thought, and I let our friendship get in the way. I revealed information I normally wouldn't."

"It's frustrating."

"I've explained before, I don't have sole control over all of this. There's the balancing of the team, there's input from HR..."

Alex smiled. "It's frustrating."

"You already said that. I don't know what you think I can do." She was on the verge of suggesting Alex look for another job if she was so damn underpaid. It was getting old.

It was truly out of her hands. Of course she felt small giving a raise that resembled a few dollars tossed on the table after a burger and fries in a coffee shop. Of course it was demoralizing to employees who did excellent work. But Alex wasn't the only one who felt demoralized. The two people on the team who were rated *five* had received only two-and-a-half percent and three percent, respectively. Of course, she couldn't tell Alex that. It was tempting, but she couldn't. She needed to stop acting like a high school girl who'd found a new best friend.

A headache crept up the back of her neck. She wanted to demand respect. Alex owed it to her. But along with lying, Tess had a gut-level loathing of the kind of respect that was forced rather than genuine. She was a good manager, she'd treated Alex with tremendous respect. She'd thought Alex was self-assured and self-aware enough to handle a relationship with blurred boundaries.

10

During my first day as a brand new employee at CoastalCreative, the entire eight hours had been consumed by new-hire training, a new-hire lunch, and tables littered with packets of new-hire printed material, handed out by every speaker from benefits to engineering. The second day, I met with Tess for two hours so she could go into more depth about what she expected of me.

Instead, she spent twenty minutes outlining my responsibilities, and the next hour and forty minutes baring her soul.

As she veered off the topic of my job and into her own life, her hunger for female companionship reshaped her face and the way her mouth moved. It started with offhand references to non-work-related topics with potential for opening a door to common ground — everything from her preferred food items offered at the company cafe salad bar to her favorite kind of wine, mentioned because one of the products CoastalCreative was preparing to launch had the code name of Cabernet. She explained that she liked starting the day early, usually with a six a.m. visit to the gym so she was in the office by seven-thirty.

After the steady drip of personal revelations, I'd interrupted. "How long have you worked here?"

She seemed eager to change the subject completely.

"Three years," she said. "And it's been a wild, exhilarating three years."

"Were you a VP when you started here?"

"Senior Director. I knew I was doing an outstanding job at that level, but when that promotion came…" She smiled and visions of the past clouded her eyes, giving them an unfocused quality.

I settled back in my chair and crossed my legs. "What about before that?"

She outlined her career path, her rapid climb, made faster by having the good luck to graduate with her MBA at a time when Silicon Valley hiring was accelerated, recruiters gulping down MBA students like ball players sucking in steroids, convinced their companies would achieve super-human strength and the ever-elusive competitive edge.

"After I got my MBA, we scattered to the highest bidder, all over the country, the world, in some cases."

I smiled and nodded. "Do you stay in touch?"

"Through email. Facebook. We have reunions, although at any given reunion, half of us can't make it. We're all in positions that demand most of our waking hours, lots of travel."

"Do you like traveling?"

She grinned for the first time. "I love it. I should have been a pilot. Of course, then you end up hanging out in the same four cities for three years. Not to mention the boredom." She mimed gripping a wheel, tweaking it slightly left and right.

Then, it seemed as if I'd stuck a nail into a five gallon jug of water. She poured out stories about the best parts of her career, the adrenaline she experienced when she talked to customers, the times she'd driven her team to design brilliant marketing campaigns or product roll-outs. She talked and talked until I had to put all my energy into keeping my eyes focused on hers, my lips formed into an expression of encouraging warmth.

"It sounds like work is my entire life. I suppose it is." She looked startled at the thought. Possibly, she'd never told the entire story of her career before in such a condensed fashion. "All my friends are work colleagues. Quite a few of my vacations are weekends tacked onto the end of an international trip — trying new food and sight-seeing with someone from work."

"I hope I can travel someday."

"It's not outside the realm of possibility. Maybe not in this role, but as you develop."

I didn't like her talking about me developing as if I were some sort of embryo she was going to shape into the employee she wanted. As if I had no mind or will of my own. I don't think she meant to be condescending. More that she was excited by my potential, but that it was wasted until she got her stamp on me.

I smiled.

She grinned back as if we'd just realized we were twins, separated at birth. "I can see you being a huge asset not just to my organization, but to me personally."

"I guess that's why you hired me."

"I feel like I can talk honestly with you."

"I feel the same way," I said.

"Not just as my employee."

"Meaning?"

"You seem like someone I can confide in." She laughed.

She clasped her hands together and leaned her arms on the desk. She laughed again, with a shrill undertone. "It's so inappropriate for me to be talking like this. Especially when I don't even know you. I just brought you on board!"

"I get what you're saying." I folded my own hands. I tried to keep my expression neutral, not wanting to look too eager, not wanting to give the impression I thought she was giving me some kind of inside access, an advantage over my new peers, most of whom I hadn't been introduced to.

"This is so inappropriate. I don't know what's wrong with me."

"You already said that."

She laughed and unfolded her hands. She placed her fingertips on the edge of the desk and pressed down, turning the skin around her pale gray nail polish bone white. She pulled her hands away and ran her palms along her thighs, smoothing her slacks that were already smooth. "I feel like we could be friends."

I waited.

"At my level, friends are hard to come by. There are men, of course. But a lot of single men don't seem to know how to be friends with a woman, and married men worry it doesn't look right. It's not that we can't all interact as colleagues, but the more personal side…it's hard." She turned and glanced out the window at a dense cluster of trees, planted to give her office shade and privacy from the parking lot stretched out beyond. "Women who aren't at my level are jealous. And women who are…well first of all, there aren't that many. It's so hard to believe that's the case, nearly two decades into the twenty-first century. I don't know what I'm trying to say." She turned back but didn't look directly at me.

I knew exactly what she was saying. She was desperately lonely.

11

San Francisco

That first conversation with Tess clung to my mind as I walked from the office to my new apartment building. I wasn't sure why the memory had re-surfaced. Maybe it was the contrast between her aggressive offers of friendship — inappropriate, as she'd said — compared with her recent behavior.

I guessed the inappropriateness had sunk in further now. Maybe she thought she'd given me too much power. I couldn't ruin her career, but I could certainly damage it. She told me things a person at my level shouldn't know, she let me see too much of her personal life. She paid for my gym membership out of her own bank account. She gave mixed messages all over the place.

The sun hadn't gone down, but it might as well have, hidden behind the fifteen- to twenty-story buildings surrounding me. The sidewalk was charcoal gray, discolored from exhaust and tens of thousands of feet. A cool wind blew up from the bay. I shivered and walked faster. I tugged my jacket around me, but it was designed to match my pants, nicely cut to look stylish inside a comfortable office building, not to keep me warm by any stretch of the imagination. I supposed I needed to buy an actual winter coat if I planned to continue walking to and from work. My leather jacket wouldn't do.

I liked the exercise of walking. And it was ridiculous to get an Uber to travel a few blocks. I wasn't sure how it was going to work out once it started raining.

City living seems so glamorous from a distance, but in reality, it has its own hardships, almost like living on a farm. I'm sure a farmer would laugh at my comparison of walking a few blocks in the rain with plowing a hundred acres of rock-strewn dirt. The difficulty of managing an umbrella in a windy storm, warm comfortable lobbies waiting at the other end were the height of luxury compared with walking through a foot and a half of mud and manure to milk a cow or repair a fence.

I pulled open the lobby door. Before I stepped inside, I glanced over my shoulder, thinking of the man in the leather jacket and 49er hat. If he had been watching me, or following, he'd already accomplished his goal. He'd infiltrated my thoughts and disturbed my tranquility by that single act. I might never see him again, and still he'd disrupted my life.

He wasn't anywhere within sight.

I stepped inside and let the door fall closed behind me. I showed the security person at the desk my ID card for the building and walked to the elevators.

Inside my apartment, the air was dry and cold. I'd left the AC set too low. I adjusted the thermostat and stepped out of my shoes. I slid the jacket off my shoulders and my pants down my legs.

Looking inside the closet was unappetizing. Clothes were smashed against each other, sleeves and pant legs stuck out at odd angles.

Every other area of the tiny apartment was clean and sparse, but opening the closet doors made me feel claustrophobic. I put on black leggings. I looked at my shorts and tank tops with open backs, my dresses and two shoeboxes containing six pairs of flip-flops. It might be a long time before I wore any of those again. I needed to find a different storage space. Even during late August, the weather in San Francisco didn't get above sixty-eight very often. When the fog came in, it felt like winter. I pulled out a long black sweater and shimmied into it. I grabbed my ankle boots and went to the kitchen counter.

After drinking a bottle of water and eating a few cubes of cheddar cheese, the apartment had warmed to a pleasant temperature. I stared at the TV, complete with a multitude of cable channels, included in the rent. A movie and a martini, followed by a pasta dinner was appealing, but I was becoming aware that I needed to limit the amount of hours at one stretch in my cubbyhole. It was too early in the evening.

Now I understood the enormous lounge with its glass ceiling and plentiful arrangements of greenery. Maybe the two- and three-bedroom, even the one-bedroom apartments allowed some freedom of movement. But the residents of the studio apartments could quickly become as tightly wound as lab mice, noses quivering as they looked for crevices to escape their tiny cages.

It wasn't that I was ungrateful for my own space. I loved it. But staying in wasn't that different from being confined to a bedroom like I had been at Noreen's bungalow. Having the place to myself was fantastic. Not paying rent was allowing me to stash all kinds of money into a virtual safe, making me feel comfortable and solid and more secure than I had in years. There was a lot to appreciate. But I needed to get out for a few hours.

I grabbed my wallet, keys, and cell phone and tucked them into a small, oblong purse. I looped the strap over my shoulder and went out.

The bartender nodded as if he recognized me. He didn't. It was a different guy from the last time, thin with black hair. I smiled and asked for a glass of Cab. He poured a liberal amount, over their pour line, from what I could tell, and placed the glass on a cocktail napkin.

"Apartment number?"

I pulled a twenty out of my purse and placed it on the counter.

"You can just provide your apartment number," he said.

"I'll pay cash."

He snatched the bill, clearly annoyed he hadn't been able to extract a small piece of information about me. Giving my apartment number would also provide a wedge for him to ask my name. He made change and I left a dollar on the bar. He didn't touch it.

I turned and took a few steps into the room. I walked closer to the windows that faced the plaza behind the apartments, putting more space between myself and the bar. I took a sip of the Cab. The Chardonnay had been better. But when it's a single pour, white wine forces you to drink too fast, trying to race against the warming of the liquid that loses its buttery taste as it turns to room temperature.

The pianist was hitting the keys so softly, I couldn't decipher what the song was. He gazed out over the room with a bored look on his face, as if his fingers stroking and skipping over the keyboard had become disconnected from his brain. The music was far enough in the background it sounded like water pinging over rocks as it moved at a lively pace down a stream.

The room was about half full. No one stood out in the crowd, no one had a look of familiarity. From my position by the windows, the room had a different appearance. It seemed more inviting, less like a holding pen for amped up urban professionals. Or maybe it was my mood.

Between two potted palms along the side of the room adjacent to the windows, was an alcove. Inside, a six foot by three foot painting hung beneath a single spotlight. On a pale pink background, the faded color of a drop of blood diluted in a gallon of water, was a woman with long whitish hair. She wore a red dress with narrow straps. Her face and the parts of her body not covered by the knee-length dress, were transparent, revealing bone and muscle, arteries and the tops of her lungs, her skull and the full shape of her eyeballs and teeth.

I stared in fascination at the jarring blend of seductive woman and garish cadaver.

12

Before I could get a closer look at the painting, my gaze shifted lower, to the couple seated on one of the sofas beneath it. Jen, and David from the elevator. They sat close, not touching but their heads bent toward each other. Two beers were on the table, standing beside a bowl of the ubiquitous nuts and pretzel mix.

I sipped my wine. I desperately wanted a close-up look at that painting. It loomed over them like something rising from the grave. And that's what it was — a painting of a corpse after the skin has fallen away. The dress looked like silk, the shade of red was rich and seductive, making you think of a woman going out for dinner in San Francisco. She wore black high heeled shoes. Her hair was glossy and thick. Everything about her clothing and hair spoke of youth and health and privilege, until the skin was ripped aside, exposing everything.

I don't know why the internal organs are considered unattractive. To surgeons, they're beautiful. But to the average person they cause uneasiness at best, nausea at worst. They make most people cringe and shudder and turn away. Maybe it's simple lack of familiarity.

Muscle and bone are the same inside any woman, or man, on the planet. There was nothing special in the depiction of this particular muscle and bone. Inside, we all look the same. Unremarkable in an individual sense, but quite remarkable in the way the body holds itself together, functioning like a machine with smooth-running precision.

The machine that all machines conceived by the human race seek to emulate, failing miserably, so far. Eyeballs useless without the optic nerve attaching them to the brain, blood vessels and arteries like tangled wires — fragile and so easy to pierce with a bullet or sever with a knife.

It was impossible to stop looking at the painting. Macabre things are like that. You want to stop, you feel uncomfortable, sometimes fearful, but you can't turn away. You have to see it, to know the worst. The hideous nature draws you. It's something you don't normally see, usually something you fear, so you have to keep looking, as if the looking will possibly make you stronger, no longer afraid, or at least ease the shock.

These things that horrify are always some type of damage to the human body, feared by every one of us above all other things — disease, dismemberment, disfigurement. All that *dis*-something. And finally, death, and the rotting that follows.

We have to look, to see how awful it could become. We have to look, to know the truth. We aren't really strong and in control and safe after all. We're a breath away from the macabre.

I took another sip of wine to sooth my thoughts. Still, I couldn't stop looking at the painting. It was a strange choice for a lounge meant for drinking wine and chatting with neighbors. For meeting people who might be beneficial to your career. An atmosphere designed for starting new friendships, offering the possibility of a new lover, a fresh relationship.

I continued to observe Jen and David. They hadn't looked up the entire time I'd been standing there. Their beers remained untouched. They knew each other well, the tilt of their heads was not the position of two people who had just met. Although they weren't touching, there was a connection. They had touched before. They'd had sex, I was sure of it.

Was he her boyfriend? He'd seemed eager to store my boxes in his second bedroom, so she couldn't be simply a roommate.

When I was given a tour of the building before moving in, I'd seen models of the larger apartments. A two-bedroom was still very tightly arranged, each room large enough for a bed and possibly a small chifforobe. Storing boxes for a stranger seemed like a huge commitment. He'd made the suggestion without mentioning another person who might not be so thrilled with indefinite cardboard storage.

His offer seemed odd at the time, too friendly, too soon. Why on earth would he want to burden himself with my boxes? If it was a ploy to flirt with me, to prove himself thoughtful and generous, there had been nothing else flirtatious about his behavior. In fact, now that I thought about it, he'd seemed disinterested compared to most men I meet. He'd briefly checked me out, maybe. It had been hard to tell with the sunglasses.

A growing cluster of people pressed around the bar, looking for refills, bowls of nuts, and a place to lean since all the seats were occupied. I moved farther away, closer to the windows, longing for a place to lean myself.

Jen and David still hadn't touched their beers or moved their heads. They didn't look like they wanted to be interrupted, not even glancing up at the two animated women seated on the sofa across from them, shrieking with laughter every few minutes.

Two things drove me over there. I was tired of standing, and I had to see that painting up close. Okay, three things. I was curious to find out what was between them.

As I approached one of the tropical plants near the center of the room, a guy bumped my arm. I turned. It was the same guy who'd been staring at Jen that first night, hovering near the bar, his presence causing her to squirm. He was tall, slender but not gangly. Moderately good looking with a very intense gaze.

"Excuse me." His eyes bored into mine.

"No worries."

"Good thing your glass wasn't full." He hovered, seeming to block my progress.

"Yes." I stepped to the side.

"Can I get you a refill?"

"No thanks." I smiled in a friendly, neighborly way, and continued toward Jen and David. Walking away from someone like that, ending the conversation before they're ready, creates a burning sensation on the back of my head, an almost physical force urging me to turn and note their expression, to see whether they're angry or hurt or have moved on. I resisted. I always do, but the burning creeps across my scalp every time.

As I approached, David reached for one of the beers. He handed it to Jen. She looked up and saw me. "Oh. Uhh...hi." She didn't smile. She shoved the top of the bottle into her mouth and swallowed some of the frothy yellow stuff.

Most people might turn away from a cool greeting like that, but I'm not most people.

13

I moved toward the table so both of them were forced to look at me.

"Hey," David said. "Tenth floor, right? Storage problems?"

"Very flattering," I said.

He winked and picked up his beer.

I turned to face the painting. Up close, it was even more alluring. The blood vessels were painted in a highly realistic fashion. As a result, the vessels and arteries seemed to throb with blood flowing through them, thick and steady. I looked into my wineglass and it too seemed to throb with the same living pulse, the same deep, secretive red.

"What do you think of that painting?" I gestured toward it with my wineglass.

"I try not to look at it," David said.

"Why?" I sat on the edge of the table and crossed my legs.

Jen looked down at her beer bottle. She raised it to her mouth and licked the opening.

"It's eff-ed up," David said. "I don't know why anyone would want to look at that. They hung it for shock value, to show how sophisticated this place is."

"It makes me think of that body exhibition," I said.

"What body exhibition?" said Jen.

"It's just called *Bodies*. They have all these cadavers, old people, young people, pregnant women... They've preserved them and dissected them so you can see inside."

"Ew." Jen wrinkled her nose and left her facial muscles contorted, as if pulling away from an unattractive odor.

"I know," David said. "The human race is one sick puppy."

"I think it's interesting," I said. "The body is amazing. The way it all works, like magic. We don't even notice how it goes about its business."

"I'd rather not notice," David said. He gulped his beer and shifted on the couch, moving his legs so they weren't as close to mine. Now his thigh pressed against Jen's leg, mostly bare with a skirt that came just a few inches past her hip bone. She wore low-heeled boots that covered her knees.

"Why?"

"I don't think you told me your name," he said.

"Alex."

"Well, Alex. I don't want to think about how my blood vessels connect to each other. I don't want to see what a muscle looks like unless it's covered with skin. No one needs to know that shit."

"It's fascinating."

"Why would I want to look at some gorgeous chick like that one," he nodded toward the painting without looking at it, "and see all that? She doesn't look hot with all that icky stuff showing."

"Is that the only reason *chicks* exist, to look hot?"

"Whatever. Don't get all feminist on me. 'Kay?"

"Absolutely not," I said.

"I don't like it either," Jen said. "It gives me the willies. I don't know why it's even here. Everyone comes down here to drink and chill out. It's a buzz kill."

David nodded.

I stood and walked closer to the painting. I touched the painted woman's tibia. It felt smooth and solid as bone. I yanked my finger away, shivering.

David laughed. "Not so fascinating after all? You felt the bony fingers of the grave?"

I turned. "That's why it's fascinating. She doesn't look dead at all. She's full of life."

"She's full of something. All kinds of gooey things."

The chatter from the women seated across from them had faded. I felt them listening to our conversation. I glanced at them. They both picked up their wine glasses and stood. They walked away without saying anything.

I sat on the vacant sofa across from the other two. Later, I'd return to the lounge when it was empty, especially when it was empty of David and Jen. The quiet would allow me to absorb all the details of the painting. Unlike them, I couldn't take my eyes off it. As they sipped their beers, their eyes jittered every few seconds, glancing at it in spite of themselves.

David stood. "Do you want another glass of wine?"

"Sure." I reached into my purse.

"My treat." He took my glass and his nearly empty beer bottle. "Jen?"

She shook her head.

He walked away, rather too quickly. I wasn't sure if he wanted more beer to shake the nerves of thinking about what beat and breathed and thrummed inside of him and every other body in the lounge, or if it wasn't that complicated. After all, his bottle was empty.

Jen continued looking down at the bottle in her hand,

avoiding my eyes, it seemed.

"Is he your roommate?" I said.

She shook her head.

"Boyfriend?"

"No."

"Lives on your floor?"

"I just know him."

I sipped my wine. "If you don't like the painting, why did you sit right beside it?"

"No other chairs." She swallowed some beer. She didn't look at me.

I studied the painting. A few minutes later, David returned with my glass of Cab. He settled across from me and put his feet on the table, crossing his legs at the ankles. "All moved in?"

"There wasn't a lot to do, since it's furnished. Just my clothes and stuff."

"So that's a *yes*?"

I smiled.

"Do you work around here?" he said.

"Near the Ferry Building."

"Cool. I'm with The Gap. A senior buyer."

"I'm a project manager."

"What company?"

"No one you've heard of."

"Try me."

"Hey, it's after hours. We shouldn't talk about work." I raised my glass toward him.

"What else do people talk about? How cool the human body is underneath all that smooth, sexy skin?" He smiled.

"Whatever you think is interesting."

"Got it." He tipped his beer into his mouth. He glanced at Jen who seemed to have shrunk into the couch, a tiny thing, a child waiting for her mother to excuse her from the dinner table.

14

Cupertino, California

In Tess's view, a woman didn't make it to Senior Vice President of a technology company if she was weak. The same was true for a man, but like everything, more so for a woman. It was rare that anyone reached that level who wasn't driven, playing at the top of her game, competitive and willing to go far above and beyond, day in and day out, month after month.

For years, she'd listened to employees complain about their performance ratings, insisting they'd gone *far above and beyond*. In some ways, they were set up, because there were no guidelines describing what *far above and beyond* meant — the criteria for a *five* rating. But when you were that person, you knew. And that was the person who made it to Director, and more infrequently, to Vice President.

Sure there were some that achieved that status by simply sticking with the same job until others around them were laid off or left for better opportunities. They hoped that by occupying a position long enough, they'd simply rise up in the organization like bread dough left covered, reacting to yeast, getting promoted becoming an organic, inevitable process. And it happened. Occasionally. When it did, those people were rarely effective leaders.

For most people, making it to the top left a lot of mess in your path. Broken relationships, betrayals. Sometimes, deeds you weren't very proud of, possibly ashamed of.

When Tess had been promoted to Director, the first step up into executive management, she lost her best friend. Even now, she wasn't sure whether to categorize the loss of Bianca's friendship as betrayal or some sort of natural evolution. Either way, an ache remained, barely noticeable, but piercing when she allowed herself to think about it.

She'd always thought there wasn't a single jealous bone in Bianca's body. She'd thought they were the same in that way. Both of them too intelligent and well-educated to yield to unattractive, useless traits like envy. They were modern women, cheering each other's successes, supportive in the face of failure. They'd been friends since their Freshman year at Mountain View High School, assigned to a debate team in their AP English class. Their first topic — *should corporations be required by law to demonstrate social responsibility* — consumed them every night for two weeks as they prepared. They'd fallen in love with the debate process. They joined the extracurricular debate team, eventually traveling all over California to showcase their skills.

At graduation, Tess was Salutatorian of their class and Bianca was one of two Valedictorians. Tess hadn't been jealous. Even though she'd studied harder. Even though she took more difficult classes. Bianca hadn't even taken Physics. But Tess also thought her enthusiastic praise for Bianca meant she'd deposited some social capital in the friendship bank.

Tess went to UC Santa Barbara, Bianca to Cal. Still no jealousy.

When Bianca got engaged mid-way through college, Tess had been thrilled for her. When Bianca decided not to go to law school after all, Tess was enthusiastic to Bianca's face, but mourned in secret.

Fast-forward a few years and Tess was a Senior Marketing Manager at HP, when HP was still an enviable company to work for. She'd submitted Bianca's resume with a glowing recommendation.

Bianca was offered the position in Event Marketing. Tess worked in Product Marketing. Two different worlds. Once a week, they met for lunch. They gossiped about their peers, complained about corporate process headaches and poor management and all the other insignificant but consuming details that forge friendships between co-workers.

For a year or so, Tess felt as if she were back in high school with a best friend who *got it*. There was nothing she couldn't tell Bianca. She told her when she thought there was a good chance she was finally going to get that Director position. She didn't mention the big chunks of stock and the perk of flying business class on international travel that came with the title. Not to mention the salary increase, and the prestige. But everyone knew about those things.

"Aren't you special," Bianca said. "Business class."

"Not really. All Directors get it."

"I know that. And it's so unfair. My legs are longer than yours. And I travel all the time. If anyone needs comfort and leg room, it's me, not you."

"It has nothing to do with fair," Tess said.

"I know." Bianca laughed. "I get it. That's why it's not fair, and it's not right. It's so arbitrary."

"It's not arbitrary. It allows executives to arrive at customer meetings refreshed."

"I meet customers at events. Don't I need to be

refreshed?" Bianca laughed louder, but didn't sound amused.

The conversation continued in circles until Bianca pressed the lid closed on her salad container, still half full of greens and steamed broccoli. "I need to get back to work. Swamped."

Tess thought it was over. A little jealousy was understandable. But Bianca wouldn't let it go. She refused to accept that it was company policy and had nothing to do with a physical need for leg room or the miles traveled per year. It was respect and consideration for Directors and VPs who met with higher level customers. An executive needed to be at the top of her game. It was an investment.

The more Bianca went on about it, the more Tess stopped talking about other aspects of her new role. It was probably a good idea to pull back, she was privy to more sensitive organizational information now, things that shouldn't be shared with lower level employees.

Once Bianca realized Tess was keeping information to herself, she resented that as well.

"You've changed. Everyone that gets to Director turns into the pointy-haired boss."

"That's not true."

"You can't see it. But ask anyone. That's what you used to think, too. I can't believe you don't remember."

"I don't recall saying that. I've always been ambitious, always wanted to be in upper management. You know that."

"Is that how they prep you for depositions? *I don't recall.* It's so fake, so self-important. I guess you need that phony distancing language now that you'll be involved in legal matters, wrongful termination suits and all that?" Bianca laughed.

She used laughter as punctuation a lot lately, a sharp, bitter tone.

"Come on, don't be like this."

But Bianca was like that. And it got worse.

At the same time, Tess got busier. They didn't meet for lunch every week. Sometimes an entire month went by. Bianca accused her of being aloof. She said Tess spoke differently, she wasn't *real* any more.

Within ten months of Tess's promotion, their relationship had deteriorated to friends on Facebook, liking each others' photographs and humorous videos and graphic images of profound yet clichéd words of wisdom.

When Tess accepted a position at CoastalCreative, she included Bianca in her farewell email blast to several hundred people. Bianca didn't respond, but she liked Tess's status update on Facebook. She ignored Tess's new position posted on LinkedIn.

A few weeks later, Tess met Steve Montgomery, the Senior Vice President of Global Sales, but she didn't put it on Facebook and she didn't email Bianca to gush over how good looking and charming he was.

15

Santa Cruz

Steve Montgomery should have been out of bounds. It was a bad idea to get involved with anyone at work. Tess had been down that road before and if there was a breakup, you were almost forced to leave the company, unless it was an enormous global corporation and you could find a position that never required interaction with your ex.

Tess had known she was vulnerable. She hadn't had a long-term relationship in three years. Lots of dates, a few multi-month relationships with good sex and great dinners out, a concert or two. Movies. But nothing that she wanted to become a permanent part of her life. Sometimes she worried she wanted the idea of a boyfriend, a fiancé, or even a husband, but not the real deal.

Being alone was fine. It was good, much of the time. It meant she didn't have excessive drama in her life. There was enough of that at work. It meant she could eat what she pleased and sleep according to her own biorhythms. And she was busy. Work consumed twelve hours a day and often ate into the weekends in a pleasant, leisurely fashion. There were all-consuming trips that satisfied her mentally and emotionally. But being single meant she felt shut out of society at times, and, occasionally, maybe more than occasionally, she was lonely.

But she hadn't started paying attention to Steve because

she was lonely and vulnerable and all those awful things she preferred not to think about because they suggested she was weak. She was drawn to him.

She and Steve lived in the same world, drank the same adrenaline of a fast-paced, brutally competitive industry.

Her last serious relationship had been with a police officer. Hearing about his job was fascinating, but he was bored to tears with the details of what Tess did all day. And the other men had lived in equally foreign worlds — a state lobbyist, a high school history teacher, a personal trainer, and a therapist.

The aphrodisiac of shared ambition, shared passion for the company's success, was powerful.

And Steve was charming. Often misogynistic, but possessing a charisma that drowned many of his offensive comments.

She'd met him when she was presenting the annual marketing plan at a sales kickoff meeting for the start of the new fiscal year. The meeting was held at the Chaminade conference center. The resort was a four-star property surrounded by trees and gardens with pools of water. It was down to earth, low-key, and offered reasonable rates for local businesses. The main building was perched on a hill with a view of the surrounding foothills. Beyond the large patio, a grassy area sloped down the hillside toward the cliff. The main building and cabins were ringed with walking paths that meandered out through a relatively untamed landscape.

Tess's presentation was immediately after lunch on the second day. The engineering VPs were given the key spots — the first day, and morning sessions when everyone was fresh and sure to be in their seats. The salesforce was hungry for new product information straight from the mouths of engineers. They weren't so excited about marketing activities. The ones who had been around a while knew the marketing plan would change several times throughout the year. They wouldn't be informed, and marketing activities sometimes came back to bite them in the ass.

When she was finished presenting, Tess left the podium and walked toward the back of the conference room. The afternoon snack was already being wheeled in on carts, even though they'd just finished lunch seventy-five minutes earlier. Coffee and bowls of mixed nuts, cookies and caramel-coated popcorn. Just what everyone needed when they were already drowsy from a lunch of grilled prawns and scalloped potatoes. A quick sugar rush and then a collapse that would have them fleeing the final sessions in droves, seeking relief from sitting in the dark, lulled by the visual drone of PowerPoint slides.

Despite her best intention, she stopped and filled a cup with caramel popcorn. She plucked out a piece and put it in her mouth. It was a delicious treat after talking for an hour. She grabbed a bottle of iced cappuccino and popped off the cap.

A moment later, Steve was standing beside her, reaching long fingers, with smooth short nails into her cup of popcorn.

He was one of those guys with an indefinable something-ness, a casual confidence that allowed him to eat food out of a woman's hands without giving her the creeps. And so she smiled, holding out the cup with an unspoken invitation to take more. Any other man in the room, any other man in the company, who reached into her food uninvited would stir up an urge to smack his hand, or grimace with disgust and hand over the tainted food. But she wasn't disgusted. She was charmed.

"Great pitch," he said. He took two more pieces of popped corn and put them in his mouth, one after the other, chewing carefully.

"Thank you."

"Steve Montgomery. Senior Vice President, Global Sales. I'd shake your hand, but now my fingers are sticky. Not to mention the spit."

"Very appealing." She smiled.

"I like to give my customers the unvarnished truth, Tess. Not like marketing."

"Ha ha. Am I a customer?"

"Everyone's a customer."

She knew that. That was how innate sales people viewed the human race.

She felt as if she were fourteen, an older boy paying attention, teasing her. She put the cup of popcorn on the table. She tugged her jacket slightly, knowing it was a habit that made her look prim, but somehow made her feel she was taking back control of a situation that was careening downhill. And it was definitely downhill if she was feeling weak, wanting. Too pleased with his attention.

"Seriously," he said. "How can you and I stay tightly aligned? It creates chaos when marketing changes direction and we're left with our pants down."

Now she felt on firmer footing. Crude sales guy bravado. Always complaining, sales challenges never his problem. Arrogant, believing that the sales force was the most important part of the company. Marketing was useless, like having six fingers, or a third nipple. Two penises. And Steve had enough swagger to fit that category, freakish as it was.

"We have a portal where anyone can register for alerts every time there's an update," she said. "And a news blast goes out weekly to the entire salesforce. If they would only read…"

"Not going to happen." He picked up her cup of popcorn. "The guys don't have time for reading white-washed info-grams."

She hated him, but still found him charming. And hated herself for feeling that way. "An educated sales force should be reading the material that's written *expressly* for them."

"They're paid to be sitting across from a customer, not reading…"

She waved her hand. "I get it. Info-grams."

He smiled. "Smart lady." He tipped the cup and poured the remaining popcorn into his mouth. He crumpled the cup and dropped it into the dishpan containing used dishware and utensils.

She pushed her fingers through her hair. It was getting too long. Nearly at her shoulders now. Maybe it invited too much flirting. She grabbed it and pulled it back in a stark ponytail, then let go.

"I suggest we meet once a week. In person, when I'm in town. You can give me the latest. Unvarnished. I like information without the spin."

"So you said."

"I did. I'll have my admin get in touch."

He pulled out his phone and tapped a reminder to himself. He pocketed it. "See you at dinner. Maybe we should meet for a drink."

But he'd left it like that, without proposing a time.

He'd shoved his hands in his pockets and turned to listen to the speaker who droned into the darkened room. A sea of chairs spread out in front of her, half of them empty. The occupied chairs were filled with people bent over their phones.

16

I sent Tess a text message.

Alexandra Mallory: *Drinks Friday? You need to introduce me to the coolest bars where locals hang out.*

Tess and I hadn't met for a Friday drink since I'd moved to San Francisco. In the past, she'd been the one to suggest meeting for drinks. A boss can invite an employee out, suggest a closer relationship, but not the reverse. It's about power, of course, but it's also about self-respect. Asking your boss to do something socially appears needy, with a suggestion of kissing up. Perhaps it's not simply self-respect, but giving her even more power than she already has, including power over your self-respect.

There was no response from Tess.

I stuffed lingerie, shoes, and an extra towel into my gym bag.

I checked my phone again. Nothing.

I crammed shampoo, conditioner, and gel, along with my zippered pouch full of cosmetics into the bag.

I missed running. I liked going to the gym after work, not in the morning. I hated getting ready for work in a public place, but I needed to intensify my weight lifting to compensate for the lack of running.

There were lots of awesome places to run in San Francisco — Golden Gate Park, trails and quiet roads winding through the Presidio, even across the Golden Gate Bridge, although that had obstacle-course potential with all the tourists strolling and taking selfies, while simultaneously herding small children. All of those idyllic running spots required getting in the car, and all of them required paying for the privilege of parking.

At some point, I had to build a routine around that, or find a place to run, maybe along the waterfront where I could walk from my apartment, although it was pedestrian-heavy. I would die without regular runs. Already my body quivered with disappointment and pent up energy when I woke in the morning and packed a canvas bag rather than heading out the door, lightweight and free — just me and my running shoes. I refused to turn into a gerbil on a treadmill.

The new gym, unselfconsciously named the Fourth Street Gym, wasn't as luxurious as the spa-type atmosphere of Tess's Santa Cruz gym. This place was slick and urban. The color scheme was industrial gray with touches of steel blue. Gone was the quiet clank of metal in a separate weight room. Now I was swallowed by a giant warehouse with weight machines and racks of free weights and a lifting cage in the back third. The treadmills were in front of the windows facing the street. A platform ran around the room forming a partial second floor. Stationary bicycles and elliptical machines lined the platform.

The noise level rivaled a four-lane road filled with bus engines, idling SUVs and trucks, and the metallic clang of cable car bells.

The lobby was all metal and black leather. The receptionist was dressed in white with slicked back dark hair, as robotic-looking as the rest of the place. She smiled with a deliberate formation of her mouth, oily with red lipstick, while her gaze fixed on my forehead to give the impression she was making eye contact.

I scanned my membership card through the reader and turned down the hall to the women's locker room. I pulled a bottle of water and my weight gloves out of my bag, hung my clothes in the locker, and pushed the bag onto the floor. I closed the door and hooked the combination lock through the hole in the handle. The lock snapped closed.

I slid my finger across my phone to see if I'd missed a message from Tess. I hadn't.

The weight area was relatively empty, most of the early morning exercisers occupying the cardio equipment.

I did a circuit of squats in the power cage, and bench press and lat pull-downs on machines. Then I worked on bicep curls with free weights. I did five sets of tricep dips and returned to the machines to work my abs.

By the time I was finished, I'd emptied the bottle of water. I was pleasantly warm without sweat pouring off me. I returned to the bench press for a final overload, setting the machine for one-hundred-thirty-five. I'd been working toward one-thirty-seven at the Santa Cruz gym, but the interruption of moving to San Francisco sent me back to my previous maximum weight.

After three sets of ten, my muscles quivered, already near exhaustion from the other work. I lowered the bars and remained on my back for a few minutes, eyes closed, breathing deeply.

I wiped down the bench, tossed my empty bottle in the recycling, and headed toward the locker room.

I wanted to beat Tess into the office. I checked my phone again, still nothing. I paused by a treadmill, abandoned by its user, and tapped out a message to her.

Alexandra Mallory: *Anything I need to prioritize over the usual today?*

That ought to get a response. Clearly we weren't having drinks. I still hadn't heard from Steve's admin about meeting him for drinks. It was funny how a meeting that hovered on the edge of sleazy when he suggested it, was now a meeting I craved. The silence from both of them felt like a plastic bag had been pulled over my head, muffling sound, making it difficult to breathe. I was trapped. I wondered if they wanted it that way.

There was no response from Tess. I looked up. Outside the windows, staring in at the vacant treadmill was the guy in the brown leather jacket. He wore a Giants hat this time, pulled too low for me to see more than his mouth. He turned and jogged across the street.

17

When I woke Saturday morning, the sun was streaming in through the balcony door.

I'd received a message from Tess at eight the night before. *Carry on. If I need something, I'll let you know. You don't need to keep texting me.*

The change in her behavior continued eating at me. I had to go for a run.

I stepped out onto the balcony. The street below was relatively quiet at seven-thirty, but it wouldn't last long. The air felt cool but that too wouldn't last long, once I passed the mile mark.

I dressed in capri spandex pants, a fitted cropped top over a sports bra, and a t-shirt over that. I drank two glasses of water and requested an Uber for Golden Gate Park. I peed and dabbed sunscreen on my face. I left the balcony door open to let in the sun-washed air. There are definite benefits to living on the tenth floor, far away from intruders, as well as casual observers trying to look inside front room windows as they pass by.

I grabbed my hoodie, apartment key, and phone.

The lobby was deserted except for the security guard at the desk. I waved and walked quickly to the entrance, shoes squeaking on the marble floor.

Outside, there were a few people, heads bent over small tablets and phones, headed toward the coffee shop on the corner. I went to the curb. Using the lamppost for support, I stretched my quads, even though I'd have to do it again once I got to the park. I pressed first one toe then the other against the dark green painted iron base, loosening the tightness in my calves and Achilles tendons.

My app alerted me the driver had an emergency but another car was on its way. Only ten minutes.

I turned toward the building, leaning against the lamppost. I scrolled through email to check whether anything had happened overnight. It's rare to get much email on Friday nights when it's the middle of the weekend in other parts of the world, but my general uneasiness with Tess kept me hunting for signs that all was okay.

The apartment building door opened and a guy wearing running shorts and a Cal sweatshirt stepped outside. He was tall with dark wavy hair and a generous smile. He waved. I smiled and tapped away from email, looking at my text messages even though I knew I'd see a blank screen.

The guy walked toward me. "Hey. I've seen you around a few times, did you just move in?"

"Sort of."

"I'm Isaiah. Isaiah Parker." He extended his hand.

"Alexandra."

I took his hand and he gave it a light shake while a smirk twitched across his face. "I guess you hang with the Greeks and I'm solidly in the Israeli circle."

It was a lame joke, but I smiled.

"What floor are you on?" he said.

"Tenth."

"I'm on the eighth."

I nodded.

"Going for a run?"

"I'm waiting for an Uber to Golden Gate Park. I haven't adapted very well to city living. It's a hassle to get anywhere that's good for running. But I don't want to dodge pedestrians."

"Along the water is nice if you get out there early."

"Do you run?"

"Not seriously. More like jogging. I like to go for a mile or so and get the kinks out every so often."

My phone buzzed. From the corner of my eye, I saw my ride — an older metallic blue Honda. "This is mine."

"Enjoy your run," Isaiah said.

"I will. See ya."

He lifted his hand in a half wave and I got into the car.

As it pulled out into traffic, I checked my email. Still nothing important. I settled back and closed my eyes.

I guessed Isaiah was about six-two, muscular and lean with a very precise way of moving. His blue eyes didn't allow you to easily look away. He didn't give off a vibe of being attached. Despite his lame joke, he seemed interesting. He came across as baggage-free.

The driver stopped across from the de Young Museum where pedestrian-only roadways split and circle large fountains. Benches face the fountains and behind them are grassy areas filled with trees. Visitors were standing near the entrance to the museum, but it wasn't mobbed like it is when King Tut or Chihuly comes to town. I thanked the guy for the ride, silently thanking him for not trying to strike up a conversation. I opened the running app to track my distance and strapped the phone to my arm.

After ten minutes of thorough stretching, I started a slow jog. The park is huge, over a thousand acres. Wide pathways weave through wooded areas, past the museum, the aquarium, playing fields, and the Japanese tea house. There's plenty of space for a long run without having to trip over throngs of pedestrians and dog-walkers.

I had no idea where the path would take me, but I'd remain inside the confines of the park and if I ended up unsure about how to get back, my running app would reorient me. Or I could simply call another Uber from wherever I stopped.

After three miles, I was pleasantly detached from concerns about work and relentlessly examining the information I had regarding my new neighbors. So far, it was a quirky bunch. I suppose most living arrangements involve people with habits that range from enjoyable to violence-inducing, and all kinds of desires and secrets, creating an eternal dance.

18

Portland

Dutifully, for over a year, I wore the supportive undershirts my mother bought me. By then I was fourteen and every girl I knew wore a bra. Most were right out of a box, purchased at a discount store — white cotton, a suggestion of lace, a tiny satin bow. They had thick elastic straps and cotton stuffed into the minimalist cups to make absolutely sure a nipple never made its presence known.

Other girls, girls my parents knew only from a distance, the ones they preferred I not spend time with and who were never invited to our home, unless I wanted to bring them to Sunday services where they could repent, wore bras that made having breasts seem like something to celebrate.

Jill Compton, the girl who sat behind me in Algebra had the best bra of all. I'd seen it when we changed into white t-shirts and red shorts for PE. Not only the best, but a collection of five that she rotated systematically throughout the week. I often wondered if she had two more for the weekends.

Jill often shared my lunch because she used her lunch money to buy cigarettes.

Even though Jill's mother didn't approve of smoking, she was *with it*, according to Jill. Ms. Compton wanted her daughter to respect her body, and she believed expensive lingerie inspired self-respect.

When Jill saw my sad little undershirt, she didn't snicker like some girls had done. She looked at me with eyes full of understanding. Her smile showed compassion not pity, and determination to fix my situation.

After PE class, she whispered that I should follow her into the last bathroom stall.

The voices of thirty-four girls as they stripped off shorts and t-shirts filled the main section of the locker room, echoing across concrete floors, up tiled walls, and down rows of metal lockers.

Jill stepped onto the toilet and bent her knees so my feet were the only ones visible beneath the door, although it was unlikely anyone would come into the restroom checking the stalls for girls trying to hide from teachers. They only worried about our presence during roll call at the start of class. They counted us when they were lining up teams for volleyball or relay races. Once we'd jumped and run and swatted balls, we were no longer their concern. Preventing potential class-cutting was now in the hands of our fifth period teachers.

Stripping off the sweatshirt she'd worn, despite the mild weather, she pulled a tea-colored bra out of its folds. The elastic straps had a satin sheen. The cups were made of silky fabric that was so soft it felt like the tender skin of my breasts themselves. Their shape was formed by thick, flat wires sewn into the fabric. Across the top was a wide edging of lace the same color as the silk.

"I'll bring you another one tomorrow. It has to be washed by hand. Just use liquid dish soap. Make sure you rinse all the soap out and hang it up to dry."

"I don't know if I can afford this."

"It's a gift. From my mother."

"Does she know?"

Jill smiled. "Of course. She gets it. I told her how repressed you are."

I laughed.

"Shh." She smiled. "My mother thinks girls should be empowered to make their own decisions."

"Then why can't you smoke?"

"She thinks smoking is a sign of weakness. An addiction."

In our health class, we'd been taught that smoking was indeed an addiction. But Jill and I didn't see it that way when we stopped at the park on the way home from school. We lit our cigarettes, crouching behind the cinderblock building housing the public restrooms. We didn't smoke because we were weak. Or addicted. Addicts had pale, yellow-tinged skin and tremors in their fingers. They were gaunt and withered with decayed and missing teeth. We smoked it because we felt grown up. We were sophisticated. Being an addict meant you had no control, and we had control. We never smoked on the weekends.

"Try it on. I think we're the same size. If not, she can exchange it."

The tags dangled from the strap. "It will fit, I know it." I bit the plastic string holding the tags and dropped them into the toilet. I pulled off my shirt and supportive undershirt in one movement and handed the rolled up cotton to Jill. I slipped my arms through the straps and reached behind but I couldn't get the hooks to meet up.

"Let me do it." Jill tucked my shirts under her arm.

I turned and she connected the hooks and eyes.

Looking down, I saw beautiful clothing on my body for

the first time in my life.

It wasn't only the undershirt that was dull and utilitarian, designed for a little girl. All my clothes were conservative and uninteresting. Jeans that covered my hip bones and navel, spacious around my butt and legs. My tops were either loose sweaters that hid my growing breasts from the world or buttoned shirts. They weren't hopelessly out of style — they came from The Gap and other stores that offered clothing designed for teenagers, but they weren't the clothes Jill and some of the other girls wore.

Inside the tea-colored silk and lace, my breasts looked rounder. They were no longer small lumps of flesh that appeared out of place, something adult on a child's body. They looked like real breasts. I could hardly breathe.

"Is it comfortable?"

I nodded.

"My mother says comfort is very important."

"It feels great. I feel..."

She smiled. She hooked her pinky finger under the strap on my left shoulder. "It feels sexy. Right?"

"Yes."

The very thought conjured up my father's voice. I closed my eyes to silence him. His voice whispered that being sexy was not a worthy objective. I'd never actually heard him say anything of the sort, but I knew it aligned with his way of thinking. He didn't have to say it.

At some point, my mother would take me shopping for a real bra. But it would be nothing like this. With my eyes closed, I saw my future, the remaining years of high school spread out before me filled with surreptitious morning laundry and damp bras hanging in the back of my closet.

Not only did I feel sexy, I felt I'd won. I might have had to do it furtively, but I was in charge of my body and it felt amazing, as if the ceiling of that dank girls' bathroom had lifted off. I could spread huge, tea-colored, feathery wings and lift myself out of the building, beyond the chain-link fence surrounding the high school, over the Columbia River, and out of the city of Portland. I could go anywhere I wanted. I was in control of my life.

19

No one at home noticed my new lingerie. Like all teenage girls, I'd developed the ability to operate in stealth mode. I filled a small plastic container with liquid dish soap. I kept it in a box in my closet, underneath my box filled with magazine clippings with photographs of houses and furnishings I liked.

Over the months, Jill's mother had supplied me with three bras — the tea-colored one, an apricot one with a satin edge rather than lace across the top of the cups, and a pale blue with sheer cups and thinner wires. I cared for them as if they were as precious as the list of commandments from God, stored in the ark of the covenant. I didn't want to tear the fragile fabric and have to ask Jill for another. Her mother had already been so generous.

In the mornings, while the water was warming for my shower, I soaked my bra under the faucet and gently rubbed detergent into the delicate fabric. I rinsed it thoroughly. After my shower, I wrapped my hair in a towel, the bra tucked inside the folds in case I ran into one of my parents in the hallway. Before I toweled my hair dry, I draped the bra over a plastic hanger at the far left end of the pole in my closet.

My mother occasionally looked through my desk and dresser drawers. I'd seen the evidence in stacks of papers or sweaters that weren't as meticulously arranged as I'd left them.

I knew mothers sometimes investigated their daughters'

rooms. A few friends told me this was true, although not common. I wondered if she did it on command from my father, or if it was her own curiosity. Her own fear.

It was so clear to me what they feared. They wanted me to be like them, and I wasn't. They were certain that not being like them meant I would have a life that was embarrassing to them, and painful for me, ending with an eternity of unspeakable suffering.

Seeing the fear in their eyes was tiring. I pitied their lack of excitement for the possibilities of the world. All they thought about were the things that could go wrong. And when you want everyone to have beliefs and lifestyles identical to your own, there's a lot that can go wrong.

I think my mother searched my room looking for marijuana cigarettes, regular cigarettes, and my diary. I no longer wrote complete thoughts in my diary. The pages were filled with codes — initials, written in reverse, of boys I thought were cute. I wrote codes for girls I wanted to get back at for being mean, and I wrote down the grades I expected to get on papers, followed by the actual results. I'd cut a slit in the bottom of my box spring and hid the diary inside. She would never find it. Since her focus was on the cigarettes and diary, it was unlikely she would look through the clothes hanging in my closet.

20

On the Friday after the last day of school, my father took the day off work for a family trip to Cannon Beach. Instead of her usual sandwiches, my mother had stayed up late the night before frying chicken thighs and breasts until their battered skins were dark and crunchy. She'd made potato salad, and cut carrots into narrow sticks to dip into olive hummus. She'd sliced heirloom tomatoes and sprinkled them with a bit of oil and balsamic vinegar.

During the drive to the beach my brothers played with their GameBoys and my sister listened to a story on CD, the foam covered headphones larger than her ears. I stared out the window and tried to catch the attention of passengers in cars going the opposite direction.

As a car approached, I set my gaze out the window. I kept staring as the front of the other car drew closer, their front bumper passing ours, and then as we moved into a parallel position, widened my eyes. Three of every ten cars that passed carrying someone in the back seat on that side of the car, turned and looked at me.

One girl flipped me off. Little kids smiled, a few of them waved. Quite a few adults frowned, as if they could chastise me from a distance, through two sheets of glass, believing their own equally intense and authoritative looks could force a stranger to stop her rude staring.

And then we were at the beach.

I was the only one of my siblings who had never learned

to swim. My father tolerated this, but not happily. I refused to even walk to the shore and allow the water to lap at my toes. The bag I carried to the beach had two magazines and a book from my summer reading list — *The Great Gatsby*. While the others splashed in the water, I would read. When they dug enormous holes trying to go deep enough to reach water, I would walk along the soft mounds of dry sand and collect polished seashell fragments. If anyone wanted to toss the frisbee, I was game, but it had to take place on dry sand. I didn't even own a bathing suit. Suntanned legs in cut-offs were good enough for me.

Although my father finally, grudgingly, accepted my mother's word that my terrified screams made swimming lessons impossible, he harbored years of annoyance that I'd *won*. He saw this as a victory over his authority, a child wresting control from the parent. I don't know what my mother told him to make him give up forcing me to accept water splashed in my face. But he continued to needle me about my fear on a regular basis.

I was lying face down on my towel, my belly pleasantly full of a plump chicken breast and two servings of potato salad. I was reading about the lovely Gatsby home. The heat of the sun on my back, the warm blanket of sand I'd dug for my toes, and the slow, easy words of F. Scott Fitzgerald were making my eyelids heavy. I put the book down, splayed beside my elbow. I closed my eyes and rested my head on my folded hands.

Gulls cried over the water and waves crashed, turning my dreamy thoughts toward mild, half-waking nightmares. I heard water moving up the beach, saw the waves swelling larger than usual, crashing and racing across the sand, dragging me into the sea.

I felt as if I was moving.

The edge of my book bumped my elbow. I opened my eyes, squinting. It wasn't a dream, my towel was moving.

I turned on my side. My father stood near my feet, holding the edges of my towel, dragging it across the sand.

I kicked my legs. "Stop!"

"You're missing the beautiful water. It's a spectacular day. Blue sky, the ocean is sparkling."

"I like the sand."

"This nonsense has gone on far too long. You'll be crippled for the rest of your life if you don't learn how to swim. You can't let fear have the upper hand. You need to trust that the Lord will take care of you."

"Let go of my towel!" I sat up and grabbed the edges as if I were holding onto the sides of a boat.

He let go of the towel, grabbed my ankles, and yanked me toward him. While I was off balance from the sudden force, he bent down, picked me up, and put me over his shoulder.

"Gary!" My mother's voice pierced the warm air, growing louder as she ran toward us. "Put her down. That's not appropriate."

"She's too old for such childish anxiety."

"Don't," my mother said. "Don't do this. She's too old to force her into something she doesn't want."

"So that's it? We let her do as she pleases? How do you think that will turn out?"

"This is different. There's nothing immoral about not liking the water."

"It's the principle. She's disobeying. She's refusing to

trust the Lord."

"Why now? She hasn't liked the water since she was an infant. And her baptism…" Her voice broke slightly. "It's cruel."

He was done arguing. He walked quickly to the water, wading in up to his knees. He let me slide off his shoulder with a splash.

I sat down hard on the sandy bottom. I managed to keep my head above the gentle waves of low tide, but the cold sea soaked my cutoffs and beige shirt. It saturated my hair, dragging my head back with its weight.

I struggled to my feet. I tossed my hair out of my face and glared at him. I wanted to spit, but I could imagine what sort of repercussions that would have. As I turned to walk back to the beach, my father grabbed my arm.

"What's this?" He let go of my arm, and snapped my bra strap, showing its fine satiny shape through the wet cotton shirt that clung to my back.

"Hannah?"

My mother stood at the edge of the water. "It's… Alexandra?"

I laughed. I unbuttoned my shirt and tugged it off, fighting the grip of wet cotton. "See? A bra, Dad. I'm a woman. I need a bra. Nothing you can do about that. My body disobeyed you." I threw the wet shirt at him.

It slapped his chin and fell into the water.

I walked out of the waves and across the sand, enjoying the warm caress of sun already drying my skin.

21

San Francisco

Once again I was hanging onto the lamppost outside my apartment building, waiting for Uber to take me to Golden Gate Park. As if he'd been standing at his eighth floor window, waiting to see when I would leave the building, Isaiah emerged through the heavy glass doors and stopped a few feet from where I stood stretching my legs. He wore running shorts and a navy blue hoodie.

"Mind if I join you?"

I glanced at my phone, hoping Uber would sweep me away like Cinderella in a pumpkin-scented carriage. A modern Cinderella, one who hires her own carriage and sits alone in the back seat. I smiled my most neighborly smile. "I like to think about things when I run. Or not think. But I don't like to talk."

"Neither do I."

I studied his face. He looked into my eyes and it felt as if his gaze was penetrating my inky black pupils, looking deep inside, searching for a pinprick of light that would allow him to see my brain.

"I'll split the cost of the Uber, obviously," he said.

It wasn't all that expensive. And with lots of extra cash now that I didn't pay rent, not to mention the savings from walking to work and the gym and restaurants, rarely driving my car, which was securely parked underground, courtesy of

CoastalCreative, I wasn't watching every single dollar that flowed out of my wallet. Still, I hated that running cost anything at all.

Running should be free. That's one of the things that's so great about it. A pair of decent shoes and comfortable clothes and you're set. It's just you and the earth beneath your feet. It's breathing in more than your usual share of oxygen, fewer things intruding upon your thoughts as your brain musters all its energy to focus on landing each step solidly, on keeping your heart beating fast enough to pump blood for the rise in activity.

It's magical. And I love doing it by myself. But I did not like having to hire a car to get to a decent venue. The city was fantastic, the energy of all those people, but all those people get in the way of a runner.

"Sure. Okay. But I'm serious. I do not want to talk. At all. Not even to discuss a route. I'll choose the path that looks interesting and you can follow along, or not."

He nodded. "Sounds fair."

As if the driver had been waiting for us to complete our transaction, the white Toyota pulled to the curb. We climbed in. To signal his goodwill, Isaiah immediately tucked his earbuds into place and began scrolling through his playlist.

At the park, I stretched. Isaiah walked to another bench and did his own stretching, keeping his eyes averted. I was growing more interested in him. A guy who listens is impressive. Anyone, male or female, who isn't a compulsive talker automatically has my interest.

We ran four miles before the path brought us back to the picnic area outside the de Young. Isaiah put in the request for another car. I walked up the stairs to study the posters of upcoming exhibits. When I turned, he was sitting on a bench, madly texting. I walked back to where he was sitting.

He didn't speak until we were in the car, keeping plenty of space between our sweaty bodies. "Do you want to meet up for a beer or a glass of wine in the lounge tonight?" he said.

"Sure."

"Does six-thirty work?"

I nodded.

He coiled the cord for his earbuds and held it in his fist. The screen on his phone darkened. He didn't talk again until we reached the apartment building. We climbed out of the car and rode up together in the elevator, silent until he said, *see you at six-thirty*, before exiting to the eighth floor.

For the next two floors, I wondered if he'd emphasized the silence a little more than necessary. Still, it was impressive. And kind of cute.

22

Somewhere around the time when she was promoted to Director of Product Marketing, Tess had begun to realize she could afford most of the things she wanted. She no longer had to keep a running tab in her mind when she shopped for clothes, making sure the total didn't exceed the arbitrary number she'd decided on for that trip.

If there were two pairs of shoes that were equally desirable, she bought them both.

She'd joined a classier gym that was more female-friendly offering a luxurious locker room, and attracting, for the most part, the kind of men who didn't think a woman lifting weights was there to flirt.

She'd bought the condo in Russian Hill and the Mercedes. She bought nice wine, and no longer set a per/person budget for holiday gifts. When she saw something that would please her brothers, a sister-in-law, a niece or nephew or a friend, she bought it.

The condo had been over-priced, all condos in San Francisco were, but for the foreseeable future, the value would only increase. And it was perfect for her. An address like hers told people how well you were doing in your career. At the same time, it filtered your neighbors to those who shared, if not exactly the same, similar tastes in music and other lifestyle choices that, in some neighborhoods, created wars among people living within shouting distance.

Having money was nice. And the shocking infusion of

money when she was promoted to vice president was even more freeing. Alongside her pleasure in having nice things, she liked knowing she could take care of herself. She liked knowing her future was secure. Nothing and no one could come in and destabilize her life.

Over the past year, as she grew more accustomed to her ability to indulge in fantasies and long-buried desires, several potential acquisitions had begun to intrigue her. Desires she couldn't fully explain, items she'd never considered buying in the past, but now viewed in a different light.

The first had stirred her interest while she sat in the hospital, waiting for her leg to be stitched up after that horrific running accident with Alexandra.

They'd been jogging through a squalid neighborhood. It was a place they didn't belong, but Alexandra had been oblivious, insisting it was safe during daylight. First, a thuggish-looking man hooted at them. Alex acted as if his crude behavior was just something to be accepted. Then, they'd passed three men who were obviously making a drug deal. In the middle of the morning. Of course Santa Cruz had a fair share of drug traffic — beach towns drew partiers, and with them came the suppliers who provided tools for entertainment.

Alex had brushed that off just as casually.

When they began their run, Tess had made an offhand comment about one of the sagging little cottages being a perfect starter home for Alex. Alex bristled. She demanded to know what Tess meant by suggesting beggars couldn't be choosers. Tess hadn't meant anything serious. She wasn't calling Alex a beggar, for God's sake. It was just a saying!

After that, Alex veered off their course, leading the way

into that rough neighborhood. Tess hadn't been able to escape the impression that Alex wanted her to feel frightened. She'd forced Tess into a situation where she felt weak, out of control. And when Tess tried to escape, which any normal woman would do, leaving the ugly area and returning to streets that were more well kept, she'd paid the price. Alex had pushed her too hard and she'd strained her ankle. It couldn't support her when she tried to make the sudden turn back to the safer neighborhood.

Tess had fallen. A rake lying prongs up ripped a gash in her leg that was going to leave a scar. No matter what the doctor said about it not being noticeable, there would be a white line. The damaged flesh wouldn't tan with the rest of her skin, drawing attention to itself when she wore a bathing suit or workout shorts. She liked wearing skirts and dresses without stockings, and the scar would mar the appearance she'd worked so hard to keep sleek and well cared for.

Worse than the scarring was the fear. An unfamiliar feeling of utter helplessness.

Sitting in the waiting room, the curtain pulled around the bed, listening to other ER patients moaning with pain, complaining about inadequate insurance coverage, and chattering over one another about all the mundane logistics of a life interrupted by a trip to the hospital, one voice had been particularly loud.

A man two beds down from hers had caught someone trying to take the toolbox out of the bed of his truck. Without stopping to think, he chased the thief. They got into a fight that left the truck owner with two missing teeth, a black eye, and a cracked rib. His complaint was one long string of curse words. For over an hour Tess listened to him.

Every few minutes, the man's girlfriend punctured the steady flow. *I know, babe. He's a fucker. I know, babe.*

Tess was sick of listening to him. To her. The cursing and rage accomplished nothing. It was maddening to those forced to listen through thin cotton curtains. She'd muttered to herself, *I wish I could shoot that guy.*

And that's when the idea had formed. And she realized it had been buried inside for several years. The foul-mouthed man and his brainless girlfriend carefully excavated it from her subconscious.

She wanted a gun.

She wanted to own a gun. A small, compact handgun. She'd get a permit that allowed her to keep it in her purse. She could even strap it to her hip if she went running with Alex and Alex pulled a similar stunt. She'd seen images of guns that were designed for women. They were sexy and powerful.

A gun removed fear. A gun put you on an even footing with a mugger, a rapist, a serial killer. A gun meant you didn't have to try to hobble away when your ankle was swollen and weak. A gun meant you weren't left helplessly bleeding on a stranger's lawn. A gun meant no creep could harass you and force you to yield out of fear for your life.

It would be exciting. Her own little secret weapon.

Now was the right time. The world was tinged with violence, erupting without warning. You felt unsafe in movie theaters and shopping malls. You weren't really safe even going out for an evening, trying to lose yourself in the music and heat of bodies at a dance club. Statistics claimed violent crime was trending down, but she didn't believe it. And what did a trend matter if you were a victim? There could be only one violent crime in an entire year, and if you were the unlucky casualty, what did an optimistic chart even mean?

The more she thought about it, the more her desire grew. She wanted a gun for the pure, well-machined beauty of the weapon. She wanted it for the explosive sound and the potential to inflict death. More importantly, its ability to give her the upper hand in almost any situation.

It was ironic that the shop she'd identified as the best place to buy a handgun was in a neighborhood filled with homeless people pissing against the sides of buildings. It was a place where you were advised never to go at night, even in a group. Most of the vagrants were harmless, but there was always one, the raving lunatic, the exception to the rule.

No one knew where she was going right now, and she liked that feeling. She liked slipping out of the office and disappearing. Not a single person on the planet knew her whereabouts. Once she had that sexy little gun in her hand, she wouldn't have to worry about being in *the wrong place at the wrong time*, a rule women were required to follow, while men, for the most part, skated free.

From now on, Tess would be in charge at work and on the street. The power would be in her hands. Never again would she be splayed on a stranger's lawn, blood pumping furiously out of her body. She wouldn't be begging someone to stay with her instead of going for towels to stop the flow of blood, because having those men notice her — wounded, helpless, alone — was worse than bleeding to death.

23

Portland

Within fifteen minutes of flinging my wet shirt at my father and parading my tea-colored bra for him, my mother, and my open-mouthed siblings, we packed up the car and left Cannon Beach. The drive home was silent. No one looked at me, although my oldest brother, Eric, home from college, poked me in the hip bone three or four times.

I was wearing my mother's zippered nylon jacket, sitting in stiff, damp denim cutoffs. My wet shirt was rolled up in the back of the mini van.

My mother shifted in her seat, adjusting the position of her legs, turning her head to look out the side window, then glancing at my father. She moved her hands on her lap with helpless, fluttering motions. My father tipped his head from side to side, snapping his neck every few miles. My siblings, even Eric, shot not very subtle looks at each other from bowed heads. I couldn't see whether they were sharing smiles or fear or a combination of the two, depending on who was shooting the look.

The silence didn't bother me at all. I liked knowing they were all thinking about me. They were remembering how I shocked them, remembering my beautiful bra. They were adjusting to the fact that I'd grown up. I smiled and faced the window, returning to the game I'd played on the drive to the ocean. This time, four of every ten cars had a passenger who felt me watching.

After an equally quiet dinner, I was told to load the dishwasher and clean up the kitchen by myself. Usually two of us were teamed for kitchen clean-up.

My parents retreated to the living room for their nightly glass of sherry.

The church leadership at Pure Truth Tabernacle taught explicitly that the Bible forbade alcohol. They glossed over the story of Jesus turning water into wine, insisting that the point of the story was not the wine, but the miracle of transformation. Wine was symbolic of a heart anointed with the Holy Spirit. And that story came about because people in that day, in the pre-Christian, or rather imminent-Christian era, drank wine at weddings. Now, alcohol was an evil influence that turned people away from Godly behavior.

Neither one of my parents explained why they flouted this clear directive. When I asked my mother, she said that sherry wasn't alcohol. I pointed out that it contained alcohol, and she simply looked away and left the room. My father told me it wasn't my place to question adults.

The dinner plates were resting between their prongs in the dishwasher tray. The silverware stood in the rack, and the pots that needed washing by hand were arranged to the left of the sink. I closed the dishwasher door, and turned on the sink faucet. As water pounded onto porcelain, I tiptoed to the door leading to the dining room. The living room was on the opposite side.

I carefully opened the door just wide enough to slip through, and not wide enough for the sound of running water to grow too loud, announcing the door had opened.

I walked quietly between the table and the windows to

the wall where an arched opening led to the living room. Standing close to the opening, I waited for my parents' voices. The only sound was the clink of glass followed by the thud of the decanter on the coffee table. So, my flamboyant rebellion had created the desire for a second glass of sherry. I wondered if it was for both, or just my father.

"You need to find a way to control her," my father said.

"I can't."

"You're repeating yourself, Hannah. I already told you, that's not a viable answer."

"You should talk to her."

"Not about women's underthings. That's not right. I told you I didn't want her wearing that kind of thing too soon. Our shameless culture pushes girls to be women before they're ready. We can't let the world control what we do."

"I didn't buy it for her. I don't know where she got it."

"You must have seen it in her…things, noticed it… women…"

"I don't know. She does what she wants."

"Not acceptable."

"Her body…"

"I don't want to discuss that. I want you to tell me what you're going to do about the situation."

"She's growing up. I can't stop that from happening. *You* can't stop that from happening. I'll buy her some modest bras tomorrow, but she needs to wear one."

"Men look at her."

"What men?"

"Men that shouldn't. And now I know why. I had no idea that's the kind of thing she was wearing. Giving off that attitude."

"What men?"

"Lots of men."

"That's sick. Stop saying that."

"It's the truth.

"I don't think they do."

"I want it to stop. She's a child and she acts like she's twenty-five."

"That's not my fault." My mother's voice wavered, growing faint. The sound of glass on wood punctuated her words. "She's always had a mind of her own. You know that."

"You need to find a way to make her understand morality."

"I'm doing the best I can." Her mother was crying now. "I don't think men are looking at her. You're just saying that to upset me. It's not true."

"I don't say things that aren't true. It's happening. Trust me on this."

"How do you even know? Do you look at girls like Alexandra?!" Her voice rose, thin at the edges, piercing.

"Please control your emotions."

"You're scaring me."

"It's what happens. Women your age lose their bloom. You know this. Girls that age...close to becoming fertile. It's God's way, but it needs to be controlled. That's your job."

For several minutes, the only sound coming from the living room was my mother's whimpering, bursts of soft choking sounds. Then she whispered, "It can't be controlled."

I heard the decanter clink on a glass again. I scurried back into the kitchen. I ran the faucet over the dishpan. I squirted in liquid soap and watched bubbles explode, rising quickly until they threatened to spill over the edge.

24

Santa Cruz

After Tess's initial encounter with Steve Montgomery at the sales kick-off meeting, she began meeting with him weekly, as he'd proposed. It was nearly two years before their relationship changed suddenly and dramatically, almost without warning.

Their weekly meetings were laced with mild flirting. Not flirting, exactly, but a charge in the atmosphere that couldn't be ignored. She looked forward to them a little too eagerly, and she soaked up the hormonal buzz even as a tiny voice, far at the back of her mind whispered that she should pull back, be less friendly. It was hard to maintain a cool approach. She felt like a teenager. Not a good thing in a lot of ways, in most ways, but it was an addictive phase of life that was hard to let go of.

She'd never thought it would go anywhere. Then, it did.

It happened in a moment when she felt weak, when Steve knew she was weak. Since then, she'd wished regularly that she could go back in time and undo it, redo it in a way that suited her.

They were at a customer site, meeting in a beautiful conference room. An entire wall was made of glass. It looked out on a lush garden with a fountain. Not one of those big splashy things, but a quiet flow of water over the sides of an enormous ceramic jug. The sound couldn't be heard inside the conference room, but every time she looked at it, she felt the calming flow inside of her.

Steve had stepped out of the conference room while she was speaking. He'd been sequestered in a room that was no more than a closet, designed for conducting private phone calls, with a desktop computer for hooking up and printing documents.

As she was explaining the service offering that would be sold as a required part of CoastalCreative's next software release, one of the junior engineers began talking while she was speaking. No *excuse me*, no raising his hand, no leaning forward to indicate by the set of his shoulders that he wanted her to pause for a moment.

He informed her the service offering she was describing was bullshit. The on-site support for which CoastalCreative wanted to charge an *obscene* amount could be done remotely. She told him there were gaps in the workflow that meant remote support wasn't completely feasible yet.

He raised his voice.

She tried to explain further.

He continued talking over her. One of his peers joined in, trying to explain on her behalf, creating confusion around the entire room.

She asked them in a cool tone, respectfully, to let her finish and provide further details.

The engineer layered his voice over her request to finish speaking. She raised her voice, telling them she could resolve the confusion when they *stopped providing inaccurate information* and let her *finish* what she was saying.

At that moment, the door to her left swung open and a gush of cool air tore through the room, touching the puffy, overheated skin of her face. Steve stepped inside. He gave her a piercing look that made her skin burn more fiercely.

When the customers were gone and she was packing up her laptop, he took her upper arm. In a rather too-loud voice himself, he told her it was uncool to blow up at a customer. She argued that she hadn't blown up.

You did. It's understandable, a lot of women have trouble controlling their emotions, but you need to learn.

She pulled away and he quickly let go of her arm. She walked past him and out the door, glad that it fell softly closed behind her and didn't suggest she was slamming out in a show of temper.

25

The hotel bar was so dark, she was surprised he'd seen her. She'd been sitting alone in a grouping of whicker furniture. She was nestled in a chair with a ridiculously high, round back, impossible to see it was occupied unless you approached from the front.

She held an empty martini glass in one hand, the swizzle stick in the other. She'd just sucked off the olive and was rolling it around inside her mouth when Steve was suddenly standing in front of her.

"Can I join you?"

She shrugged and began chewing the olive.

"What are you drinking?" He took the glass from her hand.

"Martini. Ketel One. No ice. One olive."

He returned a few minutes later. He handed her the martini and placed a glass of what looked like Patron on the table. "Don't sulk. It's unprofessional," he said.

"What gave you the impression I'm sulking? How about you don't pretend to know my thoughts or my mood."

"I can always tell when a woman is sulking."

If she'd had a momentary thought that he might be hitting on her, it dissipated.

"Now you're really sulking. Because you know I'm right."

She sipped her martini and said nothing.

He continued to toss out throw-away comments and she continued to say nothing. The trouble was, she sipped the vodka and vermouth much too quickly — it gave her something to do with her mouth so she didn't shoot it off. Obviously, Steve thought she had no control over her tongue, although he hadn't been in the room, so he had no idea what really happened. And he'd stepped out of the room again. He didn't know how the conversation came alive after that.

The kid was insulted, obviously didn't like a woman knowing more than he did, and didn't like that no one was marveling at his brilliance. It happened all the time with people fresh out of school. They assumed they were always right. And they assumed that knowing the latest technology was the only requirement for success. But once she took firm control, he backed down.

"Now you're going to freeze me out?" Steve said.

"I'm not freezing anything."

"You're not talking. Giving me the silent treatment."

She took a sip of her drink. She was pleasantly buzzed and he was so good-looking. His sexism was obnoxious, a fishbone in her throat, snagging at the tender skin each time she swallowed. And yet, some perverted part of herself found him fascinating.

"You're an incredible woman," he said. "My jokes about the fluffiness of marketing are all in fun. And you're a star at your job. One of the best I've seen. At the risk of pissing you off with a sexist comment…"

She laughed. Did that mean he recognized his comments were degrading and wrong?

"Your presentation style is seductive. You have them eating out of your hand."

Her body melted under the words that suggested she'd achieved everything she'd worked so hard for. He respected her. Better, he admired her. That admiration was something she craved. In spite of her wish to not need it, she did.

They talked about the meeting, the various reactions. They batted around their estimates of the chances the sales team would close the deal that week. He worried the tension would hurt things, but he admitted she'd been factually correct. She'd just handled it badly. He admitted he'd raised his voice with customers in his younger days. But he'd learned his lesson. Not that he was so much older and more experienced. He had three years on her, at most.

Seeing that slim, barely noticeable hint that he had a vulnerable side, combined with the draining of her martini glass, made the entire day, his condescension, slide down her throat.

She couldn't recall who made the first move. She thought it was his hand on her knee, but maybe her shin had brushed his leg first. Had she ever wanted a man as badly as she wanted him? It scared her to think maybe his caustic comments about women were part of the attraction. He was confident in what he believed, spoke with authority, didn't worry about how he was coming across. There was an appeal in that self-assurance.

Later, she worried that he'd been selling to her the entire time, maybe since the day she met him. He'd closed the deal and she'd swallowed the deadly hook with its luscious bait, like any customer does with a salesmen who is so good at his job, no one notices he's always selling.

26

Ever since that first tea-colored bra, silk and lace, delicate yet comfortable, I've never scrimped on lingerie. I shopped in high-end department stores while I still lived with my parents. Once I was on my own, I became a devoted patron of boutique lingerie stores.

A bra and underpants or thong, a camisole or night clothes, are the closest things to your skin. Lingerie is meant to caress your body and I don't want to be caressed by stiff cotton or garments with rough stitching or cheap labels that scratch and leave ugly red patches on my skin. I like silk and satin and gentle lace. I like well-designed clothes that fit perfectly.

The drawer that holds my lingerie is a rainbow of pastels and red, navy and black. Some of the black lingerie is spiced up with traces of red. I've never owned a white bra, although I do have camisoles and boxer-style shorts that are white.

Getting ready for my glass of wine with Isaiah, I thought carefully about my lingerie color. He would be seeing it soon enough and I wanted to consider what would be communicated. Not that a guy I'd just met was going to get a message hidden in a lime green bra paired with a black thong, but it would create a certain type of impression.

Illustrating the way life likes to evade your control and throw unexpected turns in your path, my phone buzzed while

I was shaving my legs.

A photo of Tess that I'd taken during one of our morning coffee meetings appeared on the screen. My first instinct was to let her call go to voicemail. I'd put in enough effort trying to connect with her, I'd sent her far too many text messages. It wasn't unheard of that she'd get in touch on the weekend, but after ignoring me for over a week, it was unfair. She acted as if her time was platinum and mine was coal. Boss or not, it was degrading.

From the beginning, the last word I'd use to describe Tess's management style was degrading. She sought my opinions, she fought for my first pay raise, she confided in me as if were a peer. In every way she treated me like her equal. She never questioned me when I had to leave work early, never expressed disapproval over a longer than normal lunch hour. When I wasn't in my office, she simply texted me, never demanding to know why I wasn't available.

But it was the weekend. I was shaving my legs. And she...

The call disappeared into voicemail, technology making my decision for me. I dragged the razor up my leg and rinsed the blades under the faucet. I made two more passes before the phone told me there was a voicemail.

I finished shaving my legs. I rubbed them with lotion. I decided to save the lime green for another time, putting on a sheer black bra and skimpy underpants — two panels connected by satin cords at the hips.

A short black skirt with calf-high flat black boots, a pale yellow sweater, a quick brush with the mascara wand, and I was ready. I picked up the phone and carried it to the couch from where I could see my entire place — kitchen, eating bar, balcony, and bed. I flopped down and put my heels on the coffee table.

Six-fifteen. Depending on what she wanted, I had plenty of time to listen to the message and call her back before it was time to meet Isaiah. Depending on what she wanted.

I pressed play and tapped the speaker icon. I placed the phone on the table.

Hey. It's Tess. I know it's the weekend…well, obviously it's the weekend, I don't have to point that out.

She laughed softly. I thought I heard the suggestion of guilt, the sudden awareness that she hadn't spoken to me in days.

Are you free to meet for dinner? My treat. There's a new French place I wanted to try. It's on Mason. Not too far. I could meet you there about seven-thirty, if that works. It has great reviews. Actually, I didn't mean to sound so casual about the time. I already have a reservation… at seven-thirty. We should catch up. There's a lot to talk about. Call me a-sap. Bye.

I stood and walked to the glass door. I slid it open and stepped onto the balcony. A stiff breeze pushed up against my face and ran down my body. I walked to the railing and looked out toward the bay. The feeling of the wind trying to shift my position and the street far below was exhilarating.

A small part of me wanted to meet her for dinner. The curious part. And the survival part. Our relationship needed to get back to its former status. I needed her depending on me, telling me everything that was going on, even if it was unrelated to me and my job. I craved the feeling of power that comes with knowing more than your peers, having an inside track that's tied to the sources of power. It's as comforting as a security blanket.

She expected me to be available, eager to see her, or she wouldn't have made a reservation.

It was hard to decide whether I was more likely to get the upper hand by agreeing to go and spending an evening filling in and smoothing out the cracks between us, or by remaining aloof.

I could call and tell her I had plans, or not respond at all, sending a text later in the evening. I wasn't sure how she'd react to any of those scenarios.

I turned my back to the railing and studied my apartment.

I wanted Isaiah. I'd been thinking about him all afternoon. It wasn't easy to silence that desire in favor of dinner, no matter how excellent the food. And I expected my glass of wine with Isaiah would turn into dinner and then sex. The meal might rival what Tess had to offer, and the anticipation of flirting over food was enticing.

I remembered her last terse, bordering on rude, text message — *You don't need to keep texting me.*

She could wait. She could cancel her reservation. She could wonder what I was up to. It was a risk, but in spite of everything she'd done and said recently, my gut said she needed me just as much as I needed her. I hoped my gut was on the up and up.

27

Even though the painting of the woman with the exposed bones and muscles made Jen feel queasy, she seated herself beside it, knowing that sooner or later, Alexandra would look in that direction. For some reason, Alexandra couldn't stop staring at the hideous image.

Jen had seen Alexandra the minute she entered the lounge, as if the gorgeous new neighbor had a shimmering aura visible to everyone. She probably was one of the best looking women in the room. Jen had noticed several pairs of male eyes following her progress to the bar with an unbelievable lack of subtlety.

There was something about Alexandra that was more than just her nice body and pretty face. An energy rising off her skin, forcing you to look at her, watching the smallest movement, her lips as she talked, the glint in her eyes. You wanted to listen to her, you wanted to tell her things that should be kept to yourself. Risky things, exposing yourself like that disgusting painting, letting Alexandra see every ugly thing about you because, like the painting, she wouldn't consider it ugly.

She wouldn't really tell Alexandra very much, but the desire was there.

Being asked so many questions had made Jen nervous. Every time Alexandra closed her mouth, Jen wanted to speak. But why did everyone think asking about your job was the most important way to start the process of getting to know someone? She hated that. In high school, everyone wanted to know what electives you were taking, what teacher you had, what bands you liked, what TV shows you watched. As an adult, it was always the job.

It seemed as if people asked because they wanted to find out how much money you made. A job shouted how much you had in the bank. They might as well tattoo their salaries on their forearms.

I'm in sales at this or that high tech company meant *big infusions of cash at the end of every year.* I'm a yoga teacher — *poor but happy about it.* I work at Sephora — *trying to improve my life, not making very much, but spending too much on cosmetics, justifying it because of the employee discount.* I'm with Morgan Stanley — *filthy rich* — why was he living in an apartment? I'm an attorney — *not yet a partner, but moving out of the building once that happens.*

It was tiresome. It was embarrassing.

Jen sipped her wine. She'd ordered wine because that's what Alexandra drank. She'd hoped to run into her and it was a huge disappointment that the minute Alexandra entered the room, her gaze met Isaiah's and she walked toward him quickly, not pausing to look around. So, they'd planned to meet.

It figured that Alexandra would get the good one.

Isaiah Parker was one of the nicest guys in the building. Hot *and* nice. David Lasher, his roommate, not so much.

Of course someone like Alexandra would get the good one. She was so beautiful and interesting and had that thing that made you want to be in her presence. Men and women both probably worshipped her.

And Jen was stuck with the not so great one. A creep, really.

David had seemed nice enough when she first met him. He'd bought her a glass of wine, treated her like a lady. She loved that, especially now. She liked being made to feel special. She liked a man looking into her eyes when she talked, as if he was really listening to her. Not just listening, but understanding what she was saying, caring about what she had to say, instead of thinking she was stupid. Or just pretending to listen until he could get her into bed.

But after a while, she'd realized it was an act. He looked in everyone's eyes when they talked, but later, especially lying in bed with her after sex, he said terrible things about them.

She's too fat for that dress.

He's a bore — this after David had spent an hour asking the guy questions about scuba diving.

She drinks way too much. What a lush.

When Jen reminded him that he'd urged the other girl — Karen — to have a fourth glass of wine before they all walked to the pizza place for dinner, he'd laughed. "She didn't have to."

"But you made her feel like she was being rude to turn it down."

"Hey. It's her brain, her body. I didn't *make* her feel a fucking thing."

Jen sighed and put her glass on the table. She crossed her legs and tugged her jeans where her boots had gripped them and pulled the seam close to her shin bone. The sides of her head itched. She raked her fingers through her hair and tilted her head back to stretch the skin.

No matter which way she positioned herself on the couch, she saw the painting from the corner of her eye. It was such an ugly painting. Most people hardly looked at it.

Why couldn't they choose something upbeat — a waterfall or people in a park. Or even a splash of color on canvas that didn't show anything recognizable.

Instead, it seemed like they wanted everyone to feel nervous, worried about what was going on inside their bodies. Or maybe they wanted everyone to freak out, to feel that life was too scary to think about so they'd better buy another beer or glass of wine. That was probably it. They didn't provide the lounge just so everyone in the building could socialize. It was extra income for them. They sold gallons of wine and beer every night, and at fifteen bucks for a glass of wine, you could be sure that wasn't what it cost them.

She picked up her glass and took a sip. The woman's exposed eyeballs seemed to be studying Jen with such intensity, they appeared ready to roll out of her skull. Jen turned again. It was uncomfortable and she had to put one leg on the couch in a half-crossed-legged position, but at least she could no longer see those eyeballs, floating in the sockets, nerves and blood vessels leading to the brain.

Alexandra and Isaiah stood near the windows at the far side of the room. Alexandra faced the painting, and she seemed to be keeping her eye on it, but her gaze never dropped to the couch where Jen was sitting. Or if it did, she wasn't acknowledging Jen's presence. Alexandra held her wine glass with both hands. She laughed. Isaiah watched her as she talked, one hand in the pocket of his slacks, the other holding his glass. When he spoke, he gestured with the glass. Any minute, the wine might slosh all over the front of Alexandra's yellow sweater.

They didn't even know Jen was here. She might as well be invisible. She drank her wine and watched Alexandra and

Isaiah, wondering what they were talking about, wondering whether Alexandra wanted to be friends with her.

28

Some of the things Tess had told Alex about her relationship with Steve Montgomery weren't true.

For example, it hadn't been just the one time that she'd slept with him. They weren't exactly having a relationship. She wasn't sure at all what they were doing, except possibly jeopardizing her career. Maybe his, but more likely hers. They'd had dinner twice, lunch a few times, and sex more times than she could count.

It was true that Steve had supported Tess's quest for Alex's first raise. It was also true he'd objected to giving Alex a *five* rating. And yes, she'd finally told him off about criticizing her for raising her voice — yelling, in Steve's words — speaking firmly, in hers — to a customer. She thought he'd respected her position more after that. Maybe.

Now, the non-relationship was getting complicated and unmanageable. He wanted to spend the night with her, to have her stay at his place every Thursday, when he was in town. He wanted to take her to dinner every week. He wanted to spend the night at her condo, which he'd never seen.

She enjoyed his company, talking about work was exhilarating. The sex was awesome. But she was pretty sure she didn't really like him all that much. She should have followed her initial instinct and not allowed her animal nature to overrule. And the more she thought about not liking him, the more he pushed to expand his presence in her life.

It was a mistake to have a relationship at work. Everyone knew that. Yet when you spent most of your waking hours, and all of your good hours giving your soul to your company, it happened. It was easy to find common ground with a co-worker. Talking about work over dinner and in bed, when you already spent most of your waking hours working and thinking about the company, probably wasn't healthy. But work was addictive. Having power in an organization, crafting strategy, helping to win new customers, growing revenue was like a game. And utterly consuming. Dealing with complex decisions and plans satisfied every fiber of your being.

When Alex had ignored her invitation to try the new French place, Tess had called Steve. If she'd gone to the restaurant alone, she'd spend the entire meal mentally picking at her irritation with Alex. She would brood about whether or not Alex was playing a game of her own. The wine would taste sour and the food weigh heavy in her stomach. She needed the distraction of Steve's non-stop flow of words and his grandiose style. But the minute he eagerly accepted, she regretted it.

Not only had she crossed another line by inviting him, it was Saturday night, which suggested they were a couple, or headed in that direction. It disgusted her that she was so confused about the issue. She was a Senior Vice President, for God's sake. She was dithering and debating with herself like she was in junior high school. And also like a pre-teen, she had a shameful desire to talk about it. Talking to Alex was out of the question. She'd already said too much. Anyone at CoastalCreative was out of the question. And her other friendships had become the type of friends you catch up with once or twice a year, not anyone you could grab a glass of wine with and pour out your relationship angst.

The food at the French place had been fantastic, her mind consumed as she'd expected, and Steve's bed as satisfying as always, even though he sulked when she left at one-thirty in the morning.

Now, she sat in her sunroom, comforted by the warmth seeping through the windows of the semi-circular room tucked between the living room and master bedroom. Her phone was on her leg, a note on the locked screen announced that she had a message from Steve Montgomery. The problem was, in parentheses after his name was a tiny number seven. Why the hell had he sent her seven text messages?

Reluctantly, she pressed the home button and tapped the message icon.

Steve Montgomery: *Last minute invite to go sailing with a guy I knew at Salesforce. Want to go?*

Steve Montgomery: *Are you free today?*

Steve Montgomery: *Hey beautiful!*

Steve Montgomery: *I need to let him know about sailing in the next twenty minutes.*

Steve Montgomery: *We'd drive to Tiburon and leave from there. Do you like sailing? Why don't I know that about you? How have we never talked about sailing? I love it.*

Steve Montgomery: *U there?*

Steve Montgomery: *Okay, now I feel like a stalker. Ha ha.*

She put her phone on the table. She loved sailing. Who didn't? And if she'd seen the first message, even the first two, she might have agreed, despite the significance of their relationship seeping further into the weekend. But the one about *how have we never talked about sailing*...what did that mean? For some reason, it made her feel claustrophobic.

She closed her eyes and pressed her thumb and index finger against the bridge of her nose, then yanked them away. She'd probably smeared her makeup. The room was getting too hot. She was overheated and she had to pee. She stood suddenly and went into the bedroom. It was much cooler.

After she peed, she returned to the sunroom. She had to answer before she lost her nerve.

Tess Turner: *Already have a commitment. Enjoy!*

As soon as she locked the screen, the phone buzzed. She tossed it on the cream and blue flowered armchair across from her. It wedged itself between the cushion and the side.

Before she talked to him again, she needed to unravel her mind. She needed to figure out how she'd gotten herself into this situation, sleeping and more or less dating a man who would, over the long term, irritate her endlessly with self-satisfied superiority.

29

Isaiah bought us each a glass of Chardonnay and we stood near the windows in the lounge. Every few minutes, I glanced at the painting of the exposed woman, letting it seep inside of me. Even so, I managed to listen attentively to Isaiah.

He started by telling me he was a foodie, in the process of turning his food passion into a career by attending culinary school. A gorgeous man and food. The perfect combination.

I smiled and urged him to tell me why he loved food. Of course, everyone loves food to one degree or another, but some of us have a religious experience at the sight of a wedge of triple cream cheese or fresh trout or a moist pork chop with a delicate, crisp ribbon of fat surrounding it. Isaiah was pretty much like me — he'd rather eat a nice dinner than just about anything. More so than me, he felt the same ecstasy when he prepared a satisfying meal.

"I feel like I'm looking into the face of a god," I said.

He turned slightly red.

I didn't smile, and he turned redder.

Quickly, he shifted topics. He liked to run, sometimes. He surfed, played basketball, and spent too much time entering other worlds via gaming.

He was lucky enough to live in a two-bedroom apartment subsidized by his uncle. So, he and I were both living on subsidies. "Since I'm into sports, serious about my education, I guess my uncle thinks I'll be a good influence on David."

"David?"

"My cousin."

"Oh." I took a sip of wine. "I met a David…from the eighth floor."

Isaiah described his cousin, and I knew it was the same guy.

David was a bit of a fuck-up, Isaiah said, but he'd met worse. David wasn't a slob and he didn't do drugs, smoked too much pot, but didn't get completely wasted, and didn't make a lot of noise.

"You describe him by what he isn't?"

He laughed. "Sometimes, what someone isn't tells the whole story."

"Absolutely." I smiled.

He touched my hand, brushing his finger across my knuckles. "Should we just have the one glass and then go to dinner?"

"Sure."

"What kind of food do you like?"

"I would describe it more by what I don't like."

"And that is?" He sipped his wine, the glass nearly empty.

"Sashimi. I do like rare beef but never uncooked fish. I also don't like eggs or radishes."

"Eggs are good for you."

"I feel quite healthy, so I don't think they're critical."

"You look healthy."

I smiled.

"It's a specific list," he said. "And very short."

"I'm not a fan of mussels or cooked celery either."

"Got it. But Indian? Chinese? Steak?"

"All of the above."

"There's a great dim sum place on Stevenson. It shouldn't be too crowded since it mostly caters to the lunch crowd. Want to try that?"

"Sounds good." I thought about steak for a moment, then sadly let go and conjured up the taste of pan fried potstickers with chili oil.

He took my empty glass out of my hand. "We'll save the steak for another time. I hope."

"I would love to have steak another time."

He put our glasses on the bar and we went outside.

"It's about eight blocks. Are you okay walking?"

"I like walking."

We started off at a good pace, talking mostly about the buildings we passed. It was cool and windy, but my new coat kept out the chill.

Along with the largest array of dim sum I'd ever experienced, we had a bottle of Cakebread Chardonnay. Isaiah said it was one of his favorites. It made me wonder if he'd planned the dinner more than it appeared, starting with Chardonnay at the lounge. He nudged me in that direction, asking if Chardonnay was *okay*, rather than asking what kind of wine I wanted.

He talked about culinary school and told me to let him know whenever I wanted to come to one of their periodic tastings, open to the public.

He kept his eyes on mine, even as he sampled dim sum, pulling apart pork buns and sliding dumplings through a puddle of chili oil and white vinegar. The chopsticks seemed to spin around his fingers as if he'd been using them all his life.

It always happens with dim sum. We kept pointing to

offerings as the carts passed by, tiny plates crowding our table, and then, quite suddenly, we'd had too much. The noodles filled our bellies and even the last of the Chardonnay couldn't stir up a spacious feeling that allowed for the remaining dumplings and the single pork bun.

Walking home, it was cold, the wind stronger. Isaiah put his arm around me which helped with the cold, but made our forward progress awkward as I bumped against him and we tried to keep our legs moving with a similar rhythm.

When we stepped into the elevator, he kissed me gently on the lips. No tongue, no rushed, fervent and aggressive passion. Just a nice kiss. He pressed the button for the eighth floor and we rose quickly. He didn't ask whether I wanted to go to his place. He stepped off the elevator and I followed.

The apartment was dark. He'd planned more than just the Chardonnay. Either David had something going or Isaiah had asked him to leave. After my two, brief encounters, David didn't strike me as someone who graciously accommodated his roommate's sex life.

"David's at a concert. He won't be home until after two."

I smiled.

He opened a bottle of Chardonnay and poured a bit into two glasses. I thought about David, curious whether he knew anything about this. I wasn't sure why that thought passed through my mind, but it did, several times. Then, I was sipping Chardonnay, putting the glass on the table, and leaning into Isaiah as we kissed.

The kissing went on for quite a long time. A half hour, maybe more.

When he stood and led me toward the smaller of the two bedrooms, I had a brief moment of wanting to check out the rest of the arrangement in the two-bedroom floor plan, and take a peek into the master bedroom, but I was led quickly into Isaiah's room and the door closed firmly.

We undressed, watching each other with tiny, friendly smiles on our faces.

As we touched each other's bodies, just before my mind became completely consumed by sensation, I thought about David's offer to store my boxes. There was no way a stack of thirty folded pieces of cardboard would have fit in this room. He'd acted as if he didn't have a roommate, just an empty room waiting to hold my overflow.

Maybe the offer wasn't genuine. One of those people who offers, making himself look generous and helpful, and then backs out, giving an excuse that only holds up in his own mind.

Then, I forgot about boxes and David and people who make false promises.

30

It was impossible to stop thinking about the painting in the lounge of my apartment building. If I thought I could afford something like that, I'd ask to buy it and hang it in my living area. I could stare at that image all day long and still not know all of its secrets.

I'd stopped by the management office and asked about the painting. The signature in the lower left was a flamboyant, slightly gothic letter *G*, but there was no card with information about the artist or the year it had been painted.

The woman at the desk didn't know the name of the artist, didn't know how much it cost, and didn't know why it had been selected as one of only three pieces of art in the lounge area. She was able to find a card from the gallery where it had been purchased.

She handed the card to me. *Herriman's Fine Art & Sculpture*

It was on Folsom, just four or five blocks away. I returned the card and thanked her.

I went back up to my apartment. I filled a glass with filtered water.

I'd completely forgotten to send a message to Tess about her dinner invite. I sent a short text, acknowledging I'd missed her call, telling her I hoped her dinner was good. I didn't apologize and she didn't respond.

I stripped off my boots, jeans, and sweater. I tied my hair on top of my head, took a quick shower, and dressed in a short black dress with a tiny jacket and ballet slipper shoes. I made my eyes up in dark shadows, lots of liner, and a bit of dark color in my brows, finishing off my face with nude lip gloss.

Outside, the air was warmer than I'd expected, a nice surprise for my tiny jacket and bare legs. I turned right and started walking along Howard Street. Like it was during most of the day, except when the sun was directly overhead, the street was bathed in thick shadows. My reflection appeared and disappeared as I passed large windows, weaving among people walking more slowly.

It wasn't that I was racing, you can only walk so fast in ballet slipper shoes and I didn't want my feet aching by the time I arrived at the gallery. Tired, sore feet don't contribute to an aloof and classy demeanor. They have a way of making your jaw look tight and your eyes tired from too much attention to your feet and too much effort looking frantically for a place to sit down.

I stopped at the corner and waited with others for the light to change. I ran my fingers through my hair, pushing it off my face. As I lowered my arms, I turned slightly. To my left was the man in the brown leather jacket, looking directly at me. He wore the 49ers hat pushed higher so I could see more of his nose and cheekbones. I faced the light, but felt I turned too suddenly. Did he realize I'd recognized him?

There was no reason not to confront him, but I hesitated. This was San Francisco — the fourteenth largest city in the U.S. — not Capitola or Aptos. There were hundreds of thousands of people. Nearly a million at the last count. Denying he was following me would be simple. He could make me out to be unbalanced. Paranoid. Harassing *him*. Thousands of men wore brown leather jackets. Millions were fans of the 49ers and Giants.

For all I knew, he lived in my building, worked on the same street I did and had a perfectly legitimate reason for being in the area on a regular basis.

But there was something about the way he was always the same distance away from me, always looking in my direction, that told me he was watching me. Possibly he wasn't following me everywhere, or following me at all, but he was keeping an eye on me.

The green light winked and the cluster of pedestrians surged into the street, spilling over the painted lines of the crosswalk. A BMW honked at a woman whose computer bag swung out from her hip and tapped his grill. She didn't flinch and continued weaving her way forward.

On the opposite curb, I saw the brown leather jacket, walking rather slower than everyone around him, deliberately lagging until he saw whether I would turn or keep going straight.

I turned left, intending to walk around the block and back to the apartment building. Even though it was only a few more blocks to the gallery, I'd get an Uber. The guy was bothering me. I didn't want him to know that and I didn't want him to know where I was headed.

There was no secret about my destination. I had no plans to buy artwork in the immediate future. I was just curious about the painting and wanted to find out more about it, read an artist's statement or something like that. See his or her other work, if there was any. I wanted to know if the other work included additional transparent figures, or if the painting in the lounge was one of a kind.

But all of that was my business. I didn't want him knowing anything about me.

If I turned to see where he was now, he'd know I was on to him, but the desire drilled into my stomach, ticked through my head, making me feel as if I'd had too much caffeine. As if I'd lost control over my own body, I stopped suddenly. I turned. He was only a few yards back.

Our eyes met. He didn't smile and neither did I.

He kept on at the same pace, passed me, and disappeared around the corner.

I stared after him. Now that he'd disappeared, I could head back to the gallery. But I didn't know the streets well enough to be sure he couldn't loop back around and find me before I reached it.

What the hell did he want? Maybe he just wanted to meet me, and he was a man with a low score on the social skill continuum, thinking he'd follow me until I made the first move. He didn't give off a creepy vibe, like some guy following me with plans to kidnap and dismember me — a too-common thought when a woman feels edgy about a man behaving oddly. The thought is far more common than the actual event, seemingly planted in female DNA.

In reality, all of womankind has been fed so much gory info about brutal attacks, gory murders that it's the first thought. Most creepy guys are not serial killers, they're just creepy guys.

I started back toward the apartment, searching my memory, trying to remember ever seeing him outside of San Francisco, thinking about other jobs and places I'd lived. I was pretty sure I'd never seen him, or I would have had some recognition of his face, even when it was half-covered by a ball cap. The only reason I'd recognized him at all was the jacket — a very nice jacket, expensive. The leather was soft and well-cared for.

No, I was almost one hundred percent certain he was a stranger.

31

Tess was lying beside Steve in his bed. Again, she'd done nothing to end things. And now there was one more night, one more orgasm, one more everything cementing the space between them. She turned on her side and looked at her clothes draped over the leather armchair in the corner. Who furnished their bedroom with a leather armchair? It belonged in the study, the living room. But a bedroom? It was too harsh. Did he ever sit in it? Why would he?

Every time she'd been at his place, he did email on his phone or his tablet, sitting in bed, pillows propped behind him. Naked. It was a horrifying image, thinking of the emails filling in-boxes throughout the company, emails sent at one and two in the morning that people read over breakfast. It probably never crossed their minds they'd been composed and sent by a man with his dick in one hand and his iPhone in another.

She closed her eyes.

A moment later, she felt Steve shift his position. He was sitting up, stuffing the pillows into place. Email now? Really? She was as diligent as anyone about staying on top of email — executive effectiveness 101 — but seven minutes after sex? She turned onto her back.

The bedside drawer slid open and Steve fumbled with the contents. She heard a click and the hiss of a flame followed by the smell of smoke.

"I don't like smoke," she said.

"It's relaxing. And I need to talk to you about something."

"I should get going."

"Why won't you spend the night? Why do you have to draw this arbitrary line? As if not sleeping here is going to secure your boundaries."

"I like sleeping alone."

"That's not normal."

"For a lot of people, it's absolutely normal. Can you put that out, please."

"It's my house."

"I'm your guest," she said.

"Just two more drags."

"What did you want to talk about?"

"Can you sit up, I need to see your face when I tell you."

She didn't want to think about what that meant. She should just get up, dress as quickly as possible, and skate out the door while he took his two additional drags. "When I sit up, I'll be getting out of bed. So tell me now or it'll have to wait." She waved her hand near the side of her head, trying to keep the smoke away. The gesture was completely ineffective.

"I did something I shouldn't have. I wasn't thinking."

A flutter of hope trembled in her chest. If he'd cheated, it would be her out. There was no way she could meet a man she might really connect with while this thing was going on with Steve. She had to end it. Pure laziness and a little bit of horniness kept her coming back. But each time, her self respect deflated a bit more.

"A few months ago, I ran into Alexandra. Right after the trade show. I mean, I talked to her at the trade show. And then I saw her again."

"Okay."

"Please can you sit up."

"I need to go home. Just tell me what it is."

He sucked on the cigarette and blew out smoke. She'd never smelled smoke in his room. Either this was a first, or he did an excellent job airing it out. Double doors opened onto a balcony with a view of the Golden Gate Bridge. She supposed when the fog blew in…still, smoke was hard to eradicate.

"I hinted around that she would do well in a sales position," he said. "It might have even been more specific than that."

Tess sat up. "What?"

"It was casual. I ran into her at the salad bar. I saw how smooth she was at the trade show, greeting customers. She was warm without gushing. She knew how to get their attention, and even better, hold it. She's incredibly confident. That woman could sell ice to eskimos."

That old cliché. Tess sighed. "Don't poach my employees."

"I didn't mean to. But she has this presence, and I suppose I'd been marveling about it and the words just came out before I could think. And she would be good, you have to admit it. Although maybe you don't. Since you've never been in sales. You don't see what I see."

"I see exactly what you see." She pushed off the covers and got up. She walked to the chair and tugged on her underwear and slipped her bra straps over her shoulders, reaching behind to fasten the hooks. "She has a lot to offer. But she's not perfect. I don't want you trying to lure her away. It's not allowed. She's hungry for advancement, spelled m-on-e-y. But there are opportunities in my group. Once she develops a bit more maturity."

"People change jobs."

"But you aren't supposed to recruit them from another part of CC, and you know it."

"You don't want someone like her to become dissatisfied and leave the company altogether."

"Tell me about it." She put on her jeans and shirt and shoved her arms into her jacket.

"Why do you have to go? What's this game with you?"

"It's not a game."

"Everything's a game. Sales is a game. Politics is a game. Men and women are a game. Life is a god damn game, Tess. I think you realize that."

She picked up her purse. It seemed as if she should walk around the bed and kiss him good-bye, but it felt so…she wasn't sure what it felt. And the taste of the cigarette. He still hadn't put it out. He could care less what her wishes were. He'd said two drags, and now the thing was slowly burning down to the filter while he continued to suck on it, blowing out smoke as if it was more pleasurable than sex. What a great image. He was blowing smoke at her. All the time. Maybe now. She should do it. Right now. Tell him good-bye for good.

But all she could think about was their weekly meeting. How awkward it would be. Quarterly sales reviews, presenting to the sales executives while he sat in front of her, looking at her, thinking whatever he pleased. How could she have been so stupid to get sucked in by a handsome face and a nice body and charisma that was so slick she was surprised she hadn't slipped and fallen on her ass? Maybe she had.

"Please don't leave. I'm putting it out. Watch me." He smashed the cigarette in the ashtray he'd pulled out of his bedside drawer.

It was like everything with him, she was already dressed and walking out the door and now he acquiesced.

"Come on, Tess. I love you. Don't you know that?"

For a moment, she lost her equilibrium. She hadn't heard what she thought. Or he was…he was what? They'd only had one bottle of wine. It wasn't as if he'd been smoking a joint. Maybe she was still half asleep, drugged with sex.

"Aren't you going to say anything?" His voice was soft, almost needy. But not really. Only for now.

"I need to get home."

"You're so cold."

"Talk to you later."

"Such a cold, cold bitch."

She walked out of the bedroom and down the hall to the front door. Her hands were like ice and she hadn't even stepped outside into the foggy two a.m. chill that fell over the city like a shroud.

32

Now that Tess owned a gun, she felt as if it was changing her relationships. Not the relationships, exactly, but her feelings toward the people who had been bothering her, manipulating her. Namely, Alexandra and Steve.

It made no sense. It wasn't as if she were going to shoot them for God's sake. But she felt more in control. She liked having a secret and liked the fact that there was a side to her they didn't know, while they deluded themselves into thinking they had her all figured out. It gave her a renewed sense of power.

With the gun, the incident in Santa Cruz had stopped haunting her. She even felt more forgiving toward Alexandra. Her feelings were illogical, but intense and unshakeable. The gun had touched something primal, buried so deeply inside of her she'd never noticed it before. The weapon symbolized her ability to take care of herself without thinking a man was required. And not requiring a male gave her a spacious feeling, as if she'd somehow made psychological room for a different kind of man to come into her life. An equal partner rather than someone to fill a shameful neediness.

She'd already had her first lesson at a target range. The instructor had said she was a natural. She accepted the comment at face value. Why not?

On Monday morning she met Alex for coffee. After they'd looked through the agenda for the alignment meeting with PR, Tess swallowed the rest of her coffee. "I need to run. But how about lunch. Friday?"

Alex nodded.

"We can have a glass of wine, linger a bit."

"It'll be good to catch up," Alex said.

Tess studied Alex's eyes. Their expression was subdued. She seemed more compliant, or agreeable than usual. Surely it wasn't because Tess had created a different dynamic, transformed by her secret knowledge of the small gun in her bag. She laughed.

"What's so funny?"

"Nothing. Sorry." She stood and picked up both paper cups. "Done?"

Alex nodded.

She carried them to the counter and dropped them through the opening into the trash container.

On Friday, they left the office building together.

They stood on the sidewalk, facing the street. The sky was soft blue and the air almost warm enough to suggest eating outdoors. Almost, but not quite. "Where do you want to go?" Tess said.

Alex put on her sunglasses, fiddling with the arrangement of her hair over the sides. "I tried a good dim sum place last weekend."

"Too much carb, what else?"

"Thai?"

"The one near Embarcadero?"

"Yes."

"Okay." They turned and started walking. Alex talked about the difficulty of finding a place to run that didn't require driving somewhere. They walked quickly past a few boutique clothing and shoe shops, a mobile phone store, and a bakery.

The Thai restaurant was dark, making it seem like evening in the middle of a bright Friday afternoon. The walls were covered with tapestries and each table had a small shelf cut into the wall beside it holding a piece of artwork — sculpture, vases, glassware. The red tablecloths and a ceiling with gold crown molding, as well as the tapestries, gave a warm feeling. The acoustics were good and despite the room being nearly two thirds full, the noise of diners talking and dishes being cleared from tables was muted.

Because it was after one o'clock and the lunch crowd was thinning, they were given a table at the front, near a street-facing window. Red curtains hung from a gold bar at the center of the window, preventing them from being on display.

After they placed their order and took a few sips of a light Pinot Grigio, Alex leaned back slightly. She crossed her arms, giving the impression she was about to speak, but she said nothing.

Tess talked about work. They talked about the different energy level working in San Francisco. The food came, and they talked about healthy eating and working out.

Tess nudged her plate to the side without finishing, the healthy eating conversation weighing on her. "So, what's new?" she said.

Alex shrugged.

"Well I have something new." She took a sip of wine. In less than sixty minutes, she was ready to blow the secret that made her feel so confident. Alex's unnerving silences, her willingness to sit through conversational gaps had a way of forcing people to say things they wished they hadn't. Tess hated her lack of control, and now, unless she could think of something else, she'd end up telling Alex about the gun. She could feel the secret clawing its way to the surface.

"Changing jobs?" Alex said.

"Why would you ask that?"

"I haven't seen you around much. Maybe you've been interviewing."

"Meetings."

"There are always a lot of meetings. I meant more than that."

"Are you keeping tabs?"

Alex smirked. "Of course not. I'm not your EA."

"I'm not really sure what you're referring to."

"It's not important." Alex took a sip of wine. She picked up the bottle and topped off her glass. She didn't offer any to Tess. Alex drank her wine with tiny sips. She plucked puffed rice noodles off her plate one at a time and eating them as if they were an imported delicacy.

After several minutes of silence. Tess was annoyed. Alex could never admit when she'd made a mistake, couldn't admit that she was nervous about the minimal communication between the two of them. And now, refused to ask what the news was once her first guess was proven wrong. "Do you want to know my news?"

"Sure." Alex picked up the bottle and poured a small amount into each glass.

"I bought a gun."

"Why?"

"I think I've always wanted one."

"You *think*?"

"Shooting at targets, improving your accuracy, is very

satisfying. It takes your mind off work, and other things."

"I'm sure. But why do you need a gun?"

"I don't *need* one. I wanted one. I just said that."

"Do you shoot at those black silhouettes of men, like the ones you see in movies?"

"Yes."

"So you're imagining killing a man. A shadow."

"Don't dramatize it. The reason I pulled the trigger now, ha ha, is your fault anyway."

"My fault?"

"I suppose fault is the wrong word, but you pushed me in that direction."

"How did I do that?"

The server came to the table and began stacking plates. Tess waited for her to finish, sorry to see the plates go. She was still a little hungry and wished she'd ordered another dish — the asparagus stir fried with prawns, maybe. "When I fell and gashed my leg."

"That wasn't my fault."

"I said that was the wrong word. But it was your idea to run in a bad neighborhood."

"That's not why you fell," Alex said.

"In a way, it was. I felt uncomfortable. I cut across the yard because I needed to get out of there. I don't ever want to feel that way again. Especially the way I was sitting there, completely helpless. It was awful."

Part of her didn't want to reveal her vulnerable feelings to Alex, but another part of her longed for empathy. And she wanted to return to how they were before. Friends, almost. Before Alex was upset about her performance rating, before the injury.

They had equal fault in the fracturing of their relationship, she just wished Alex could see that. It wasn't good for a manager to be so subservient to her employee, but she missed their easy talks, the feeling that they understood each other. She regretted being so aloof, avoiding Alex because she was afraid she would spill her guts about the trap she'd fallen into with Steve.

"How would a gun have helped you?"

"It's the idea of it."

Alex laughed.

"It's strange. It makes me feel like I'm in charge. It wouldn't have kept me from falling, but it would have kept me from being so scared of those drug dealers. And that other guy."

Alex shrugged.

"They didn't make you uncomfortable? Not at all?"

"I don't have a lot of fears," Alex said.

"Maybe you should."

"Why? What did it ever get you — being afraid?"

Tess didn't have an answer. She felt a sliver of weakness, regret that she'd revealed the thing that was gently shifting her view of the world, even if it was extremely unlikely she'd ever use it to defend herself.

Alex swallowed the rest of her wine. "There's a painting in the lounge of my apartment building. It was purchased from a gallery on Folsom. Do you want to walk over there with me? I want to find out more about it. Get the name of the artist."

"Sure." Tess put her credit card on the table. "My treat."

"Thank you." Alex smiled.

The smile looked genuine. Tess wasn't sure if the smile

was for the meal or that Alex felt she'd won a point, luring Tess into her plan to visit the art gallery.

33

As they walked toward the art gallery, neither of them spoke. Tess was glad. She needed to get her thoughts properly arranged again. The powerful, secretive feeling she'd had over the gun had collapsed under her own need to fill the space between her and Alex with words.

What was wrong with her these past months? She seemed to be losing control of herself, no longer gliding confidently toward her goals, no longer knowing with absolute certainty what she wanted from the world. Was this some weird, premature mid-life crisis? Maybe it was an incredibly delayed response to the achievement of her goal, her overwhelming drive to get to executive management, and here she was.

Reaching the pinnacle of Senior Vice President was a remarkable feat. Not a lot of people managed it.

In order to reach that level you needed top-line skills in a lot of areas — sterling work delivered year after year, almost without fail, proving yourself as a manager that could drive a team of people to do the same. You had to understand and be articulate in technology even if you lacked an engineering degree. And you needed working knowledge of finance, sales, product development cycles, and even human resources. You needed to know how to deal with the media and industry analysts, never allowing them the upper hand. It wasn't easy.

The rewards were fantastic, and she'd set her eyes on that goal when she was a Sophomore in college, possibly earlier.

Secretly, something she hardly admitted to herself, she craved a CEO position. It was a long shot. Not all, but most CEOs had a technical degree. It would have to be the right kind of company. It definitely wasn't achievable at CoastalCreative.

So, there was nowhere else to go at this company. Maybe that was the problem. Or maybe it was just no longer having something challenging and all-consuming to work toward. She was done. She was at the top of her mountain, looking around and seeing the things she'd left scattered beside the path during the climb to the top. Things that weren't important at the time, suddenly looked larger, and farther away. Impossible to retrieve.

She felt threatened by Steve's offer to Alex, whetting Alex's appetite for a position in sales. But Alex hadn't said a word about it, and that was a greater betrayal.

Knowing Alex, it was surprising she hadn't used the potential job offer to ask Tess for yet another pay increase. But that omission was what made it feel like such a betrayal. Clearly Alex was more interested in keeping the secret from Tess than she was in getting a raise. And she wanted more money so badly, the desire oozed out of her skin, dripping from her eyes like tears.

Not that wanting more money was bad. Everyone wanted to be well-compensated. For the tangible reward as well as for the satisfaction of knowing your work was so valued the company was willing to part with cash.

Alex wanted money. She frequently asked boldly, hinted about it even more.

Instead, Alex had decided to start a secretive relationship with Steve, keeping him on the back burner if she found working for Tess wasn't getting her where she wanted to go.

If Alexandra wanted advancement, she should be talking to her manager. Asking for more projects, expanding outside the realm of what she currently did. She should not be having side conversations with a sales executive.

No wonder she'd looked so startled, and Steve so guilty, when Tess had seen them outside the conference room a few months ago. No wonder Alex's behavior had changed, no longer quite as passionate about her job. She recognized the jackpot that can come to a top sales person. She didn't realize that those big bonuses and accelerators weren't guaranteed, weren't easy to get. You had to fight like a shark to win those prizes.

If Alex had simply sought her guidance, she could have told her all of that. Sales was a fantastic opportunity for a lucrative income, if you were good. If not, you'd be spit out of the system within two years. She doubted Steve had mentioned that little fact to Alex.

As they walked, she felt Alex deliberately not looking at her, keeping her gaze ahead, completely comfortable with the silence between them. As she thought about Steve and Alex, the Thai food burned in her esophagus. She needed to tell Steve more firmly that he'd better keep his hands off. Literally.

When they were a few yards away from the gallery door, Alex suddenly spoke. "Hey. You said there was a lot to talk about. In your message about going to dinner last weekend. What did you mean?"

Tess waited. She'd honestly forgotten. "I don't remember," she said.

34

The gallery was small, as most of them are. San Francisco real estate is beyond expensive. And with so many high tech companies leaving Silicon Valley, setting up camp in the city in order to provide the urban living their twenty- and thirty-something cream-of-the-crop college grads desire, prices were climbing every month. If they weren't careful, all the establishments that made it cosmopolitan and sought after for a rich offering of food and entertainment, art and culture, would fold up and move to Albuquerque. Or something like that. I've never been to Albuquerque, or New Mexico at all, but it's an inexpensive place to live and manages to have an artistic flair.

I held the door for Tess. She hesitated for several seconds before she stepped inside.

As the door closed slowly behind us, she sighed.

I looked at her. She gave me a smile that suggested the thing she'd wanted all her life was to walk into *Herriman's Fine Art & Sculpture*.

A super small woman in super tall heels with super short hair clicked toward us with the ease of a woman wearing tennis shoes. She was smiling as if she'd been waiting all day just for us. "Welcome. Welcome." She extended a skeletal hand. "How can I help you?"

"We just want to look around," Tess said.

I actually wanted help, but decided waiting a few minutes, looking around, was worthwhile.

The narrow space made it difficult to move farther into the gallery without pressing up against the manager. She positioned herself in the opening between two displays, leaving inadequate space on either side. To the left, were pedestals bearing sculptures of naked women — the ubiquitous choice of sculptors throughout the entire history of *man*kind. These were seductive in a way that had nothing to do with sexual appeal — smooth bronze lines that drew your eye gracefully across the skin, holding you so you didn't even want to look at the next sculpture, much less turn away to look at work by another artist.

The sculpted women were reclining, standing, a head turned looking over a shoulder, hands clasped loosely at the base of her spine. All of them gazing into eternity.

Tess had moved to the opposite side of the gallery where several free-standing walls featured acrylic cityscapes. She walked quickly past each one. As she did, the manager's smile stiffened, then sagged. "Let me know if I can answer any questions," she said.

Tess ignored her.

I moved from the sculptures to a group of smaller paintings, also done in acrylic. These featured women addicted to heroin and crack, the implements of their downfall lying beside the dirty toenails of naked feet splayed on cracked pavement. The work was so realistic I felt I was looking out the window at a street in the decaying, hidden corners of the city.

Despite the dark subject matter, I couldn't stop looking. I guess we all have a ghoulish side. That's why we're drawn to macabre art and photography, movies and TV, news and reality shows.

Tess had zipped through the cityscapes to a small alcove with abstract paintings where she was moving with equal speed past each one.

The manager walked over to Tess. "I forgot to introduce myself. I'm Celine."

Tess said *hi*, keeping her back to Celine.

"What are you interested in seeing? We have more work in the back."

"She's the one with the question." Tess nodded her head in my direction.

In a moment, Celine was beside me. "Yes?"

"I live in the dual tower apartment building on Howard. There's a painting in our lounge of a woman in a red dress. Her body is..."

Celine nodded once. "Garth Gilbert. His *Interior World* series."

"So there are more?"

"Yes."

"Are they in the back too?"

"Unfortunately, we don't have them in the gallery right now. Are you interested in purchasing one?"

"I haven't seen them."

She gave me a thin smile. "You seem very taken with the artist, since you came in to ask about it."

"I am."

"For serious buyers, we can arrange a private display."

"I'm quite serious." I smiled.

"Excellent. And you know he's very hot right now."

"How *hot?*" I shifted my gracious smile into the suggestion of a smirk.

"*The Woman In the Blood Red Dress*, the one you referred

to, was sold for seventy-five-thousand."

"It's very compelling," I said.

"I feel the same way. Why don't you give me your card. I'll talk to Garth and see when we can arrange something."

I touched the heroin needle in the painting to my left. It was so life-like, I expected it to pierce my fingertip.

Celine frowned.

"I don't have any cards with me. Why don't you give me yours, and I'll call."

Her smile went away. "Of course you don't." She clicked over to the round counter, nestled between the abstracts and the cityscapes, barely large enough to hold two glasses of wine. She returned with a business card and handed it to me. "When you're ready…"

"Also, do you have any kind of artist's statement about his work?"

"As I told you, his name is Garth Gilbert. You can look for his website online."

Tess had disappeared.

Celine looked around, jerking her head from side to side, as if it was imperative she locate Tess before she slipped out the door with a five-by-eight foot, seventy-five-thousand dollar painting tucked under her arm.

"Where's your friend?" Celine said.

"I don't know."

Celine clicked toward the back of the gallery. "Oh. There you are. Still no questions?"

Reluctantly, I pulled myself away from the addicts and followed Celine.

Tess stood in a small room with a low, cushioned chair. On each of the three half-walls was a portrait of a woman —

first as a child-like young teenager, then a woman in her thirties, and the final one, a woman in her early sixties, on the cusp of crumbling into old age.

I gasped.

"I know," Tess said.

The colors were soft and the strokes so delicate they pulsed with life. The skin and the eyes were as real as photographs, yet transcending mere photography, rich and vivid. I moved closer.

"Exquisite, aren't they," Celine said.

"Who is she?" Tess said.

"The artist's lover. He knew her when she was a young woman."

"His name?"

"Xavier Holland."

"Thank you," Tess said.

After several minutes of silence, Tess turned to me. "Did you get your questions answered?"

I nodded, looking past her at the center painting. The woman wore a low-cut black sleeveless blouse. Her brown and gold streaked hair fell to the tops of her shoulders. Hazel eyes gazed back at me with a look of utter contentment, her lips reflecting the same tranquility.

"Well then, let's go," Tess said.

Celine followed us to the door and wished us a good afternoon. "Do come back," she said.

Tess nodded. "I will."

When we were outside, before we started walking, Tess turned to me. "I've always wanted to have my portrait painted."

"Holding your gun?"

She seemed to not hear me. Her voice was low, almost a whisper. "I've wanted that for a long time."

35

As beautiful as Golden Gate Park was, as idyllic as my runs along its Eucalyptus-lined paths, I was fed up with Uber-ing to a run. Going for a run should be spontaneous, uncomplicated, not hamstrung by the necessity of accessing an app, requesting a car, and waiting around for a driver. In some cases, with the added effort of silencing a chatty driver. Then, topping it off by climbing back into a car and sitting in traffic for thirty minutes.

It sapped most of the pleasure. The purity of me and my legs and the fresh air and the silence or sound, as I chose, inside my head.

The solution was obvious, once I thought of it. Dodging pedestrians wouldn't be a problem at four-thirty in the morning. The sidewalks would likely be empty even at six, but for the first try, I wasn't taking any chances. I'd miss the park and the settling presence of grass and trees and birds, but once I lost my body to movement and my head sank into my classical piano playlist, it would all be good.

It was forty-eight degrees outside, so I put on leggings. I still wore a sports bra because no matter how cold, eventually my body would scream for fewer pieces of cotton and spandex clinging to it. I covered up with a long-sleeved t-shirt and a hoodie.

Standing on the sidewalk, stretching against the lamppost that shone above me, I felt the buildings like so many granite cliffs reaching into the black sky, their summits hidden for another hour or so.

I was holding my right foot, pulling my heel toward my butt, when I saw the first pedestrian. Unbelievable. It was twenty to five. Where on earth was she going?

As I peered through the watery illumination of streetlights, I saw that she wasn't going anywhere. She stood near the entrance to a building halfway between me and the corner. After a moment, she took a few steps back, moving to the center of the sidewalk.

I let go of my right foot and grabbed my left.

A man stepped out of the entranceway. He was tall, nearly a foot taller than her. His hands were shoved into his jacket pockets. He was talking with a great deal of head and shoulder movement. The hands remained motionless, unable to emphasize whatever point he was making.

I heard his voice rise and fall, but couldn't make out the words.

The woman turned slightly.

I squinted. Something about her looked familiar.

She took another step back, landing in the pool of light coming from the streetlight behind her.

Jen.

From where I stood, in the darkness, the man appeared to be the one who'd been watching her in the lounge the night I first met her. He had the same lean shape, the same intensity. It hovered around him as if light emanated from his skin, searching, watching everyone with raw hunger. It had been the same when he jostled my arm as I carried my glass of wine. Jen had said she didn't know him. Based on her stance and the way she was listening to him now, she clearly did know him. Rather well.

I didn't have any body parts left to stretch. I spread my legs a few feet apart and did some side stretches, reaching my arm alongside my ear, clasping my hands as I bent left, leaning into the stretch. Jen and the man continued talking. Mostly, *he* continued talking. She nodded occasionally, spoke a few words, then he carried on.

Once I started running, I would go right past them on my way to The Embarcadero.

I didn't want to linger too long while the city was still waking up, but I wanted to continue watching, trying to get a read on what was happening between them.

Questions surged through my arms as if my reaching up into the darkness had pulled them out of the sky. Why had she said she didn't know him? Why had she told me she thought he was looking at her, as if she had some kind of telepathy when she knew for a fact he *was* looking at her? Why was she standing on the street before dawn letting him go on like that? What was he talking about? How did they know each other?

All unanswerable, but I couldn't stop watching. I hoped they would raise their voices, allowing me access to their drama.

I don't know what it is about me. Possibly it's the ghoulish interest in our fellow human beings that a lot of us have, but I have in spades. Curiosity has a way of derailing every plan, yanking me off course and forcing me into situations where I don't belong.

It's especially powerful when I perceive anger or jealousy, despair or hatred or desire coming from another person. Something builds inside of me, almost physical, like a desperate hunger. The same desire that responds to the aroma and taste of a perfectly grilled steak. I pick up that scent from a mile away and follow it no matter where it leads. Then, it goes beyond the normal curiosity others possess. Feeding on the emotions of other people's experiences is my life blood.

The man moved into the pool of light, standing only a foot or so from Jen. He put his hand on her shoulder, giving the impression of a father speaking to his child, but there was no warmth. There was no change in her posture or rearrangement of her stance. Her voice rose slightly.

The man moved his hand to the back of Jen's head. He pulled her toward him, pressing her face into his coat. His fingers became one with her hair, burying themselves in a very intimate gesture, as if he was feeling the shape of her skull, trying to memorize its contours. And yet, they didn't seem like lovers. He held her there for so long, I wondered whether she was having trouble breathing. Her body was motionless, and her head slightly bent.

I lowered my arms and began a slow jog toward them.

At the sound of my footsteps, the man let go of Jen's head. He moved back. He turned and walked quickly to the corner, turning right.

"Jen." I slowed. When she turned, I waved.

She said nothing.

"Why are you out so early?" I said.

"No reason." She looked at the pavement.

"Who is that guy? I thought you didn't know him."

She shivered. "It's really cold. I should get back inside."

"But I…"

She moved around me. "Are you going jogging?"

"Yes. But I…is everything okay?"

She nodded. "Have a good run." She tugged her coat more tightly around her and turned.

"Was he bothering you?"

"Leave me alone." She walked quickly away, headed toward our apartment building.

I watched her go, that tantalizing aroma of something intense stirring my hunger.

36

Portland

A few months before my fifteenth birthday, a guy from my civics class started smoking with Jill and me. He followed us once or twice, and then, without an invitation, he was standing beside us as if it had always been that way.

It was exciting to think of a boy following me...us. The sound of footsteps made me slow my own. I kicked through yellow leaves scattered on the sidewalk, and then made my footsteps softer, waiting to hear if he followed my lead and kicked at the fallen leaves. I didn't know which of us he was interested in, or if he just wanted smoking companions. While we smoked, he watched us with a very attentive expression, so it seemed like he thought we were cute.

He brought his own pack and he didn't limit his smoking to one cigarette like Jill and I did. That was our rule. We were sure the rule protected us from ever getting lung cancer or leathery skin. We felt virtuous with our strict obedience to the rule. No matter how much Denny pushed us to have a second, we never yielded.

No other girls I knew had boys following them. It made me feel fascinating, knowing I was the center of someone's attention. His interest turned me into a different person, a person who stood out from others. It also made me newly self-conscious. Suddenly I was on stage, every gesture a performance calculated to keep his gaze focused on me. I tucked my hair behind my ear and saw his eyes widen ever so slightly. I smiled and watched his lips unconsciously mimic the curve of mine. I put the cigarette in my mouth and felt him lean closer. Even if I didn't see his body move, the warmth between us increased, telling me he'd moved.

The cinderblock wall of the park restrooms hid us from passersby, mothers watching their children on the playground equipment, and people walking their dogs. Beside the building was an Aspen tree that dropped even more yellow leaves than those covering the sidewalks. Our feet sank in the soft leaves, and our ashes fell on them, turning dark and damp — charcoal gray on yellow.

We talked about school and music. Denny told us about his annual summer trip to his uncle's farm in Eastern Washington state. He got to do whatever he wanted on that farm. The adults ignored him, believing he couldn't get into trouble because there wasn't a single person for miles around. There was a small fishing cabin beside a creek that ran through one corner of the hundred-acre property. He was allowed to spend the night alone in the cabin. He fished and pan-fried his own trout on the ancient white stove that stood in the corner of the single room.

Jill's lips parted slightly. She glanced at me, her eyes shiny. I thought of us staying in our own cabin, almost adults. We wouldn't go to sleep until after midnight. We could talk and smoke whenever we wanted, ignoring our rule for a while. We might drink beer. I imagined we would go outside in the darkness, no city lights. We'd walk and look at the stars and shout and no one would hear us.

Denny blew out a stream of smoke. He smiled at me as if he knew what I was thinking.

Once she realized Denny liked me, Jill didn't get jealous or tell stories about me like some girls would if a guy picked you instead of her. She didn't suddenly decide to eat lunch at a table where there was no room for me, leaving me standing like a too-small fish tossed back into the water with a jagged tear in the side of my mouth, holding my lunch tray, frantically hoping to catch someone's eye and generate a smile. The longer you stood there, the more everyone knew you were stupid or boring.

Jill shrugged and said, "Maybe I'll pick a guy myself, instead of waiting for one to pick me."

That's why I liked her.

Denny started walking me home from our smoking place. He'd walk with both of us until Jill turned off onto Arrow Drive to her house. My house was four blocks farther. He'd talk about unimportant things — homework or the houses we were walking past, or what he'd watched on TV the night before.

At my house, he kept talking. We sat on the stone wall that surrounded the raised front lawn, arms stretched behind us, palms and fingers pressed into cool grass. I wished we had another cigarette, but we couldn't sit in plain sight and smoke. It was also a risk sitting in plain sight, period. I wasn't allowed to go out with boys. I wasn't allowed to go to parties that included boys. The only time I could associate with boys was when neighbors or church members were invited to our house, or there was an event at church.

I knew my siblings wouldn't mention Denny. We watched out for each other, mostly by keeping our mouths shut and minding our own business. Keeping your mouth shut was important to my father, and I guess we learned the lesson well. He never considered how we'd use it to thwart him.

My mother was busy cooking dinner in the late afternoon, and since the kitchen faced the backyard, I wasn't worried she'd see me. But then, she did.

I came into the house, closing the front door softly, hoping to avoid a lot of questions about school and my friends. I was thinking about Denny's way of saying good-bye the past two days — taking my hair in his hand and letting the strands slide across his fingers.

"Alexandra?"

My mother's voice was clear and firm. It wasn't a tone that allowed for me to say I was going upstairs to get started on homework. I dropped my backpack on the hall floor and went into the kitchen. It smelled of fresh bread, but the onion and garlic browning in the frying pan were starting to drown out the bread.

"Can I have some bread?"

"*May* I have some bread," she repeated.

"May I?"

"It's too close to dinner. Why do you always ask when you know the answer?"

"I'm hungry."

"Didn't you eat your lunch?"

I got out a glass and filled it with water.

"Who was that boy?" she said.

"He's in my civics class."

"What was he doing here?"

"He walked home from school with me."

"Your father doesn't…"

"I know."

"Then why did you let him?"

"He just started walking with me. What am I supposed to do, tell him to get lost?"

"Yes."

"That's not very Christian."

"You have to say it nicely."

"How do you say *get lost* in a *nice* way? It's not a *nice* thing."

"You know what I mean." She ran water over a dishrag and wiped it across the cutting board where she'd chopped the onions.

I did not know what she meant.

"You can't have boys over."

"I didn't have him over. He walked home with me. Followed me."

"Do I need to call the school and complain?"

"No."

"If your father saw him, he'd be very upset."

"He doesn't have to know."

"There's plenty of time for boys when you're older. Boys from church, from Godly families."

"How do you know his family isn't godly?"

"It's safer to be friends with boys at church. Your father will like that better. When you're older."

"Can I go? I have a lot of homework."

She smiled. "I'm glad we had this talk. It's important to share things with me now that you're growing up. I'm always here to listen." She widened her smile and moved toward me.

I didn't want a hug with her onion-smeared hands. I backed up quickly. "I know." I hurried out of the room, grabbed my backpack, and went upstairs.

There was no way I was going to tell Denny to get lost.

37

San Francisco

I walked into the lobby lugging my gym bag, and my pants, jacket, and shirt on hangers, holding onto my apartment key and building ID. I flicked the ID up facing the security guard and turned toward the elevators, shifting the hangers to be sure the clothes weren't coming close to the floor. It was mopped daily and swept regularly between moppings, but when I'd walked across it in a new pair of shoes, the soles were already dirty by the time I reached the doors to the street.

Before the elevator chimed, Jen appeared beside me.

"Hi." She had a coffee drink in her hand. She stuck the straw in her mouth, took a long slurp, and moved it away. "Sorry if I was kinda bitchy to you the other morning."

The elevator chimed.

"No worries," I said.

"I don't mean to be weird, but I thought maybe we'd get to be friends, and I...that's not how a friend should act."

The doors opened and I stepped inside, hoisting the clothes higher on my shoulder. She followed me in. I pressed the button for the tenth floor. She didn't press any.

"What floor are you on?"

The doors closed and the elevator began gliding upwards.

"I was wondering." She sipped her drink. "Could I come over for a glass of wine or something?"

"You have a coffee."

"I guess it's not cool to invite myself, but…"

"Do you like martinis?"

"I've never had one."

"Then this is an excellent time to lose your virginity."

She laughed. "That's not really funny."

"Probably not, but it just came out."

The elevator chimed, the doors opened, and we stepped into the hallway.

"Can I carry something for you?"

"I got it." I dangled the key. "You could unlock the door."

"What apartment?"

"Ten-twenty-three."

We walked down the hall. She unlocked the door and we went inside. I dropped the gym bag near the front door and laid the clothes and their hangers across the back of the armchair.

"You haven't decorated much," she said.

"No."

"How come?"

"No time."

"Too busy with Isaiah?"

"Why do you say that?"

"I saw you with him. I could tell he likes you."

She sounded like a high school kid. I wondered how old she was. Another item on the list of things I didn't know about her.

"I'm going to take a quick shower and then I'll make martinis. You can finish your drink. And if you don't mind, you could get out some cheese and crackers. There's cheddar and brie in the fridge, a few kinds of crackers in the cabinet over the stove."

"Okay." She put her drink on the counter.

I hung my clothes in the closet, grabbed a pair of gray leggings, a charcoal gray tank, and a long white sweater. After my shower, I dressed fast, realizing I'd been a bit naïve to leave a secretive woman I hardly knew alone in my living room slash bedroom. I flung open the bathroom door.

Jen was slumped on the couch, looking at her phone, sucking on the long straw coming out of her clear plastic cup. A plate with thinly sliced pieces of cheddar cheese and a fan of square wheat crackers sat on the coffee table.

I went to the kitchen and took out the shaker. "How many olives do you want?"

"How many are you supposed to have?"

"There's no rule. Most people get two, I have three because I like olives."

"I'll have three," she said.

I filled the shaker with ice, measured vodka, and stabbed olives onto stir sticks.

When the drinks were finished, I carried them to the coffee table.

"I always wanted to try one. It looks sexy," Jen said.

"Doesn't it? Cheers." I raised my glass.

She pursed her thin lips over the edge of the glass and let the liquid touch them. She shivered. "Wow." She took another sip, more confident this time.

"You get used to it."

"Why would you want to drink something you have to get used to?" she said.

"Didn't you have to get used to coffee when you first

started drinking it?"

"I guess so."

"It's called acquiring a taste."

She took another sip and placed her glass on the table. "It's good."

We ate cheese and crackers, sipped our martinis and talked. She was much freer than she had been in the lounge, but she still didn't reveal much. Just so many words. We talked about movies and TV shows, shopping and guys. However, the tall thin guy she'd met at four in the morning didn't come up. Neither did David. Her conversation centered around the kind of guy she wanted, and the amount of creeps in the world. She mentioned kissing a lot of frogs. Several times. She seemed to have adopted the cliché as some sort of personal challenge. Almost as if she'd find a guy she cared about if she determined to seek out and kiss, and I think she meant fuck, as many creeps as she could.

It was a strange philosophy. But she was a strange woman.

"Is that guy I saw you with the other morning one of your frogs?"

She laughed and sipped her drink quickly. "It's nothing like that."

"Who is he?"

Her phone buzzed. She looked at it and put her glass on the table. She stood. "I should go. Sorry."

I walked with her to the door and said good-bye

Despite her aloof behavior, or maybe because of it, I could see that we might be friendly on a regular basis.

38

After Jen left, trailing her mystery and vagueness and uncertainty behind her, I messaged Isaiah.

Alexandra Mallory: *Want company?*

Isaiah Parker: *Sure. What time?*

Alexandra Mallory: *Now. I'll bring vodka. Do you have vermouth?*

Isaiah Parker: *The door's already open, the vermouth and shaker are moving to the counter as we speak.*

I smiled. I went into the bathroom and brushed my hair. I grabbed the vodka and a jar of olives, just in case he didn't have enough.

When the elevator stopped at my floor, there was a group of three women and a man crowding the center. I stepped inside and they laughed and joked about kidnapping me to steal the vodka bottle I was holding by the neck. When I got out on the eighth floor, the man said, *Come back any time. As long as you have vodka.* I gave them a half-hearted smile.

Between the lounge and occasional partiers in the elevators, it sometimes felt as if I'd moved into a dorm designed for people who were between college and settling down. A holding pen for the twenty- and thirty-somethings, all of us waiting for life to start, not fully realizing it already had.

Isaiah's door was indeed standing open. I pushed it farther and stepped inside. He was sitting on the couch, waiting.

I made martinis while he stood behind me, hands on my hips, his body tracking every movement I made.

We went onto the balcony. Standing near the edge, the wind hit our faces, cold and slightly damp. We stepped back from the railing after a few minutes. He pulled out two simple wood chairs that were tucked in the corner and we sat down. Sitting, it was impossible to see the view, but the sky with a few glittery stars was still visible and a view all on its own.

We drank our martinis without talking, simply feeling each other's warm presence, sliced by the icy cold of our drinks.

When my glass was empty, I put it on the concrete floor and climbed onto his lap, I started to kiss him. He slid his hands up inside my sweater, found the edge of my tank top, and his fingers made their way up inside of that as well. He pulled the top edge of my bra below my breasts. He rubbed and massaged and played with them until I was a puddle of liquid. Finally, we stood. Leaving the glasses on the ground, he led me inside, across the living room and into his bedroom.

As he was about to close the bedroom door, the front door opened.

David's voice wasn't extremely loud, but it managed to fill the living space and follow us into the bedroom. "Shit! It's freezing in here. Did you leave the patio door open again?"

I heard the front door close. A moment later, David was standing in the bedroom doorway.

Isaiah started to close the bedroom door. "Kinda busy. Sorry about the patio."

"Hey," David said. "I didn't know you two…"

"Busy," Isaiah said. "It's not a good time for you to catch

up with our neighbor."

"It looks like you've already done quite a bit of catching up with our new neighbor. Hi, Alexandra. How's it going?"

I smiled.

I heard someone else moving around in the living room. The sliding glass door to the patio closed. There was a quiet cough.

David gestured, sweeping his arm in Isaiah's direction, then mine. "So when did all this happen? You're the stealthy dude. I had no idea."

"Why would you?" Isaiah said.

David took a few steps into the bedroom. "What's new with you, Alexandra?"

"Not much," I said.

"And yet, it seems as if there's a lot that's new."

"Come on," Isaiah said. "Leave us alone."

David grinned.

Isaiah grabbed the hem of David's sweatshirt and gave it a sharp tug.

David continued grinning, not bothered by the stretching of his shirt, the way it tightened around his neck. He leaned forward slightly. He studied my face, then raised his eyebrows at the condition of my sweater which probably revealed my twisted bra beneath.

There was another cough from the living room.

"You're being rude to your guest," Isaiah said.

"She's not a guest."

Isaiah gave him a look I couldn't interpret. He held it for several seconds. He let go of David's sweatshirt, gripped his arm below the elbow, and pulled him toward the door. "Get lost."

David punched Isaiah's shoulder with his free hand. Not hard, but enough.

"Hey!" Isaiah said, but he didn't let go of David's arm.

A woman's voice came from the other room, louder as she moved closer. "Don't fight."

It sounded like Jen, but there weren't enough words to know for sure.

I stood and adjusted my sweater over my hips. Fixing my bra would only invite more leering from David, so I left it alone.

Jen appeared in the doorway. "Sorry." She gave me a timid smile. She looked tired. Much older than I'd originally guessed. She was definitely in her thirties, not the twenty-year-old she seemed to play at times. "Come on, leave them alone."

David twisted, trying to break Isaiah's grip. "You don't need to prove you're the man," he said. "You already got the hot girl…"

Jen's face turned into something like a crumpled piece of aluminum foil.

David went on, "…you have the bright shiny future. Let go of me and quit trying to prove something."

Isaiah let go.

David moved to the doorway. He put his hand on Jen's neck. "Don't start sulking. You know how it is."

"Don't worry. I'm not." She ducked and slipped away from his loose hold on her neck. She disappeared into the living room. David gave Isaiah another unreadable look. "Enjoy." That part was clear enough.

He went out and shut the door.

Isaiah went to the other side of the bed. He took off his

shoes and shirt and collapsed onto his back. "What do you want to do?"

I peeled off my sweater and tank top. I adjusted my bra and walked around to his side. I straddled him and put my hands on his shoulders. "What do you think?"

"They kind of wrecked the mood."

"It's easily re-captured." I unhooked my bra and bent over him, kissing him until he closed his eyes.

39

When Tess invited me to go for a run on the Golden Gate Bridge, I hesitated for a very long time before responding to her message. Facing my fear of water in Soquel Creek, when I allowed my body to be submerged, this time by my own hand, had been a turning point. Never again would water choke me with its promise of death. It wouldn't keep me from some day vacationing at the ocean or beside a lake.

Preventing it from haunting my dreams was probably too much, too soon.

Knowing I'd conquered it once didn't mean I was eager to run across a bridge with miles of water spread out on both sides, touching the horizon to the west, and fingers of it creeping around the San Francisco peninsula and surrounding land formations.

I'd seen photographs of people walking on that bridge. The railings were woefully inadequate. Most people feared the moderate height of the railings because looking down from that height was terrifying. The distance to the water didn't trouble me at all, but the water itself...

Tess Turner: *If you don't want to go, just say so. I'm not in the mood for a game.*

Alexandra Mallory: *It's not a game. I was thinking about my schedule...I'll go.*

Tess Turner: *Good. I'll pick you up at six-forty-five a.m. Hopefully we can get across before it's too crowded.*

That night, I dreamed I was hanging from the side of the

bridge. My fingers began to lose their grip on the fat cable they'd been clinging to for hours. Above me on the bridge were Tess and Steve Montgomery. They were both slowly shaking their heads as if I'd missed some very important, very obvious point. Their arms were folded across their ribs, their shoulders tight. They made no move to help lift me out of the precarious position, to save me from certain drowning.

An obvious dream. A dream that was almost embarrassing to remember, it was so unoriginal.

That didn't stop it from waking me with enough sweat on my body to force me out of bed and into the shower. Then, I couldn't get back under the covers with wet hair. So the day started at three-forty-five.

Tess arrived on time, as she always does. We drove with eighties music turned up just loud enough to discourage talking. I took the hint.

At the bridge, she drove across and parked on the Marin County side. We stretched and started our run. There were a surprising number of pedestrians out already, but there were other runners too, and most of the walkers were gracious about not scattering around and clogging the sidewalk. It's wide enough to hold four people abreast, more in some sections. The bridge is about three miles long.

We ran to the second tower at an easy jog. Her leg was healing well, a thin line showing the place where she'd gashed it. I resisted the urge to ask whether she'd brought her new little toy. Her tight running clothes didn't provide any place to conceal a gun, no matter how small, but I was still tempted to ask, just to see her face.

When we made the turn and started back across the span, I said, "Are you seriously thinking of getting your portrait painted?"

"Yes. Those portraits were unbelievable. I hope he does commission work."

"Why?"

"Because his work is brilliant."

"I meant why the portrait."

"It's something I've always wanted to do." She slowed and paused by the railing, looking directly into the sun that was rising higher over the Bay Bridge to the east. She opened the water bottle attached to her waist and squirted water into her mouth. It didn't all make it in, running over her lips and down her chin. She swiped her fingers across her face to get rid of the moisture.

She held out the bottle. I shook my head.

"Why not get a formal photograph?" I said.

"There's something longer lasting about a painting. Something more…I don't know…meaningful."

"Why is it more meaningful?"

"I can't explain it. I suppose because it's art?"

"Good photography is art."

"I said I can't explain it."

"Commissioning a painting sounds expensive. And you have to sit for hours."

"It feels like the right time to do it."

"You want to memorialize your face?"

She looked at me.

"Do you?"

"Maybe I do. While I'm still in my prime. A painting lasts forever."

"But who…"

"I think painted portraits are interesting. They show

something a photograph doesn't. I'm in awe of painters who can capture the essence of a person — their appearance and their personality, everything about them. They take standard paint colors and a few brushes and make you come alive on a canvas. It fascinates me and I want to have it done."

"I never thought of all that."

"Well I have. A lot."

"I'm not criticizing you. The way you describe it makes it sound very cool. Transcendent."

She swallowed my words as if they were heartfelt, hearing what she wanted. "Exactly." She smiled as if someone understood her for the first time in her life.

I did, but I didn't.

40

The strip of sand near the foot of the Golden Gate Bridge was empty on a Monday morning. Jen loved sitting alone by the edge of the water when the rest of the world was racing up elevators into high-rise buildings filled with offices. The weekend sailboats were gone and it was just her and the massive base supports of the bridge, the rocks, and the water. A few gulls scavenged for discarded food. On the weekends, she felt out of touch with the hives of people around her as they reveled in their two free days. She felt adrift in the world, unconnected to any real job, unconnected from a mate, childless, and therefore unable to find a pathway into the lives of other human beings.

On weekday mornings, with the sun glowing like yellow glass on the water, or even in the fog, feeling it falling down on her, making the world appear silent even when it wasn't, she felt alive. She felt like a member of the human race because the rest of them weren't around to disprove her existence.

The last time she'd been truly happy was four years ago. The day after her twenty-eighth birthday. The moment everything came apart in a single day. How was that even possible? To have your whole life unravel in the space of thirty hours?

Then, unlike now, she had a job. A real job. A respectable job. Her two-year degree from a Junior College had secured her a position as a pre-school teacher. Daycare, really, but the parents liked calling it preschool, liked knowing their children, even if they didn't have the money for pricey early childhood education, were learning to count and read and share their toys. From eight in the morning until six in the evening, Jen helped the three- and four-year-olds play simple math games and practiced printing the letters of the alphabet. She read stories and listened to the make-believe tales.

They were so precious. Their faces plump, the texture of their skin like vine-ripened tomatoes. Their eyes unblemished with pain. The only pain they'd experienced were falls from tricycles and monkey bars, pain that went away with a parental kiss or a hug from a teacher.

The job didn't pay a lot, but Jake made enough for both of them, working in technology. Jake — the love of her life and soon-to-be fiancé, he swore it would be *soon, very soon. Stop bugging me and it would happen faster. Of course he loved her. How could he surprise her with a ring if she kept bringing it up?*

Jake and Jen were so cute, even their matching names were adorable, everyone said. And they loved all the same things — cheering for the San Francisco Giants, going to the beach, hiking local trails, and gaming. They were meant to be together.

Then, Jake forgot his laptop at home. It was Presidents' Day. Jen's pre-school was closed, Jake's company was not. Was it ever? He worked constantly, evenings and weekends.

She sent him a text that he'd forgotten his laptop. He'd rushed out of the apartment, late because Jen hadn't set the alarm. He didn't answer but she figured he was still in the car. She stared at the dark screen, trying to decide whether she should drive to his office and give it to him. She didn't want to spend her day off driving there and back, but he lived with that laptop. His entire brain was on that laptop, he always said.

When she yanked the cord, the laptop woke up. Usually he set the screen lock, but he'd stayed up late, working on PowerPoint slides, complaining that every time he went for a soda, the screen locked. He must have unlocked it.

Instead of PowerPoint slides, she saw his Gmail account. She didn't mean to look, but it was right there. Filling screen after screen were emails from someone called Jordanna Michaels. One after another, Jen opened them. She didn't need to read them all to understand that not only would Jake not be asking her to marry him, he would be gone from her life in the very near future. Still, she read every single one, as if she took some perverse pleasure from feeling the words cut shreds across the surface of her heart.

Was it possible to feel numb at the same time your heart was bleeding?

Jake wrote about needing time to *let Jen down carefully*, as if she were a fragile vase and the care was required because there was something wrong with *her*, not because he'd betrayed her, torn his heart out of her hands and given it to someone else. He wrote about how *hot* Jordanna looked in her leather dress, how no-one at the club danced the way she did. He *couldn't control* himself when she danced. He wrote about how much he loved Jordanna — she was his soul mate. Even their names matched — *two J's*, proving it was meant to be.

There were emails filled with erotic descriptions of what they would do with each other, how desperate they felt to be together and how they ached for days at a time, separated and alone.

She closed the laptop. She showered, washing tears and mucous off her face. She left her underwear in the drawer. She dressed in a tight, low-cut black leather dress. The one Jake used to love because she looked so *hot*. She put on a pair of stilettos with silver heels, shoes she'd bought to spice up the dress when he seemed tired of it. She put on dark eye shadow and thick eye liner. She spread bright red creamy color across her lips.

When she arrived at his office, she walked into the lobby with the laptop. The receptionist stared without trying to hide her shock. Jen settled in one of the armchairs and sent a text to Jake.

Jen: *I'm here in your lobby, babe. I have your laptop.*

Jake: *You're an angel! You saved my life. I'll be there in two secs.*

When he entered the lobby, he stopped. He jerked his head, looking toward the reception desk where the middle-aged woman sat smirking. He turned and looked at a group of visitors sitting on two couches who were more interested in Jen than in whatever they'd been discussing a moment earlier.

Jen stood and slowly pulled down the zipper on the front of her dress. "Is this what you're looking for?"

He yanked the zipper but it wouldn't go up. He didn't understand you had to hold both pieces of fabric stable to maneuver the zipper tab back up along the heavy teeth. He grabbed her arm and half-dragged her out of the lobby to the parking lot. He opened her car door and pushed her into the passenger seat. "What the hell is wrong with you?"

"I thought this is what Jordanna gave you." She smiled.

His face turned pale. He grabbed the guilty laptop, backed away, and walked into the building.

He didn't come home that night.

The next morning, Jake showed up at the pre-school. Jen was reading *The Very Hungry Caterpillar* to thirteen wide-eyed children. The rest of the class was sitting at a low table, printing their numbers under the guidance of the head teacher. Jake grabbed the book out of her hand and threw it on the floor.

"Thanks for getting the entire company laughing at me." He slapped her face.

She cried out and shoved him. He stumbled back, half-falling onto a small boy with white-blonde hair.

"Fuck you!" He kicked out at her and managed to land the heel of his shoe on another small boy who began crying.

The entire staff of Precious Care Pre-School was appalled. A letter of apology was sent to all the parents. Jen was asked to leave that day. A final check would be mailed.

With that kind of reason for termination on her resume, her career in childcare was over.

No fiancé. No job. No home.

Now, here she was, in San Francisco.

She dipped her feet in the icy water. At least now she could breathe, for a while. David was gone, visiting his father in LA. For three glorious days she could be herself, more or less. Not constantly waiting for the next text message from David: *Come here.*

41

Pinning down Steve Montgomery was a challenge. I hated it that the situation had done a complete one-eighty and now I was seeking him. Once a week, he worked out of the San Francisco office. Once a week he was in Santa Cruz meeting with the engineering teams. The other three days he spent visiting customers, when he was in the Bay Area. Nearly fifty percent of the time he was on an airplane heading to customers on the East Coast, Europe, and Asia.

Disinterest is much more profitable than neediness. I continued resisting the temptation to call or text him, proving I was anxious to consider his offer. His admin was located in Santa Cruz, so I couldn't casually pass by her desk, hoping to lure her into a conversation, sharing pieces of tasty gossip until she felt obligated to share her own with me. Like sharing a few tastes of your cheesecake compels your dinner partner to offer a spoonful of chocolate mousse. Bites of little known information, I didn't know what, that might have given me additional leverage with him, if she was the gossipy type.

When he was in San Francisco, it was usually for all-day meetings, but I would need to lurk outside a conference room for hours, since I wasn't privy to their agendas and couldn't guess when a break might come. The standard routine was a working lunch, food wheeled in on carts, arranged on tables at the back of the room, served buffet style so they could carry on meeting without interruption, food growing cold on their plates when an argument proved more stimulating than curry chicken over rice or beef stroganoff. This meant another avenue for casually wandering by was closed to me.

He'd said his admin would set up a time for us to meet for a drink. In San Francisco, it should have been easy. Upscale bars with luscious towers of alcohol reaching to the ceiling were everywhere. I've been told there are more than thirteen hundred bars in less than fifty square miles.

How was it that he'd been so keen to invite me for a drink, so convinced I'd be a good fit for sales, and then completely forgotten about it? Or changed his mind. That was possible, but why? Part of me wondered if Tess had found out he'd talked to me, but I couldn't think of a way that might have happened. He'd insisted I shouldn't mention it to her, so surely *he* hadn't.

And then Tess gave me a chance to make the first move without appearing too eager.

For her next executive review, she needed to know how marketing leads were distributed to the sales teams — how many per person, whether they were handed out across the board or to a select group. Steve wouldn't have such trivial information, but it was legitimate to ask him who was the best person in his organization to give me the data I was collecting for her.

I shot an email to him.

Fifteen minutes later, he was resting his elbow on the top edge of my cubicle wall.

"We broke for the afternoon, so I decided to stop by," he said.

"Perfect. Do you have a name for me?"

"First, a question. Why do you need to know?"

"For Tess. For the review with Hutchins."

"And why does she need to know."

"I just told you."

He looked annoyed, as if he thought I was being deliberately obtuse. "Why is the information important?"

"They're wondering if we would get a better return if select sales people were trained specifically on how to follow up on a lead from an event or direct mail," I said.

"Rick Esperanza."

"Thanks."

"How are you liking the change of venue?" he said.

I pushed back my chair and stood.

"No need to get up."

I did need to get up. It put us on a slightly more equal footing. "I'm loving it."

"Good. Talk to you later." He began walking away.

He behaved as if he'd never suggested a job of any kind. He behaved as if he hardly knew me and all the conversations between us were figments of my imagination.

What the hell was going on?

I walked out of my cubicle and followed him down the hall. He was about thirty feet ahead of me already and I was on the precipice of making a fool of myself. But I needed to know. If he'd changed his mind, I needed to talk to Tess about expanding my job into something that attracted more money, or think about other options.

I was beginning to realize that getting ahead in a good-sized company, in any company, would take years. I was impatient for larger salary increases, determined to find a way to accelerate that process. My goal is a home with property in the next five years and at the rate I'm going, I'll be lucky to have enough to purchase a condo, unless I move out of California. I have lots of huge dreams, but no clear-cut plan for how I'm going to acquire the cash needed to implement them.

Steve had reached the elevators. From where I was, I could see the lights above the doors advancing to our floor. I picked up my pace even though I had no idea what I'd say when I reached his side.

Just as the doors opened, I touched his sleeve.

He turned quickly. "What's up?" He stuck out his arm to prevent the doors from closing.

"I…" It's so rare that I'm at a loss for words, I froze even further, marveling at my lack of planning.

He stepped into the elevator, keeping his hand on the door.

"What's Rick's title?" I said.

He stared at me as if I was a complete idiot. And I was. Three key strokes and I could have looked it up. If I even needed it. Chasing Steve down the hall and grabbing him out of the elevator was not necessary.

"Director of Sales Operations."

"Thanks."

"Is that all?"

"Yes, I…"

"I have another meeting."

"Sure. Thanks."

He moved his hand and the doors closed with painful slowness so that I was forced to stare at his expressionless face for several seconds.

When the doors were finally shut, I felt my face steaming as blood pumped closer to the surface of my skin. All I could think of was the woman in the painting with all of her internal organs on display.

42

Going for a run was critical. Steve had tipped me so far off balance, I wanted to kill him. That's not something I say lightly. He hadn't done anything to deserve it, not really. But his nonchalance had a threatening undertone. He'd undermined my last raise and he'd dangled an opportunity he'd now withdrawn. He'd turned things around so completely, if I was paranoid, I'd think he was trying to mess with my head, to put me in my place. But why? It was possible he realized he'd offered something he couldn't deliver. Or maybe his responsibilities truly were so consuming, he'd forgotten.

Instead of expanding as they should have, my options were shrinking. Instead of seeing more money and a place of my own shimmering on the horizon like the green flash that signals to soulmates they've found each other — if you believe that sort of bullshit, heavenly signs and soulmates — I saw nothing but fog. Thick, unrelenting fog that destabilizes your equilibrium.

I took off my shoes and dress, tossing the dress on the couch to be properly hung later when I didn't have tremors in my fingers, adrenaline demanding I run as fast as I could for as long as my lungs held out to push all my nerve endings back into submission. I put on capri running pants and the rest of my usual gear — topping it with a neon yellow hoodie and a matching sweatband.

After drinking a large glass of water and emptying my

bladder, I hurried out to the elevator, hopping from one foot to the other as it descended to the first floor. I jogged across the lobby and out onto the sidewalk. I wove among groups of people headed to bars and dinner, or up to the Muni station for their commutes home.

I'd run two miles, back and forth along the waterfront from Howard to the Ferry Building, and was starting my third pass when I saw him.

My stalker. Calling him a stalker was a slight exaggeration, but everything about my day was over the top.

I wasn't sure why I hadn't noticed him earlier. Maybe he hadn't been there, although he looked fairly hunkered down on a bench beneath a fluorescent light, a copy of the San Francisco Chronicle open wide in front of him. This time, his hat advertised the Golden State Warriors. If he thought he was hiding behind the change in sports teams, he wasn't very bright. And maybe the fact that I'd noticed him several times was telling me the same thing.

I passed him and continued to the end of the path. When I turned, I thought about how disturbing his presence was, and then remembered how thrilled I'd been at the age of fifteen to know a boy was following me. It's fascinating how something looks one way at a certain point in your life, and then, as if your life is a circle, and you're slowly moving around every event as time goes on, you see a different side that shocks you.

What kind of person was I at fifteen that made me thrill to a boy following me? Of course, he was in my class, so I hadn't viewed him as a stranger. But why not? It was a delusion that because he lived in the same school district and occupied a chair on the other side of the classroom, he was somehow safe, a known entity. I knew nothing about him. Such a false sense of security comes from attending the same school or working at the same company or living in the same apartment building. You assume there are no serial killers or rapists, no thieves or con artists, no generally undesirable people at all.

It makes us sitting ducks, sometimes.

My body felt calm. My soothed muscles were starting to infuse my brain with the same pleasant feeling of chaos drained out, replaced by steady thoughts, fed by steady nerves.

When I reached the stalker, I slowed. I cut past some small trees toward the bench where he was sitting. He folded the newspaper haphazardly and tossed it beside him in a way that made me realize he wasn't reading the paper. What an amateur.

I smiled. I put my foot on the bench. I untied my shoe and began re-tying it. "I've seen you watching me." I gave him a coy, sidewards glance.

"You're confused."

I put my foot on the ground with a firm thud. "No I'm not."

"I've never seen you before."

"Well I've seen you. Do you work around here?"

"Yes." He stood.

"Where?"

"None of your business."

"Just trying to be neighborly," I said.

"Is this an awkward attempt at flirting?" He laughed. The sound was rough and phlegmy. He cleared his throat.

"Is that what you want it to be?"

"I don't even know you." He frowned and took a few steps away.

"Maybe you're following me because you want to know me."

"I'm not following you. I've never seen you in my life."

How dramatic. *Never in his life*. I wanted to laugh. He was bad at concealing his presence and bad at lying. "So what should I do if I see you again?"

He shrugged.

"Should I start keeping a record of how often I see you? Report to the police what's happening?"

He laughed more softly. "If you want to prove you're unbalanced. Go right ahead."

"I think they'd believe me."

"Maybe if this was 1953. But it's not. Far from it. *Far* from it."

He took a few steps away from the bench.

"You forgot your newspaper."

"I'm finished with it."

"So you just leave it for someone else to pick up?"

"That's right." He started walking.

I grabbed the newspaper and jogged after him. "Take it."

He shoved his elbow at me, brushing it against the side of my arm. He walked faster.

I dropped the newspaper in a trashcan and watched him disappear around the corner onto Howard Street.

43

Despite my mother's intimidation, I let Denny continue walking me home. Instead of sitting on the stone wall with me, he now stopped at the corner. I walked to my house and around to the backyard where the lawn sloped down to a wooded area. I went a few yards into the trees, sat on a fallen log, and waited.

About ten minutes later, Denny would saunter through the woods, having accessed the area from a house a few doors down from ours. It was the house where a woman whose son had murdered her violently abusive husband lived as a recluse. The drapes in her home were always drawn. This made it easy to use her backyard to access other yards and the wooded area, as well as providing a place where kids occasionally hung out after dark, smoking or making out. Her yard was party-central and her drapes blinded her to that fact.

Once Denny and I had the privacy of the wooded area, making out became our top priority. We spent the late afternoon until close to sunset with our arms around each other, our tongues twisted together, and our hearts thudding with slow, heavy pleasure.

About a week after we settled into our new meeting place, my mother came out to the backyard one afternoon. She walked along the porch, arms squeezed across each other in an effort to keep herself warm. She walked down the steps and hovered around her garden, plucking absently at dead leaves.

For a few days we didn't see her, and then she was there again. This time, she went to the edge of the porch and stared into the wooded area as if she knew we were there. And maybe she did. Maybe she'd known all along. She quickly descended the steps, walked across the lawn, and down the sloped section to where we sat.

Of course, we'd not only stopped kissing, we'd put two feet of space between us on the log. Because she'd seemed to look directly at us, I wasn't sure if she'd observed the kissing or not.

She walked right up to Denny. "Who are you?"

He stood and extended his right hand. *Point one.*

She stepped back with an apologetic smile. She slowly extended her hand.

"I'm in Alexandra's civics class. Denny Baker. Pleased to meet you, Mrs. Mallory." He took her hand. *Point two.*

She giggled.

I stared. Who was this woman?

"Nice to meet you, Denny. Do you live around here?"

"On Harrison."

"Oh, that's nice. That's a nice area."

I waited for her to ask where he went to church. She didn't. I waited for her to invite him to our church. My parents were always inviting our friends to visit our church. Despite my parents' rather extreme, and harsh beliefs, they worried. Those extreme beliefs meant they felt with their entire being that anyone who didn't believe the same was destined for eternal separation from their creator. They wanted to be sure every single person they met had a chance to escape the horror of living in utter darkness, filled with unimaginable pain for eternity.

They were diligent and heartfelt. They couldn't bear to think of people suffering without an end in sight. They had no problem with people suffering on earth — that's what earth was *for*. Time on earth was for the sole purpose of recognizing the need to accept short-term pain in exchange for long-term gain.

My mother seemed unconcerned with Denny's soul. She couldn't stop staring into his eyes.

He was a very good looking guy with blue eyes and dark hair that he wore slightly long. He had beautiful curls but they didn't make him look feminine — they somehow managed to look rugged. He was tall, almost six feet and still a Sophomore in high school. He was lean with broad shoulders and long legs.

My mother looked up at him. She combed her fingers through the ends of her hair. She glanced at me and frowned, then moved slightly so the back of her shoulder faced me, effectively closing the space between them, leaving me on the outside.

"Do you play sports?" she said.

"I like to ski."

"Oh. I always wanted to try skiing, I never got the chance."

"There's no reason you can't try it now," he said. *Point three.*

"I might be too old for that."

"Not at all," Denny said. "You're young, you're fit. You should try it." *Point four.*

"Maybe I will. Does everyone in your family ski?"

He nodded.

"Maybe our families could go together. You could teach me." Her voice rose with excitement.

My stomach churned. I tasted the bologna sandwich from lunch mixed with cigarette smoke that clung to the back of my throat. What was wrong with her? It seemed as if she was flirting with him. I'd never seen her like this, and I wasn't sure what had flipped the switch. It was embarrassing. Because of the way he was speaking in such a warm, exaggerated tone, his words coming out more slowly than usual, I knew he was half teasing. He recognized the flirty smiles and the way she tilted her head for what they were.

I wanted to crawl under the log. Instead, I stood up. I took a few steps and wedged myself between them. My mother refused to take the hint. She rooted her feet deeper into the soft earth and let her hip bone press against mine. I wanted to shove her out of the way.

I didn't know Denny very well. There was a good chance he was so entertained by her ridiculous behavior he would tell his friends. It would fly around the school that Alexandra's mother thought she was the kind of woman who could attract the interest of a high school guy.

"It's cold. We should go inside." I looped my arm around hers and tugged gently.

She pulled her arm away. "I'm not cold at all. I'd like to learn more about skiing."

Denny smiled at her. He didn't even give a sideways glance at me. *Point five.*

At least I wasn't in trouble, but I was not going to fight with my mother for a guy's attention.

44

San Francisco

Finding a place to smoke in San Francisco, a very progressive city in every way, including an aversion to cigarette smoke, is difficult. Across the entire state of California, smoking is banned in restaurants and bars, often in parks and outdoor concert venues. Most buildings have smoke-free zones around their entrances, and the zone is enforced by doormen and parking valets, occupants and patrons.

A smoker is made to feel like a fugitive. In some areas, smoking pot is more acceptable than smoking a cigarette. A smoker is no longer simply blackening and hardening her own lungs into a sticky mass of tar that eventually chokes on itself. She's inflicting the promise of death on anyone who is forced into regular contact with the smoke streaming out of her mouth in seductive silvery ribbons.

Smoking on my apartment balcony wasn't viable. The space was narrow — basically a concrete box open on one side to provide a view. Smoke layered itself over the concrete walls and would eventually find its way into the apartment. The odor of smoke inside the apartment meant a forfeited cleaning deposit. I hadn't paid the deposit, but CoastalCreative would surely deduct it from my check.

Around the corner from my building was a shabby liquor store. The shabbiness didn't let on that they were well stocked with a decent general selection as well as top-shelf alcohol. Smoking was tacitly tolerated in the vicinity of the entrance. A higher than average percentage of people shopping at a liquor store are occasional smokers, if not full time. The clerks seemed to be under instructions not to inhibit business in any way.

It wasn't the glamorous experienced I craved — standing in front of a magnificent building, smoking and watching passersby in those few moments before I'm asked to take my filthy habit elsewhere and the imagined glamor is ripped away. Outside the liquor store, I felt a little shabby myself. But smoking, in a slightly different way than running, helps me think, and I needed to think.

I wore dark brown riding boots, cut higher in the front to cover my knees, and my new hip-length wool coat since standing outside in San Francisco can feel like you're in the arctic when the wind kicks up. I've never been to the arctic, and I suppose that's a gross exaggeration, but the penetrating nature of that damp cold coming from the ocean and the bay at the same time has a way of cutting through to your bones. I also wore a hat — a coffee colored beret.

The cigarette was half gone. Cold was seeping through the soles of my boots and stiffening my fingers. I was contemplating whether I could stand the chill long enough for a second smoke. So far, my lazy contemplation of my career and the stalker had been circular — a snake eating its tail.

I felt someone approaching on my left. I turned and saw David.

He walked toward me, stopping about a foot too close.

I took a step to the side and exhaled.

"Can I bum one?"

Smoke hung in the space between us. His shoulders were hunched, hands shoved in the pockets of a thin jacket.

"You look cold," I said

"I'm not."

I pulled the cigarettes out of my pocket, removed one, and touched it to the tip of mine until it caught. I handed it to him.

"Thanks." He inhaled and blew out a stream of smoke. "It's funny how we know this is so bad, but we all need it sometimes."

"Agreed."

"And we're desperately hoping that the occasional smoke won't kill us."

"Depends on how you define occasional," I said.

He nodded and took a slow drag.

"Headed to the liquor store?" I said.

"Yes and no."

I tapped the ash off my cigarette and put it to my lips, inhaling slowly.

"Don't you want to know which it is?" He smiled, shifting his demeanor from jerk to maybe-I-initially-misjudged-him.

I dropped my cigarette on the ground and stepped on it. Until I saw which impression was correct, a second smoke could wait.

He sighed. "I do need a bottle of vodka. But I saw you go out. I was curious."

"You followed me?"

He smiled. "I'm not stalking you, don't worry."

"I'm not worried."

"Good. Because I'm honestly not stalking you."

"Did I look like someone sneaking out for an illegal smoke?"

"No. But you looked like a woman with a purpose. I like that."

"Do you?"

"Did you live in the city before you moved to this place?"

"No."

"New job and new apartment?"

"Same company, but they opened a new office."

"Remind me the name of the company?"

"I never mentioned it."

He smiled. "And you're not going to tell me now, either. You seem like a very private person."

"I am."

"Are you this non-talkative with Isaiah?"

"You'd have to ask him."

"Why can't I ask you?"

"Because I don't know whether he finds me talkative or not."

"Fair enough." He took a drag on his cigarette and tapped the ash off. "Are you two a couple?"

I shrugged.

"Or just close friends? Really close?" He laughed, a single note.

"It's too early to say."

"I'm sorry he made the first move. Since the day I met you, I wanted to talk to you more."

"About what?"

"Nothing specific, just to get to know you." He moved

the cigarette to his left hand and took a step closer.

"I thought you were with Jen," I said.

He laughed.

"Why is that funny?"

"How well do you know Jen?"

I shrugged. "Not well."

"She's a whore."

I moved away. "That's disgusting." I stepped around him and started toward the corner.

I had not misjudged him after all.

45

David's sharp, degrading voice pierced my brain as I walked quickly toward the corner.

That word stirs up something inside of me that makes me feel like the character Maleficent in the Disney version of Snow White. I feel my entire being change shape, my body growing huge and fierce, daggers coming out of purple-shadowed eyes, sickly green skin, horns sharpening — black and purple robe turning to flames.

Whore.

It's always a certain kind of man who loves to throw that word around, a suggestion that it defines women. And to use it toward a woman he was in a relationship with?

"Alex! Wait."

He was running after me. I walked faster. I turned the corner and lengthened my stride.

"Wait. You misunderstood."

I stopped and turned. He came up too close, pulling back suddenly, stumbling to avoid plowing into me. His eyes suggested he was afraid of angering me further.

"I didn't misunderstand anything."

"But that's what she is. What she does. Maybe I should have used a PC word. I'm not sure what that is — Prostitute? Hooker?"

"Stop."

"Did she tell you what she does for a living?"

She hadn't. In fact, she'd slipped around the question.

Changed the subject quickly. But she was evasive about everything.

"Maybe she didn't want you to know. She's embarrassed about it, I think."

I remembered the guy watching her in the lounge. The certainty she felt that he wanted to talk to her. His mad gesturing followed by pulling her close to him in the darkness when I saw them outside the apartment. But he'd cradled her head like he cared for her. I tried to reform the image, shaping this new information around it.

Being embarrassed made sense. Especially when you're meeting someone knew. Even more when you're talking to another woman. If men look down on prostitutes, categorize and dismiss them as so much trash, women are worse.

Women hate prostitutes. Their perception is that sex workers lure men to indulge their worst inclinations. They hate them for spreading disease and for turning something that should be an equal exchange into a business transaction. They hate them for making it easy for men to get sex without responsibility. It was something that's rarely discussed, but when it is, opinions are strong and angry. Some women might accept the reality of sex workers, striving to improve their conditions, but that's definitely the exception. Most women think prostitutes are scum. Maybe they're terrified some men can't tell the difference.

David took my arm.

I stiffened. "Let go of me."

"I'm trying to explain."

"Let go."

He removed his hand from my arm.

"I shouldn't have told you. It just...I know it's shocking.

I was shocked too. She doesn't look like the type."

He had no clue that he was pissing me off further.

"She has a sweet face, not that hard look you expect," he said.

"The hard look of a whore?"

"Yes. You know how they are."

"Do I?"

"You've seen them. Their skin is kind of rough and they have this dead look in their eyes. I guess they are dead inside. Because of what they do. Maybe Jen hasn't been at it long enough."

A couple walked past us, the woman leaning into the man, looking up at him as if he was the most luscious thing she'd ever laid eyes on. She leaned against him with so much force, he stumbled every few steps.

I waited for them to pass out of earshot. "A woman who's probably been beaten, abused, degraded in so many ways you can't even imagine?"

"I guess. I don't know anything about it. I was just trying to say, she seems like a nice-enough person."

"And whores aren't nice people?"

"Look what they do."

"Have sex?" I said.

"With strangers. For money."

"You've never had sex with a stranger?"

"Come on. I didn't mean to get into an argument about...hookers."

"I'm sure not."

"Can we start over?"

"I'm not finished."

He sighed. He looked at his feet, a boy about to be chastised.

"I thought she was with you," I said.

"She…"

"So you pay her? Really. When I've seen her with you, I had the impression she didn't want to be there. Now I get it."

"Not true. That's not at all true."

"It was my impression."

"You mis-read it."

"Do you want to tell me anything else about my mistaken perceptions?"

He laughed, nervously.

"Are you two a couple or not?" I knew the answer. Based on how he felt about whores, he sure wouldn't allow one to be his girlfriend. Maybe he was her pimp.

He must have seen the change in my eyes. "I'm not a pimp. It's not like that at all. We're just…friends."

He seemed to be circling around something. If they were friends, why had he called her a whore in such an ugly tone? If that was truly Jen's livelihood, it wasn't as if she'd planned it from childhood, like a little girl announcing to her family she wants to be a lawyer when she grows up. If it was true, forces in her life had sent her in that direction, into one of a handful of jobs that women do when they've run out of choices.

I started walking.

"How about another smoke?" David said.

"It's cold."

"Do you want to come over or something?"

"I'm with Isaiah."

"I know that." He smiled. "For now. You can't blame me

for trying. It's not like you and Isaiah are something solid."

"You don't have a lot of respect for your cousin."

"I do. I just…"

"Whatever. It's cold." I walked quickly to the door of the building and pulled it open. He didn't follow, which I appreciated. Riding up with him in the elevator would have been too much.

46

The stunning portraits of the woman in three phases of her life had not been the first thing that prompted Tess to think about commissioning a portrait of herself. The desire to acquire a portrait of herself had developed around the same time as her thoughts about buying a handgun.

There was a certain snob appeal to having your portrait painted. It was something done by the upper classes. A painting was something that lasted through generations, not that she had another generation to value her portrait. Although that wasn't completely out of the question yet.

There was no Turner clan with portraits hanging on the dining room wall of an ancestral home. That didn't mean she couldn't start her own. It was a legacy. It was…she wasn't sure where the idea had even come from. She wasn't a snob, just proud of her achievements and happy to enjoy the financial rewards. She had money to spend on acquisitions that others might consider frivolous. It was part of success. There was nothing wrong with it.

Seeing Xavier Holland's work bought her desire to the foreground. Xavier Holland. The name rolled around in her mind, slid across the roof of her mouth, even when she only spoke it in her thoughts. He was supremely talented and if he could make her face as sublime as his lover's… The three paintings were so clearly the same woman, demonstrating his talent for capturing the essence of his subject.

Her feet were icy cold, but she was too comfortable to

get up from the love seat and go into the bedroom for a pair of socks. She folded her legs and tried to wedge her feet under her right hip. The city was draped with heavy fog. It always made her feel colder, even though the temperature inside her condo was comfortable.

She cradled the phone in her hand, trying to arrange her thoughts in case Celine asked why she wanted a portrait. It didn't seem like an important question for a gallery manager, but it was possible the artist had some sort of pre-screening process that Celine managed for him. Tess liked to be prepared for all possibilities.

She couldn't say it was part of her legacy. How grandiose to think of a legacy at her age, in her situation. But why did a desire like this have to be explained? Even to herself? Why did it matter? She wanted it. She could afford it. *Why* wasn't a factor.

She unlocked the phone, opened her contact list and found Celine's number.

Celine answered on the second ring.

"Hi." Tess uncurled her legs and stood. She wanted her voice strong and firm. Sitting squashed your diaphragm and lungs, thinning your voice into a meek tone. "This is Tess Turner. I was in the gallery last week and..."

"I remember you."

Tess smiled. "I wanted to ask about commissioning a portrait from one of your artists. How do I go about that?"

"Which artist?" Celine sounded distant, her voice cooler and less excited.

"Xavier Holland. His work is unbelievable. He..."

"I'm so sorry. Xavier only has one subject."

"What do you mean?" She knew what it meant, but the

disappointment poured through her, clutching her throat, refusing to let her believe the desire had brushed its fingers across her heart and slipped away so easily.

"He only paints his lover. That's all. The three you saw are only a few from the collection, but..."

"He only paints her? That's his entire portfolio? How does he make a living?"

"The rest of his work is abstract."

"Such a waste," Tess said. "Has anyone ever asked him directly whether he'd reconsider?"

"Yes."

"Recently?"

"He isn't interested. I'm sorry."

Tess was silent for several minutes.

"Hello?" Celine said. "Are you still there?"

"I'm here." The words were slow to emerge... "I suppose...can you recommend another artist?" She felt her vision of a painting that would leave viewers breathless was being shredded with a box cutter before the suggestion of lines and shape were even placed on the canvas. A painting that would allow people to see her soul within a few brush strokes, revealing its power and complexity, yet not exposing vulnerability.

"Oh. Yes. Absolutely. I could give you several, but let me recommend Joshua North."

"He's not the one who paints the figures with their bones and organs exposed, is he?"

Celine laughed. "No. I can arrange a private showing with Joshua. He's done a wide variety of portraits. I think you'll be intrigued."

"That sounds good," Tess said. "Can you give me his

website so I can take a look?"

"I think that would do him an injustice. The real deal is so much more impressive and you don't want to come in with a certain expectation. Let me call him. Can you give me a few dates?"

"Tomorrow evening, or Thursday after four both work for me. Do you need more choices?"

"No, that should be fine. He's usually quite flexible."

"So other people have commissioned him for portraits?"

"Of course."

When Tess finished talking to Celine, she opened the browser on her phone and tapped in *Joshua North*. Four artists named Joshua North in the Bay Area appeared. She closed it. Celine was right. Better to view them in real life. And meet him. She had to get a sense of him, observe how he responded to her. Feeling comfortable in his presence was an important factor. It might be part of why Xavier's portraits were so remarkable.

Right now, she needed to swallow the disappointment that continued to squeeze her throat. If she saw Joshua's work online, she'd compare it too quickly with Xavier Holland's brilliance. She needed a few days to adjust, to let go of her expectations so she was ready to be swept away by a different style.

She went into the kitchen and uncorked a bottle of Chardonnay that was sitting on the top shelf of the fridge. She poured a glass and took a sip. She carried the glass to the sunroom and returned to the love seat.

Closing her eyes, she took several sips of wine, trying to empty her mind of all thoughts but the sharp cold wine on her tongue, along the insides of her mouth, sliding down her throat. She let the silence settle around her.

Once she saw the work of this new guy — Joshua — her original excitement would return. It had to. Because she'd gone from wanting the portrait to needing it. The result would be stunning, she was confident, even though she had no rational basis for feeling that way.

47

I saw him again as I was walking up to my apartment building after work. The brown leather jacket. Faded blue jeans. Giants hat. He watched me approach, not looking at the building, and not faking it with a newspaper. I waved.

He didn't respond, but neither did he turn away.

I opened the lobby door and went inside.

Jen was standing near the windows. She wore tight jeans, boots, and a low-cut tank top under a black leather jacket. Very low cut. I looked at her outfit with new eyes. Her dark hair and dark bangs gleamed under the fluorescent lights. She wore dark makeup smudged beneath her eyes and across her lids, but no lipstick. There was nothing that made her stand out from any other woman passing through the lobby.

The disdain in David's voice had made me think of a prostitute that worked a street corner. It hadn't occurred to me maybe she was more of a discreet, highly-priced call girl, if what he said was even true. Despite his attempt at sincerity, there was still something disturbing about the guy.

Jen was looking out at the street as if she expected someone any minute. Or maybe, she was watching the guy who couldn't stop staring at the entrance to our building.

I walked up to her.

She smiled and greeted me.

"Do you see that guy in the Giants hat across the street?" I said.

"In the brown jacket?"

"Yes. Do you know him?"

She shook her head.

"Are you sure?"

"Yep."

"I see him around a lot. I think he's following me."

"Why would he follow you?"

"I have no idea. But he's bothering me."

"That's scary." Her eyes widened as if fear was the only possible response.

"More irritating."

"Are you worried he's a serial killer or something?"

"There really aren't that many serial killers, even though TV and movies make it seem like there's one on every block. The odds are against it I think. And serial killers are usually smart, methodical. This guy doesn't do a very good job of hiding it. I asked him why he's following me, but he denied it."

"You talked to him?" Her voice rose slightly.

"Yes."

"That's crazy." She glanced out the window. "He's still there."

"So you've never seen him?"

"I don't think so. But you never know. Lots of guys dress like that, so it's hard to tell."

"Okay. He's annoying the hell out of me and I want him to stop. If I see him again, I'm going to be more aggressive. He accused me of flirting with him."

Jen laughed. "Sorry. I guess that's not funny. But isn't that what a lot of guys assume, no matter what?"

"Yeah. Are you waiting for someone?"

"David."

"Are you going out?"

"I doubt it," she said.

"You don't seem thrilled with him. Are you two a couple, or what?"

"Are you and Isaiah?"

I laughed. "Okay, that's fair."

"He's just a friend."

"I get the impression you don't really like being with him."

"You do?"

"Yes."

"Sorry."

"Why are you sorry?"

She shrugged.

"So why are you waiting for him here, if you're not going out?"

"You ask a lot of questions," Jen said.

"I'm a very curious person."

"Okay, maybe we're not really friends. Sort of. He's helped me out a lot. And I owe him."

"Owe him what? Money?"

"No."

I don't know why I persisted. Sometimes you just do things, motivated by some unseen, pre-programmed part of yourself. Maybe a simple drive to action over inertia.

There was no reason for David to lie about her, unless it was some elaborate way for him to back away from calling her a whore, assuming I'd never have the nerve to ask her directly. I absolutely had the nerve. I just wasn't sure it was the right time, standing in the lobby with people going in and out, our conversation open to the entire room as voices bounced off the windows and marble floor and high ceiling.

She glanced at the street and back at me.

I waited half a minute.

She turned her head again, staring intently, as if searching for a particular face. It seemed like she was watching the flow of foot traffic for someone other than David. Maybe, she was watching the man watching me. Maybe the man was watching Jen, not me. If Jen was what David claimed, the man in the brown leather jacket might be wanting to hire her. But then, when I was running, she was nowhere around, and there he was.

"How long have you known David?" I said.

She shrugged.

"A few weeks? Months?"

"Two years."

"Oh." I swallowed my surprise. "You should never feel like you owe people."

"That's not true at all." She didn't look at me as she spoke. "If someone loans you money, or helps you. If they give you a ride or water your plants, if they babysit your kids or your pets for free, don't you think you owe them something in return?"

"No. Someone isn't really a friend if you think you *owe* them. You might want to do something to thank them, but it shouldn't feel like a debt."

"Whatever." She tipped her head back and moved it from side to side. She straightened and rubbed the back of her neck.

"Do you trust him?"

"As much as you can trust anyone. Which isn't much." She laughed.

Dancing around the subject was ridiculous. I was either going to ask or I wasn't. "Do you think he talks behind your back?"

"He better not."

"He does, you know."

She turned slowly, her gaze lingering at the sidewalk outside, but finally shifting to my face. "Like what?"

I decided to flatter as much as I could, ease into the conversation respectfully. "He said you're an escort."

Her lips parted and turned soft. A sheen covered her eyes and although they were directed at me, they seemed not to see me. "I doubt that's what he said."

"It's not."

She shrugged. "Great. That's just fucking great."

Her eyes filled with tears. She blinked and tilted her chin up. When she lowered it again, the liquid was gone, but they glimmered with rage. The teal color piercing, like deadly shards of glass.

48

Jen pulled out her phone and checked the time. "I guess he's not coming."

"Maybe that's good."

"I need to talk to him."

"Do you want to go upstairs, get a beer or a glass of wine?"

She unlocked her phone and tapped around, her finger moving faster and faster. She wasn't texting so I wasn't sure what she was looking for. After a few more taps, she slipped it into her back pocket. "I suppose now you want to know all the icky details. About what a disgusting person I turned out to be."

"I don't think you're disgusting."

"Yeah, right. You'll wait until I try to explain and then tell me I'm a low life."

"I'm not like that. We do what we have to do. Lots of men want sex without strings and you provide it. I don't think it makes you any kind of person at all."

"Are you bullshitting me?"

"Let's get a glass of wine."

We walked to the elevators and went up to the second floor. The lounge was only about half full. We went to the chairs where we'd sat the first time — separated a bit from the other groupings of furniture. "Red, white, or beer?"

"White wine," she said. "Chardonnay, thanks." She gave me a watery smile.

When we were seated with our wine and a bowl of nuts and pretzels, I raised my glass. "Cheers."

"I'm not feeling very cheerful."

"To future cheer."

She laughed softly and took several sips.

"So what's the deal with David?" I said.

"Don't you want to hear my long, pathetic story?"

"If you want to tell it, sure."

Talking fast, almost faster than I could follow, swallowing some of her words, she told me about a humiliating break-up, getting fired and shut out from her career in childcare. "I guess I could have become a waitress or something unrelated. But no matter what kind of job I applied for, they wanted contact information for previous employers. And I didn't want any future boss knowing my whole personal life before I even got the job. If I got a job."

She scooped up a handful of nuts, picked out the pretzels, and dropped the nuts back in the bowl. "I was at a party and this guy thought I was a hooker. When he offered me five hundred bucks, I felt like it was the first good thing that had happened to me in months. And it was so easy. He was hot, he wanted normal sex. It was so easy, almost fun. To be honest, it *was* fun." She smiled. "It's not always. But most of the time, it's not too bad."

The lounge was getting more crowded, the noise level swelling as if we were trapped inside a hive of bees. I wished we were sitting by the painting of the woman with the exposed body. Something about her grounded me, but the way the couches were positioned near the painting, a private conversation was impossible.

I found myself shifting in my chair, trying to manage an

angle that would allow me to see the painting. No matter how I moved, plants and people standing in groups blocked it. "And David's okay with your job?"

She shrugged.

"A lot of men wouldn't be."

"We aren't together. Not like that."

"Is he a…"

"No. I mean…" She sipped her wine. She turned and looked across the room, searching.

I realized now, she was always scanning the crowd. Possibly she was assessing the men, not looking for one in particular. I'd never known a call girl and I was curious. There were so many things I wondered about, but unlike other jobs, it seemed like I'd be wriggling through a puddle of prurient slime if I started bombarding her with questions about the how and the when.

She spoke in a soft voice, too low for me to hear.

I leaned forward. "What?"

"They don't like it here."

"Who doesn't like what?"

"The management. This is a classy place." She looked into her wine glass.

"Oh. I get it."

She looked up. "So you can't say anything. Please? Okay?"

"Never."

She put down her empty glass and pushed her hair away from her face with both hands, letting them linger on the sides of her head as if she was holding her cheeks. "I don't understand why he told you. I'd be evicted, if you… It's illegal."

I stood. "Do you want another glass of wine?"

"Sure." She held up her glass.

I wove my way among people and chairs, plants and sofas and tables to the bar. Three men and a woman were ahead of me. I turned and looked at the painting. Even from across the room, it grabbed me, holding my thoughts.

"Are you next?"

I turned back and put down the glasses. "Chardonnay, thanks."

The bartender filled them and I picked them up, turning slowly. I walked past the windows, moving slowly, keeping to the outer edge of the crowd. When I reached the wall where the painting hung, I paused and took a sip of my wine, then moved closer.

Four women sat on the facing sofas beneath it. One was turned sideways, her back to the painting, looking as if she was determined to keep the image behind her no matter how awkward her position. It fascinated me that people were either drawn to it or sickened by it. Surely that said something about their view of the world, although I hadn't quite figured out what. I wondered whether the artist was aware of the polarized reactions. I wondered if he was aiming for that division. A lot of art is intended to shock, or unsettle, I just wasn't sure if his intent fell into that category.

Celine had directed me to his website for insight into his vision, but I'd never looked. I sipped my wine and studied the painting.

One of the women caught my eye. "Creepy, isn't it?"

I smiled. "I love it."

She raised her glass to me in a silent toast. I did the same, then continued back to where Jen was sitting with her heels pulled up onto the seat cushion, hugging her shins. I put the wine on the table.

She spoke through the space between her knees. "You seem like a nice person. Since you already know about me, I'll tell you the whole thing."

I took a sip of wine. She ignored hers.

"He, David, overheard me talking to someone about my, uh...my services." She laughed roughly. "He said if I have sex with him whenever he wants, he won't rat me out to the building management."

I took several sips of wine. I thought about David, betraying her as casually as her boyfriend had. Using her. Terrorizing her, really. The best thing for him, the thing he was deserving of, was having his skin slowly peeled off until he looked like the woman in the painting. Stripped of dignity and life.

49

Jen and I left the lounge after the second glass of wine. We walked two blocks to the Pho place she liked and sat at a tiny corner table. We slurped Pho and talked about movies we liked. I told her a bit about my job, but none of the drama.

She didn't ask what I thought of David's behavior and I didn't offer my rage.

It was another three days before I ran into David while I was stretching for a pre-dawn run. He came out of the building carrying a garment bag, wheeling a small suitcase behind him like a pull toy.

"Hey." He walked to where I stood, his plastic wheels rattling on the rough spots in the concrete. "I didn't know you were a runner. A smoker and a runner. That's eff-ed up."

"I don't smoke that often," I said.

"Whatever you say."

"Where are you headed?" I smiled and unzipped my hoodie.

He studied the skin exposed by the open zipper. He shifted the garment bag to his other shoulder. "Manhattan. A two-day review for next year's styles."

"Nice. I'd love to visit New York."

"You've never been?"

"Sadly…"

He waited for me to say more. I smiled.

"Too bad you're with Isaiah. I'd invite you to go with me."

"We're not a couple or anything like that."

He frowned slightly. Clearly confused. "I'm not gonna invite a girl who's…seeing my cousin to hop on a plane to New York with me."

"I don't think Isaiah has any illusions about what our relationship is."

"Better safe than sorry, but you're very tempting."

"Do you travel a lot?"

"Once a month, more or less."

"Maybe next time?"

He grinned. "Sure. Wow. The other night I thought…"

I waved my hand to shush him. "Come on, haven't you ever been snappish after a bad day?" I tilted my head to the side and gave him a tiny smile.

"I thought I offended you."

"Oh? Why did you think that?"

"You seemed pissed."

"I said I had a bad day. A terrible day."

"I thought you were upset about Jen, or something. I don't know."

Such an astute guy. He was brimming with sensitivity, thinking I might be upset he'd called a woman a whore, and broken her confidence to make himself look less slimy for calling her that. Also ignoring a major point — he was blackmailing her.

Now that I'd hinted at a future something, he was even happier. Gleeful.

I took a few steps toward him and put my hand on his wrist. "I told you I had a bad day. Don't you ever have those?"

"Yep. Too many of them."

"We all do. And it was fun smoking with you. A lot of people get all wound up when they find out you smoke once in a while."

He nodded. "Yeah. It's crazy."

"People love to tell you what you're doing wrong."

"No shit."

"Have you been friends with Jen a long time?" I said.

"I hardly know her."

"Oh. I thought you were close."

He grimaced and shook his head. "Here's my cab."

"Why don't you take Uber?"

"My company pays for a cab. It's easier."

I couldn't fathom how it was easier. "Have a good trip."

"I will. Looking forward to my return." He grinned.

"And you haven't even left. Bring me a souvenir."

"Okay. What do you like?"

"Surprise me. Something New York-y."

He laughed. "Sure."

I took a step closer. I leaned toward him and kissed his lips, softly, almost like a friend, just at the sides, without full contact, a quiet suggestion of more.

"Mmm. That's nice." He looked sad.

"Don't forget my souvenir."

"I won't."

He climbed into the cab and it wrenched away from the curb.

Clearly, peeling off his skin and watching him die was only a fantasy. But he did need to be removed from circulation. He was a disgusting excuse for humanity, using Jen like she was some sort of plaything. He might as well be her pimp, taking what he wanted, terrorizing her into doing what he said. Turning her into a sex slave.

A building that allowed prostitutes wouldn't attract the right residents, not to mention the illegal aspect. And I honestly didn't want to live in a place like that. But Jen wasn't bringing men into her apartment. She met them in hotels. All she did was live there. She had a right to live where she chose, regardless of what anyone else thought of her lifestyle. Surely the building housed a drug dealer or two. And it was surely home to unethical attorneys. I knew it had a large percentage of employees from the financial services industry, several of whom were likely paying their six or seven thousand dollars a month in rent out of profits skimmed from the home loan fleecing that unraveled in 2008. In fact, one of the occupants was extorting sex rather than cash.

There were men and women who had cheated on spouses and partners, there were people who cheated on their taxes. It would be difficult, impossible I think, to find an apartment building that didn't house people who had some kind of corruption or shady corners in their lives. When you come right down to it, finding a human being without some ethical or moral compromise is pretty difficult. Many won't admit that, we like to dismiss our lapses with justified excuses, but no one is perfect.

We choose to minimize the minor crimes of betraying friendships, sabotaging co-workers, mistreating clerks and servers…the list goes on.

Contemplating the idea of killing David in New York City was appealing. The fantasy swept me away during the first mile of my run. I pictured myself checking into a luxury hotel, perhaps brushing shoulders or hips with the famous people that wandered around the streets of New York.

A bellhop with a Bronx accent would take me to my room. On the elevator ride up, he would tease me, even though he knew he should be staid and aloof, in keeping with the hotel's reputation. I'd tease right back, knowing that when I left the hotel for the final time, my makeup would be washed away, my hair a different color, and my classy dress exchanged for yoga pants and a baggy t-shirt, high heels for casual sandals. I would slip through the lobby unnoticed.

Left behind in my gorgeous room would be the very beautiful corpse of an unidentified man. Possibly with a piece of skin from his arm cut off — a symbolic gesture. Maybe not, I don't like blood.

The painting with exposed muscle and bone and blood intrigued me, but in reality, I stay as far as I can from the stuff. Not only because I'm squeamish, but the mess. And its ability to tell people you've been up to no good, tying you to someone's death.

The upside of this fantasy was the delay before they identified the body — it would give me a fair amount of anonymity. But the airfare and the cost of the hotel weren't in my budget. I wanted to be saving for more important things.

And David didn't warrant that expense.

50

No one was going to know Tess planned to move forward with having her portrait painted. She wasn't discussing it any further with Alexandra and she was not mentioning it to Steve. Definitely not Steve. She wasn't sure why she'd even thought of him. None of her other acquaintances or friends knew anything about it. Talking about her desire opened the door for slight ridicule and a strong dose of pity. At least that's what she'd seen in Alexandra's eyes, that's what had echoed in her voice.

This was something that was just for her. It wasn't vain. It was historically important. Not that she considered herself a historic figure, but she had an interesting life and it was worth noting.

The importance of history had collapsed in the twenty-first century. Everyone was racing so madly into the future, they cared less about preserving, or even acknowledging the past. Unless it was digital preservation. And what was that? Who looked at the gigabytes of photographs and terabytes of videos in their cloud accounts? Who played even a fraction of the music they'd purchased?

And what if there were a global energy crisis? The planet was burning up, the arctic melting. Warehouses full of servers were humming around the clock, sucking in dwindling energy forms along with wind and solar. At this moment in time, wind and solar were limitless, but the human race had burned up every other resource, or was well on its way to that point.

Who was to say humanity wouldn't figure out a way to suck the very life out of the sun?

Someday, the whole networked infrastructure might disappear. And then where would all those digital images reside? They'd be vapor.

Even if that didn't happen, once your life was over, those images occupied their little bits and bytes in cyberspace and no one ever looked at them.

Tomorrow, she'd see Joshua's work, and assuming she liked it, they would arrange her first sitting. She was confident she *would* like it, confident in Celine's recommendation. He'd tell her what to wear, how to arrange her body, what to think about to create the most interesting expression, a look defined by her interior world rather than by everything external to herself. She'd thought about hiring a makeup artist to be sure her face was perfect, but then realized the painter would focus on capturing her soul and would surely be forgiving and inventive with the palette on her face.

Tonight, she was supposed to have dinner with Steve at a place on Pier 39. Cheesy and tourist-riddled, but he thought it would be fun to behave like tourists, experience the city as outsiders. His idea was completely unappealing. She was so done with him. In fact, she didn't feel like eating dinner with him no matter what restaurant he chose. She didn't feel like listening to him drone on about how brilliantly he'd saved the day, closing deals when the reps were floundering, in danger of losing a sale. She definitely didn't want to wait expectantly through the meal, as if on the alert for a wasp hovering just out of sight, wondering when he'd slip in a casual dismissal or denigration of women.

His parting comment the last time she'd had sex with

him — *don't you know I love you* — had forced her out of complacency. She wasn't in love with him and she never would be. He wasn't in love with her either, he just said it to keep her in line. He said it to get her to spend the night, so she'd be conveniently available for morning sex. Steve loved morning sex. It gave him an *edge* when he walked into a meeting and looked around the room, assessing who had gotten some in the past twelve hours and who hadn't gotten any in the past twelve days. He thought that tactic for achieving psychological superiority, for subtly dominating meetings, positioning himself as the alpha male, was brilliant and funny. He couldn't stop talking about it.

Some day, she did want to be in love. And, if it wasn't too late, she might want a child. Someone who would cherish her portrait. She laughed. She didn't want a child simply to value the painting. It sounded so wrong, even in her own thoughts. But a child *would* value it. If the child never materialized, the painting might be something that could be gifted to a museum. Or a library. So many possibilities.

Right now, she should be getting dressed for dinner. If she wasn't going, she should be calling, or at least sending a text message that she wasn't up to it. But then, he'd want to come to her place. Order takeout. No message was easier.

Standing him up was cold, and not good for her career. She just couldn't figure out how to deal with the love thing. Was she supposed to break up with him like a teenager? *Sorry, I met someone new?* That was a lie. Why had that been the first thing to come to mind. *Sorry, I'm...* what? *It's not you, it's me.* She laughed.

How did you break up with someone? At her age? A colleague?

She went into the kitchen. After the soft carpet, the tile chilled her bare feet. She opened the fridge and took out the ever-present bottle of Chardonnay. She poured a glass and took it into the sunroom. She stood at the window and looked out at the city. So lovely. Santa Cruz had been nice, but she was made for a city. The anonymity, the culture, the variety, the clothes.

God, the clothes they wore at CoastalCreative. Jeans and t-shirts, sandals. A few people even showed up to the office in flip-flops. Shorts. Tank tops. They thought because they sat in their offices writing code all day, or attending virtual meetings via conference calls that their appearance didn't matter. She should have realized, going to work for a company with a name like that, what the culture would be like.

Maybe it was time for a lot of changes. Time to stop taking crap, to regain the confidence that she'd allowed Steve to leach out of her. Time to be rid of a casual love affair and time for the next step on the career ladder. The problem was, the rest of the ladder disappeared in the clouds. She had no idea how to find that rung. She was in danger of stepping out into nothing, falling forever.

51

The stalker wasn't there for three days.

Then, I saw him.

In the dark, he was always more unsettling. Anyone in the dark is more unsettling. Darkness hides the familiar contours of a human face, puts a shadow over the eyes, making the most innocuous expression appear sinister. Darkness makes a large person take on a mammoth proportion. Darkness stirs up animal instinct, the assumption that a man or woman using it to conceal their presence has malevolent intentions. In the dark, every paranoid thought runs freely. Details are stripped away and fear assumes that what's hidden is not good.

Possibly because of the darkness, my patience ran out.

He stood under the awning of the building across from my apartment. I couldn't read the logo on his hat. He made no attempt to disguise the fact he was staring at the entrance to my building, and even less attempt to hide that he was studying me as I walked toward the lamppost I used for stretching my legs.

I put my hand on the post and turned so I was looking directly at him.

He adjusted his cap and put his hands in his jacket pockets. He took a few steps back, concealing himself beneath the awning from the chest up.

I grabbed my left foot and pulled the heel close to my butt. After counting to sixty, I released it and grabbed my right foot. A moment later, I let it go and darted across the street.

Rather than walking away as I'd expected, he stood his ground.

Stepping inside the space that most consider their comfort zone, I looked directly into his eyes, the pupils enlarged to cover almost the entire iris. "What are you looking at?"

"Nothing."

"What are you doing out here at five in the morning?"

"Same thing as you," he said.

"Going for a run?"

He laughed. "Get on with it then."

"Why are you following me?"

"When did I follow you?"

"I want it to stop."

"It's a free country."

I smacked the bill of his cap, bringing the rim down on the bridge of his nose.

"You're a bitch, you know that?"

"So I've heard."

He adjusted his hat, but kept it low so I could no longer see the black holes of his eyes. "Just pretend I'm not here."

Although I could no longer see his eyes, I stared at his face. I put my hands in my pockets. I stood there, not moving, taking soft, shallow breaths that were impossible to hear, that didn't cause my chest or shoulders to move. The lack of movement allowed the chill to creep through the cotton hoodie. A breeze, gentle but damp brushed across the backs of my legs.

He took a step toward the doors behind him.

After three or four minutes, he coughed. "Go ahead with your exercise program."

I said nothing.

He moved his shoulders and resettled his hands in his pockets. "Do you have something else you want to say?"

I remained silent.

"What's wrong with you? Either speak your mind or get lost."

I took a half step closer.

When I'd seen him those other times, I'd leaned toward the assumption his intent was sex, a disturbing interest in some sort of relationship, or an obsession with watching a certain kind of woman, and I was simply his latest target. Now, I wasn't sure. Because I'd been focused on his constant presence, I'd never thought much about the vibe he was giving off. Now I realized it didn't seem directed at me as a woman, but more…analytical. If he wasn't solidly in his forties, I might think he was a student doing behavioral research.

He turned and began walking away. It should have pleased me, but I wanted him gone for good, not just on a single morning.

I jogged after him, passed him, took a few steps backward, and turned to face him. "I know you're following me. I don't like it. I *will* file a police report if you don't stop."

"I'm not breaking any laws. I've said nothing to you, I haven't touched you."

He was right. But there had to be some kind of law. I could still complain. A cop would talk to him, wouldn't he? Not that I'm inclined to go around making myself and my problems known to cops. I keep as far away from them as I can manage. I don't want them knowing anything about me, don't want to inadvertently get myself on their radar in a significant way.

But what stalker isn't at least a little concerned about the threat of police?

My confidence wavered. Maybe, this guy was a police detective himself. Maybe…I'd been meticulous with the murders in Santa Cruz, in Mountain View. I cleaned thoroughly. There's no law enforcement record of my DNA, so even if something were found, they'd have to test me to get the match. There were no legitimate records of me at any of the places I'd lived. There was no way in hell a detective could have tracked me to a slick, high-rise apartment building in San Francisco. No way.

A chill ran up my spine and across my scalp. It took all my will power not to shiver. I stepped around him and began jogging. I didn't look back.

52

Portland

As I grew into my teens, I had the normal arguments with my mother. In all of those arguments, my father was the shadowy figure hovering over us. I heard his voice in the words she chose, in the rules she established, in her opinions of my behavior.

Beneath his voice, dominating her entire being, there was a faint whisper of her view of me. It came out in small ways, easy to miss when I wasn't looking closely. Even the embarrassing and foolish undershirt bra hinted at her care. I saw it when she took me shopping and admired some of the clothes I liked, even though we both knew we'd be sent back to the store to return them if we dared making a purchase.

I saw her opinion of me when she pinned my reports and test papers with bold, red *A*s to the bulletin board. I saw it when she gazed at my school photographs, her eyes studying my face, slowly losing focus, gazing into the future, a tiny smile on her lips. A natural smile that wasn't the smile she wore for church, or the smile she wore when she spoke to my father. It wasn't the smile she gave to my friends or the one she adopted talking to clerks when we were running errands.

Flirting with Denny transformed her into someone I didn't recognize. I'd never seen the smile she gave him.

Did she seriously believe Denny found her attractive?

Why couldn't she see that he stood up to greet her, shook her hand, smiled at her, gave her warm attention to distract her, to save me from punishment? When she'd marched across the yard, it was clear I was going to get a lecture at the very least, and most likely told to get inside the house. From then on, she'd be watching the wooded area and there would be no more making out among the silent, gently swaying trees.

He was playing her like a pro. And not only did she fail to recognize that, she took it as something else entirely, acting like a fool. I wanted to slap her face.

She talked to him about skiing and school and grilled him pleasantly about his other interests for twenty minutes while I stood beside her, trying to catch her eye. She studiously avoided my gaze. Her eyes were sipping flattery out of his, her lips were soft, looking like she wanted to be kissed.

Finally, Denny decided he'd exercised enough charm. She was solidly on his side. If she'd seen us kissing, she'd shoved it to the back of her mind. She was more concerned with the finer points of snowboarding versus skiing than she was with finding out the details of why we were hiding behind trees, using a dead tree as a bench.

"I should get home," he said. "It's getting dark. My mom will be wondering where I am."

My mother looked displeased that he'd mentioned mothers. She seemed to have forgotten she was one. A mother with her teenage daughter standing beside her, giving her dirty looks. He'd made her forget, for quite a few minutes, that she had a husband. She had five children. She had dinner to cook and beds to make and laundry to fold and bathrooms to scrub.

She put out her hand. "I'm sorry you have to go. You're a

fascinating person. I didn't even realize how cold it was getting." She gave a little shiver and rubbed her arms. "I bet you're not cold." She smiled at Denny.

"I am."

"But you look strong — well-developed muscles like yours keep the body warm."

"If you say so."

He extended his hand.

Slowly hers came out to meet his, and she gripped it hard. Finally, she let go.

When he was gone, I started walking toward the house.

She trotted after me.

"What a charming..."

I turned. "What's wrong with you?"

She looked shocked. "Nothing's wrong with me."

"You were flirting with him. It was weird. Creepy."

"I wasn't flirting."

"You were."

"Don't pervert this." She had a vague smile on her face, one that told me she absolutely knew she was flirting. One that told me she was not only trying to change my perception of what I'd observed, she was lying.

"He doesn't think you're sexy, just in case you were wondering."

The pink in her cheeks disappeared suddenly, as if it had been sucked back inside her skull. "I didn't..."

"You think he's attracted to you? You're old. Even dad said so. You've lost your bloom, to quote him." I laughed.

"That's disgusting. What has your father said to you?"

"You're married. Denny does not think you're hot and sexy. He doesn't have a thing for you." I almost said worse, but managed to control my wildly racing mind, forcing it to think of consequences rather than venting.

"I'm your mother. You don't talk to me like that."

"You sure didn't act like my mother for the past half hour."

"Stop using that tone with me."

"He's laughing at you."

Her lip quivered. She hardened her face, getting control of her wobbly flesh.

"You're a mother and a housewife."

"I know what I am. Trust me," she said. She looked angry and very, very lost.

53

Joshua North lived in one of the Painted Lady houses that line lower Haight Street. The Painted Ladies were scattered throughout the city. They populated neighborhoods that featured late nineteenth century architecture spared from the 1906 earthquake that crumbled much of the city and caused fires that leveled even more, leaving half its residents homeless.

Nearly fifty thousand Victorian and Edwardian style houses were built in San Francisco in the second half of the nineteenth century and early twentieth century, and quite a lot of them had been painted with brilliant colors. Toward the end of the nineteenth century, journalists bemoaned the *loud colors* that were in fashion, the *uncouth panels of yellow and brown*. During World War I and II, many of the houses were re-painted with battleship gray war-surplus paint. About sixteen thousand were demolished, and others had the Victorian decor stripped off or covered with tarpaper, brick, stucco, or aluminum siding.

In the sixties, an artist began combining intense blues and greens on the exterior of his Victorian house. He was criticized, but then a few of his neighbors copied the bright colors on their own homes. Other artists started to transform dozens of gray houses into Painted Ladies, a term coined in the seventies.

Joshua North's house was a yellow-gold and burnt orange with forest green accents that oddly complemented one another, rather than clashing as would be expected.

Tess would never choose to live in such a gaudy home, but she was charmed by the homes' detailed embellishments and bright colors. She was foolishly nervous about meeting Joshua. Her cheeks were warm despite the low-hanging fog, blowing as if it had somewhere important to go, sweeping through the streets, searching, and moving on without finding what it was seeking.

In order to not look too eager, as if she was exaggerating the importance of her meeting and the portrait itself, she'd worn faded jeans, scuffed boots, and a white v-neck sweater.

Beside the door was a brass button, but when she pressed it, there was no sound. She pressed a second time in case it was ringing somewhere deep inside the house, inaudible on the front porch. After a minute or two, she knocked firmly. It was another few minutes before Joshua opened the door.

His eyes were sharp, dark beads, assessing her before he spoke. He was thin and tall. He wore jeans and a faded yellow t-shirt with a logo even more faded, impossible to read. His feet were bare. A few coarse dark hairs grew along the metatarsal bones and on his big toes.

"Tess Turner." He moved back and waited for her to enter.

"Hi." She stepped inside and closed the door behind her. The house smelled of coffee — fresh, expensive coffee, rich and dark and warm. The narrow hallway and what she could see of the front room were crowded with too much furniture.

"Thank you for coming here," he said. "It's easier than

dragging my paintings to the gallery for a viewing."

She thought immediately of viewing the deceased prior to a funeral. She'd only been to one viewing in her life. In fact, she'd only been to one funeral. Every other death was acknowledged with a memorial service, and a private scattering of ashes well after the fact. At her age, she felt she'd experienced more death than was normal. At least for someone living in the United States, raised in an upper middle class suburban neighborhood. The deaths she'd experienced compared to someone in Syria or the Philippines or a hundred other places, was nothing.

She smiled, too widely, trying to turn her thoughts to the purpose of her meeting, working to prevent them from tripping off down a dark alley filled with people who had died and the horrors of viewing a nicely-dressed, cosmetically enhanced corpse.

"I'll show you the work I have that's relevant for what I think you're envisioning. I'll leave you alone with the paintings. I don't like to hover when someone is viewing my work. It helps them relax and focus on their response rather than being distracted by feeling they have to verbalize their thoughts." His expression was solemn.

"Sure. That sounds reasonable." She followed him down the hall to the back of the house. He opened the door to a large room, lined with tall, narrow windows. On a clear day, the sunlight streaming in must be gorgeous. Easels were set up around the perimeter of the room, a few taller ones in the center.

"I'll come back in fifteen minutes, if that's enough time for you?"

"Yes. Okay." She stepped into the room and he closed

the door.

She swallowed. Her hands turned cold. She tucked her fingertips into her pockets to still their sudden trembling. She'd walked into the home of a stranger and he'd shut her into a back room. She had a desire to rush to the door, checking whether he'd locked it. She hadn't heard the clunk of a lock turning, but she'd been admiring the windows, thinking about sunlight, taking in the easels and paintings.

It was simple animal instinct gone overboard. Celine had recommended this guy. Celine knew him personally. Or did she? Now, Tess wasn't sure. She hadn't felt any kind of anxious vibe when he answered the door, but even working her mind through all of those factors, a tremor of anxiety continued fluttering inside her chest.

She swallowed again and forced herself not to check the door.

The painting in the center of the room drew her first. It was larger than the others and she knew before she even got close, that Joshua would do her more justice than the promise suggested in Xavier's portraits of his lover.

The woman depicted here looked to be in her mid-forties. The assessment of style and color, the shape of her face, and the pose of her body were immaterial, the eyes dominated the painting. They were filled with life, making you forget they were formed from paint and brush strokes. It was almost incomprehensible to think this man had managed to create such life with a tiny sable brush and a finite variety of colors, blended to create the hazel hue of those eyes. It gave the impression that this woman's eyes were the most extraordinary color ever seen, that hazel was the most mesmerizing eye-color that existed in the human race.

But maybe…maybe he hadn't done it at all. Just because the gallery knew his work and just because Celine had provided his address did not mean he was the artist. It was a wildly paranoid thought, but at the same time, possibly a wise thought suggesting the buyer should be wary. In the lower right of the portrait, tiny brush strokes indicated a *J* and an *N*. But that could be anyone.

He'd had a strange demeanor, not holding the door for her when she stepped into his home, as if he was cautious about not accidentally brushing against her. And closing her in this room, no matter how light and welcoming it was. His insistence that she look at his work without feeling compelled to speak to him about it. But still. The painting.

She thought she could stand there for another hour, gazing at those eyes, expecting a sparkle of recognition as the woman shed her painted shell and began to breathe and move.

There was a soft knock on the door. She turned, glancing at a few other paintings, all exhibiting equally breath-taking talent.

Rather than making an agreement with him now, she should be cautious and finalize the arrangement via the gallery. She should talk to Celine and describe the work, just to reassure herself he was genuine. This was going to cost a lot of money and she didn't want to invest that, and her time, in an imposter. She had no solid reason to believe he was such a thing, but the thought gripped harder with every breath.

What would be the point in tricking her? In posing as someone else? What kind of artist would do something like that?

The door opened and she stood there staring, still uncertain about what she should say.

54

The minute she saw David, Jen was going to rip him a new one. Not only had he put her home at risk, his blabbing about how she earned money had a trickle down aspect. All of her clients worked or lived in the area. They wouldn't want to travel across the city for half an hour or an hour of sex with her. There was no way they'd follow her to another part of the city, or worse, the suburbs. They liked her, none of them saw other hookers, as far as she knew, but she wasn't stupid about her value. In all price ranges, ninety-five percent of the time, one hooker was as good as another.

Most of her clients were regulars, which made her life safer than some. She knew what they wanted, knew what to expect when she walked into a hotel room. Despite insistence from most of the married or coupled guys that they loved, *craved*, variety and excitement in their sex lives, they almost always settled into a predictable pattern after three or four hook-ups.

Even the ones who liked to act out fantasies always wanted the same damn scenario. It was funny, really. They wouldn't see it that way, but she giggled about it when she was alone.

She'd left two voice mails and sent five text messages to David, demanding to see him, hoping it didn't sound like begging. He'd ignored the voice mails and responded to three of the text messages with vague answers about needing to see her soon but he was busy. Of course he was. He expected her to build her schedule around his unpredictable desire for sex. It didn't matter whether she was tired. It didn't matter if she had an appointment with a client, she had to reschedule when David decided he wanted her that night.

His last message had said simply: *maybe*.

In the hope that she'd hear from him at some point this evening, she'd rescheduled one of her longtime clients — an attorney. She took a shower, closing her eyes as the steaming water streamed over her face and through her hair, turning it to warm, soft silk. She shaved her legs and spent a few more minutes letting the hot water sting her skin. She dried her hair and put on makeup — dark shadow up to her brow bone. Thick eye liner smudged under her bottom lashes. Black mascara. She dressed in a short red skirt that David liked. He would be coming to her place, so she could get a bit crazy with the kind of clothes he liked.

When she was in the public areas of the apartment, going out to eat, even headed to a bar, she dressed like other women her age, slightly more conservative, careful that none of her outfits suggested *whore*. People who saw her should never have that word even enter their minds.

She chose a red bra and a white, low cut top that showed most of the bra. For now, she'd leave her feet bare and comfortable for walking around the apartment, repeatedly checking her phone for messages.

By ten-thirty, she was lying on the couch watching TV, her head on a pillow, angled forward so the fabric didn't smudge her makeup. The phone was in her left hand where she would feel it buzz, and the remote was in her right. A bottle of beer, only half empty, stood on the table. She hadn't wanted to down too many of them and fall asleep, dulling the rage and making her forget the things she needed to say to him.

The phone buzzed.

David Lasher: *On my way over.*

Ten-thirty. Why couldn't he *ever* ask if it was a good time? He never asked if she was asleep, or eating, or running errands, or simply didn't feel well. Nothing that had to do with her life, as if she didn't have a life. She belonged to him. She didn't exist when he wasn't horny. Of course, that was part of their deal — total availability. But would it kill him to at least check? Once? Maybe change the time he came over by even twenty minutes? She stood up and stepped into her high heels.

A moment later, there was a knock on the door. She opened it. "Why didn't you use your key?"

"Nice outfit." He put his hands on her butt and pulled her toward him. "Mmm. Now that I've seen it, time to take part of it off." He elbowed the door closed and trudged sideways, tugging her toward the bedroom.

"I thought we could have a drink, first," she said.

"Since when?"

"Since I thought it would be nice. I had a crazy day, and I want to relax."

"What does that mean? You had back-to-back sex?" He laughed. "I hope you showered."

She pulled away. "I have vodka and OJ."

He slumped on the couch and bent forward to untie his shoes. "Okay. Sure. I'm not gonna refuse a drink." He pulled off his shoes. "It's hot in here. Can you open the door?"

She walked around the couch and unlocked the sliding door. She slid it open a few inches. "How's that?"

He was looking at his phone and said nothing.

She went to the kitchen and dropped ice into glasses, poured two shots of vodka over the cubes in each glass, and filled them with orange juice. She took a sip of hers. She took a few more sips to steady her nerves. The idea of telling him off for exposing her to Alex had sounded easy inside her own head, but now that he was sitting on her couch, acting like he owned her, the reality of his physical presence scared her. He would laugh it off. She had to think of a way to get him to understand, but her mind was blank.

He took the drink, swallowed some, and put the glass on the table. She liked him to use a coaster, but he ignored her and he laughed at that too.

She settled in the chair across from him.

"Come over here." He patted the sofa cushion.

"I'm pissed at you," she said.

He pouted. "Aww. Now what am I gonna do?"

"It's not funny. You told Alex about me."

"Oh. Yeah. It sort of slipped out."

"The whole point of this…" she gulped her drink and waved her free hand between the two of them, "…is you weren't supposed to tell…*anyone*."

"It's not like I reported you to the management company."

"You don't know her, she might say something. Or tell someone else…and pretty soon everyone knows and then they find out and I'm screwed."

He picked up his glass and stood. He walked to the TV and ran his finger along the top. "You need to dust."

"Thanks for the FYI," she said. "Don't ever tell anyone again. You promised!"

"Or what? What will you do?" He laughed. "I said it just slipped out."

"Well it can't. I could lose my apartment, I *would* lose my apartment, and…"

"Don't worry about it. Alex won't tell. She seems like a chick with secrets of her own."

He leaned against the doorframe leading into the tiny bedroom. He picked up a purple-tinged bud vase sitting on a small table between the TV and the bedroom. "Expecting a rose?"

Her eyes watered. She took a few more sips of her drink. "How do you know she has secrets?"

He crossed the room and put his arms around her. He slid his hands up under her skirt. "I've had enough to drink. Let's get busy."

"How do you know she has secrets?"

"You can tell by looking at her. She doesn't talk a lot, and she won't say anything about her life. All questions get this look like she just slammed closed a cast iron door."

"Well it doesn't matter if she has secrets. We don't know them." She pulled away.

"What are you doing? You owe me."

"Not if you're going to blab about me."

"If it makes you feel better, I'll try to find out some of her secrets."

"Maybe."

"Now, come on."

He grabbed the hem of her shirt and pulled it up, forcing her to raise her arms as he slid it over her head. He took her wrist and led her into the bedroom, walking too fast. Her heel caught on the carpet and she lurched toward the bed. She kicked off her shoes and wriggled to the center of the mattress. She closed her eyes and tried not to think about Alex telling Isaiah, and Isaiah telling the guy he played tennis with, and, and, and...

55

As Joshua crossed the room to where Tess stood, he held out two sheets of paper. In spite of the extreme social awkwardness she couldn't seem to control, she took several steps back. Her shoulder bumped the painting on the easel and it wobbled.

"Careful!"

A wave of cold sweat spread across her back. What was wrong with her? He looked perfectly normal. The house wasn't cheap, worth easily $1.5 million. Unless he'd inherited it, he was obviously doing well. It was clean, there wasn't a hint of decay or aberrant behavior revealing itself in odd collections or too many closed doors along the hallway they'd walked down to reach the back of the house.

"Before we discuss my fee and arrange the other details, I need you to complete this questionnaire." He handed the papers to her.

"What for?"

"To see if you're a suitable subject."

She laughed. "You're kidding, right?"

He didn't smile.

"You're serious?"

"Art comes from the creative core of our being. I need a connection to my subject matter. I have to feel passion for the journey we're taking together."

She folded the papers in half, not looking at them, trying to decide what to say. Subject matter? What did that mean?

And passion? He couldn't be suggesting…

"The connection needs to be deep, and encompass more than the physical. I'm painting your form and features, your hair and the lines of your body. But to capture the lasting essence of you, the utterly unique nature of a portrait, I need to know what's inside of you."

It was weird, but that sounded better than passion. More bizarre, but at least not sexual. She let her breath out slowly. "I…"

"If you can't do that, you'll have to find another painter. But then, you won't get this." He swept his arm around the room, gesturing toward the circle of paintings.

As they stood looking at each other, neither moving toward or away from the other, her mood began to shift. She realized he might not only be a deep-thinking artist, he might possess savvy marketing techniques. Holding the papers, thinking about his requirements, she found herself no longer questioning his talent or the authenticity of his work. Instead, she longed for him to choose her. Knowing the decision wasn't in her hands had turned the room sideways, everything sliding toward the place where he stood, waiting for… Her eager agreement to fill out his forms? A handshake with a promise to return the forms later?

It wasn't clear what he expected, but suddenly she was desperate for him to paint her portrait. More than she'd felt after seeing Xavier's work, she experienced a visceral desire for him to find her worthy, to choose her, to need to paint her as much as she needed the painting done.

If he was looking for a connection beyond the physical, this was it. Needing something that couldn't be defined, or captured on two sheets of paper.

"Should I do that right now? Or bring them later? Mail them?"

He smiled for the first time. "If you have time, you can sit at my desk. They do require a lot of thought, so be sure you have time. It's nothing to be rushed."

She unfolded the papers.

At the top of the first sheet was his name in a large scripted font. The first question read — *How do I want to be remembered?* The second — *What secret defines my life?*

She stared at the questions. They were indeed not something she could dash off in a few minutes. The first was almost more intimidating than the second. Almost.

"I'd like to do it here, if you don't mind."

If she left, he might decide she wasn't a worthwhile subject. His schedule might get booked with other women, other projects.

"Come with me." He went to the door and stepped into the hallway. "Would you like a cup of coffee while you work?"

She nodded. What she really wanted was a glass of wine. After the past twenty minutes, a martini would be even better.

She followed him down the hall and around a corner to another shorter hallway. He opened a door and showed her a small room with an armchair near a narrow window that went almost to the floor. In the opposite corner was a writing desk. The desk was empty except for a glossy black pen and a leather pad to prevent the pen from gouging the wood of the desk.

"Do you want sugar or cream?"

She shook her head. She went to the desk and pulled out the narrow oak chair. She was a student taking a test under the sharp eye of a teacher who didn't allow the slightest opportunity for cheating. She felt naked without a computer, internet access. Her phone was in her purse, but she realized now that she'd left it on the floor near the painting, too busy clutching the sheets of paper in both of her clammy hands.

She put the papers on the leather pad and sat down.

A moment later, Joshua appeared with a cup and saucer. Like the aroma she'd first noticed, the coffee smelled divine, possibly the best coffee she'd ever smelled. He put the cup and saucer on the desk and left without speaking. The door closed softly.

She smoothed her hand over the papers and picked up the pen.

56

Tess had no idea how she wanted to be remembered, so she left that question blank for the moment. The answer to the second question was easy, but almost impossible to write down. She knew what her secret was without a moment's thought. It consumed her dreams and ate at the back of her mind. When she wasn't consumed with working, it made her weepy and melancholy.

The last thing she'd said to her father, her beloved Daddy, the man who created the driven, successful woman she was, who praised and cheered and bragged about every tiny achievement, and all of the big ones, had been a lie. The man who urged her to get her MBA and blew the loudest party horn at her graduation, shattering his dignified persona, left the world on a lie from his daughter's lips.

She loathed herself for what she'd done.

The lie wasn't the kind of secret that could get her into trouble. It wasn't a secret that mattered to anyone but her. But Joshua's criteria was a secret that defined her life, and this secret defined the shape of her existence in so many ways, she wasn't sure she could trace all of its slender cracks.

Her parents had asked her to come for a two-week visit during July. They knew business usually settled down for her after the close of the fiscal year. It was the best time to catch her with flexibility in her schedule. They'd rented a house near Lake Tahoe. It would be just her and them, unless she wanted to bring a man? The hope in her mother's voice was enormous, as she tried to sound casual but failed. *Was* there a man to bring?

Tess didn't want to deal with the unspoken questions about men, the concerned look in her mother's eyes.

And despite the promised pleasure of hiking with her father, there would be long hours in between. Hours of eating every meal together, watching more television than she liked, isolated and cut off from her adrenaline-driven life.

"Usually, July is a great time to get away, but this year is different. We have a huge product launch coming the first week of September, and we're practically living in the office. I'm so sorry."

Later, she would tell them the announcement had been delayed due to an engineering bug. Lying turned her hands clammy and pierced her throat with something sharp. She prided herself on blunt honesty. Too many women coped with the challenges of a competitive career environment by using white lies to navigate the demands of family relationships and friendships, valuing niceness and the preservation of feelings over being direct.

But in this case, what could she say? If she told them she didn't feel like it, they would be so hurt. Crushed. Protecting the feelings of co-workers and friends and lovers wasn't her job, but her parents? She couldn't possibly tell them she didn't want to spend so much time with them.

As a result, instead of taking her father's SUV up to the Sierras, they took their silly little smart car. A migraine headache had debilitated him, so her mother was driving. The collision with a drunk driver totaled the insubstantial car and her father died instantly.

Not only had her final words been a lie, she'd effectively

killed him.

Her rational mind ran incessantly over the rules of logic — the nature of accidents, the psychological imperative to place meaning on something after the fact, to create meaning and cause and effect where there was none. Accidents and the course of events are more random than not. But the lines were so clear, she felt she was lying to herself even now when she tried to explain away her culpability.

In her dreams, she was accused by her brothers and her mother. Occasionally her father showed up, not as an accuser, but to quietly express his disappointment in her failure to own her desires and choices, to put misplaced sensitivity above ethics. To not be willing to live with the consequences of her choice — the hurt they would feel.

She couldn't write about the guilt. She cut half the story and wrote that she'd lied to her father on his deathbed. Another lie. She answered the remaining questions quickly and briefly.

What makes you smile? A well-trained dog.

Where do you go to escape? Hiking.

What is your greatest passion? My career.

Who is your closest friend? Alexandra.

The answer shocked her. It was frightening in the speed with which it came. She moved on quickly.

Are you in love? No.

What will you fight to the death for? Pretty much anything I feel strongly about, assuming *death* isn't to be taken literally.

Why do you want a portrait of yourself? For posterity.

She returned to the first question and wrote — I want to be remembered as a woman with intelligence and integrity, passion and drive.

As she stood, she hoped he wasn't expecting elaborate answers to the more straight-forward questions. She didn't want to be sent back to the desk, a child who hadn't completed her assignment. Posterity was confusing, and inadequate. There was more to it, but she still couldn't explain it in her own mind, much less on a form.

She hoped the lie in the second question wouldn't show in her portrait.

57

On the spur of the moment, I invited Jen to be my guest at the gym. We're allowed to bring one guest a month, and it can't be the same person more than once every six months. I don't think they really track it, but I try to follow the rules. Besides, I wasn't going to bring her more than once.

She always looked a little tired, and if nothing else, I thought she'd like sitting in the hot tub after a workout. When I mentioned the hot tub, she smiled like a kid who was offered a popsicle on a hot summer afternoon.

"I don't really exercise," she said.

"You should."

She shrugged.

"Especially weights. A woman in your line of work needs to be strong."

"I'm strong."

"Getting stronger never hurts. And if you don't work out with weights, you'll get less strong in a few years. Your muscles start to lose mass if you don't stay on top of it."

"I can't afford a gym."

"You could get some ten and fifteen pound weights and work out in your living room. I could help you with some exercises."

"Let's see how the gym goes, first."

We went on Saturday morning at seven. She wasn't thrilled about the early start time, but waiting until eight or nine on Saturdays means spending the next hour waiting for a treadmill or the bench press.

Jen ran on the treadmill, earbuds tucked in her ears, her dark hair in a short ponytail that bounced as it kept time with her pace. While she ran, I did a complete weight circuit. It took me almost an hour, and she ran without stopping that entire time. For never exercising, she was in pretty good shape. I guess walking instead of always sitting in a car does that.

By the time I finished, the gym was packed. I led her to the rack of free weights and showed her how to do bicep curls and shoulder presses. I demonstrated kneeling on a bench and lifting her bent arm while holding a weight to work her back. My muscles were spent from my circuit, so I used five pound weights just to give her the idea. "Your back's important. You want to look good in cocktail dresses, right?"

She shrugged. "I don't go to clubs that often. But I do like doing this. It feels good."

"It's addictive."

"I feel my body's buzzing with energy. It makes me want to get stronger."

I smiled and popped the top on my water bottle. I took a long swallow. "Hot tub?"

"Definitely."

"Hi, Alex."

I turned. Tess was standing a few feet away, her black clothing further emphasizing her black hair. I turned and looked at Jen.

I think I'd seen the resemblance when I first met Jen — the black hair, the heavy eye makeup they both favored. But because their mannerisms were different, because Tess's face was carved with authority and confidence, and Jen's was slightly lost at times, I hadn't focused on the similarities. Tess was slightly taller, her eyes more piercing.

But if they wore the same clothes, and you didn't know either of them well, it would be easy to mistake one for the other.

I turned back to Tess, studying her face, then glanced again at Jen.

It was eerie. There was something besides the black hair and the eye makeup, but I wasn't sure what. Their eyes were a similar blue. Jen's teeth were smaller, but neither one was smiling now, clearly wondering why my head was snapping back and forth.

"Jen, this is my boss, Tess Turner." I looked at Tess. "This is Jen. She lives in my building."

Neither stepped forward to shake hands. It didn't surprise me that Jen didn't, after just finishing a workout, and also because she's fairly casual. But Tess? They both murmured hello.

"What are you glaring at?" Tess said.

"I didn't realize until just now how much you and Jen look like each other."

Tess wrinkled her brow. She lowered her eyebrows, narrowing her eyes. "No we don't."

"Not exactly, but a lot. Enough that I can't stop comparing."

"Well stop," Tess said. "Nice meeting you, Jen." She turned and walked toward the line of treadmills.

"She seems very pulled together. In charge," Jen said.

I smiled. "She's definitely that." We started walking to the women's locker room that housed a sauna and a hot tub large enough for ten or twelve people.

We stripped off our workout clothes, took quick showers, wrapped comfy towels around our bodies and strolled down the hall to the hot tub room. I dropped behind her slightly and studied the back of Jen's head. Of course with wet hair the similarity wasn't as obvious, and the way they moved was nothing alike, but still, I couldn't stop thinking about the resemblance. Possibly, I was reading too much into similar haircuts and makeup choices, striking dark hair and crystal blue eyes.

58

Spending the evening with Steve had not been in Tess's plans, but she was walking out the main exit of the building that housed CoastalCreative's offices, headed toward the parking garage and Steve was suddenly behind her, shouting her name. She hadn't even seen which direction he'd come from.

He caught up and walked beside her, sliding his arm around her waist.

"Don't do that," she said.

"Don't do what?"

"Touch me in public, especially right near the office."

He let go. "You stood me up."

She said nothing.

"No text? No call?"

"Apologies."

"That's it?"

She lengthened her stride.

"Hey, what's the rush? Do you have a date?" He laughed.

"No."

"Then how about dinner? Indian?"

It was six-forty-five. She was hungry, and she couldn't avoid forever what she needed to say. Delaying was making the situation worse. Telling him in a restaurant was cleaner. And the more she thought about Indian, the more she salivated, already tasting butter chicken and aloo gobi. "Sure. Okay."

"Wow. I thought you were going to say no."

She smiled.

"My car's parked in the Mission Street garage. I'll drive and bring you back tomorrow."

She sighed. Did he really think she was going to fall for that? "I can't go back to your place. I have work to do tonight."

"It can wait 'til tomorrow."

"No, it can't. Does the invitation still stand?"

"Of course. What kind of guy do you think I am?"

She knew what he was. She'd known the moment she met him, and yet, she'd played around, not thinking about where she was going, making a mess of their professional relationship. She hoped he'd be mature enough to leave it alone when they were forced together in meetings — cool and cordial. It wasn't too much to expect.

The restaurant was warm and the aroma of beef made her even hungrier. There were five dining rooms, separated by arched openings. The rooms were dimly lit, decorated with tapestries and luscious photographs of unique architecture and rural areas of India. Enormous brass pots stood in the corners, some filled with twisted dried wood, others containing live plants.

They were seated in a room filled entirely with two-tops, six of the ten tables occupied by couples obviously enjoying romantic dinners. Tess looped her purse over the back of the chair and sat down. She put her phone on the table, a not-very-gentle signal that she had other things on her mind. This wasn't a romantic dinner and she wasn't changing her mind about the rest of the night. She tried to find a place to fix her gaze that didn't involve a couple with their heads close together over the small table, or holding hands. Not the best atmosphere for the message she needed to deliver, but it was too late now. She picked up the menu.

They ordered a bottle of Pinot Noir and studied their menus. She suppressed her desire for food, thinking of the logistics of leftovers between a man and woman with different destinations, no longer a couple. She suggested the butter chicken, aloo gobi, and rice.

"Okay, and I'll get…"

She interrupted. "I'm not very hungry, and I know you like butter chicken and aloo gobi, so that's plenty."

"Not for me," he said.

"I don't want leftovers."

"You're not required to take them home." He winked.

When the server returned, Steve ordered the dishes she'd proposed, along with a basket of garlic naan, raita, chicken biriyani, chana masala, and lamb kabobs.

He talked about his meeting with a large bank. The customer had insisted on delaying a purchase, offering only a vague reason for waiting. Between rapid sips of wine and repeated phrases, it became clear Steve was working hard to keep his mood level, to let go of his frustration. The wine seemed to be helping that process more than his attempt at self-control and the effort to adopt an all-in-good-time attitude.

Their food came and Steve piled his plate full, adding two pieces of naan to the side where they balanced precariously.

As she dribbled sauce from the butter chicken over her rice, her phone buzzed.

Before she could put down the spoon, Steve said, "Who's

Joshua North?"

The phone buzzed again. She wanted to answer it, she needed to answer it. This must mean he'd agreed to paint her portrait! Surely if he'd declined, he'd send email. Although, he did seem a bit old fashioned — his writing desk and pen and paper — maybe he would call with a formal dismissal. She put her hand on the phone, then removed it.

"Who is he?"

His tone was sharp. Was he jealous? She couldn't imagine that. But his face was twisted into an unhappy expression. The foot-dragging customer, or the phone call?

"I don't recognize the name. He's not from CC," he said.

The screen went dark. "No, he's not."

"I thought we were…"

Just because she received a call from a man who wasn't a colleague didn't mean he was a lover. God. What was wrong with him? But she didn't want to reassure him, that seemed false, with what was coming next. And then there was the butter chicken and aloo gobi. She couldn't break it off now, not before she ate. Not before she finished her lovely glass of wine.

"What's wrong?" Steve said.

The phone buzzed with a voicemail alert. She put her hand on it again. She was absolutely sure he'd chosen her. She smiled.

"What's going on?" Steve said. "What's that smile for?"

She ate a piece of butter chicken with some rice. She sipped her wine. "I really should listen to this message."

He glowered but said nothing.

She picked up the phone, stood, and walked to the waiting area, out of Steve's range of sight. She pressed play.

Joshua North here. Tess, your answers make me feel I've caught a glimpse of your soul. Call me at your convenience so we can arrange the first sitting. Cheers.

Blood rushed to her face. She imagined the color blossoming across her cheeks. She took a few steps to the door and walked outside, letting the cold air wash over her. She listened to the message again.

When she returned to the table, Steve's plate was half empty, as was the wine bottle.

She sat down and picked up her glass. She took a sip and ate a piece of cauliflower.

"Can you explain what's going on? I think I've been patient."

Against her instinct, she decided to divert the conversation away from his obvious distress. It was the only way to avoid offering false reassurance. "I'm having my portrait painted. That was the artist."

"Are you kidding?"

"Of course not."

He laughed. "How pompous can you get?" He gulped some wine. Gesturing with his glass, he went on. "Do you think you're some kind of royalty? I guess that would explain your condescending attitude. I guess that would explain a lot of things."

She didn't want to know what it would explain. She couldn't care less. The painting was important. She'd known he wouldn't understand. She continued eating, quickly now, eager to move to the final conversation. She no longer cared about the butter chicken.

"A portrait? This isn't the nineteenth century. You work in high tech, you're not the matriarch of British landed gentry. God, you are too much. You aren't serious, right? This was a joke. Ha, ha." He laughed and drank some more wine.

Tess took a sip of wine. She unhooked her purse from the chair back, pulled it onto her lap, and took out her wallet. She removed two fifty dollar bills. She held them below the edge of the table where he couldn't see. "It's not a joke."

He held up his hand. "Okay, okay. Don't get all offended."

She looked at him. "Steve. If you think about it, you'll agree that we're not right for each other. We need to stop pretending this is going somewhere." She put the bills on the table.

"What the fu…"

She spoke quickly. "I apologize for not telling you sooner."

"You've been…"

"I think, given our positions, we can find a cordial way to work together. I know I can." She stood. "I'm sorry to leave in the middle of dinner, but I really do have a lot of work to do."

"Is the painting nude? Now that would make sense." He gave her a soupy grin.

"Please," she said. She touched his shoulder, turned, and walked quickly to the exit before he said something else to disgust her.

The next few weeks might be rough, but she'd find a way to handle it, eventually move past it. She smiled and walked out the door into the cool night, the texture of her skin returning to normal.

59

Portland

My mother flirted with Denny on a Friday afternoon. That evening, she avoided me completely. At nine-fifteen, I was sitting in my room waiting for the nightly torture of her eavesdropping presence on my hypocritical prayers. The knock on the door was firmer than usual.

"Yes?" I scooted forward, ready to drop to my knees.

The door opened to reveal my father. "Your mother and I have decided you're at the right age to pray by yourself. It's probably past due." He thrust his head and shoulders over the threshold, as if fully entering my room might weaken his words. "I hope you'll take this trust seriously and spend concentrated effort. I hope you'll include time for contemplation." He moved back into the hallway and closed the door.

I went to the window and shoved it open. I removed the screen and took my usual spot sitting sideways on the sill. It was cold, but the chill and my new-found freedom excited me. I felt as if I could fly out the window. I'd never have to kneel on my bedroom floor again. I'd never have to invent false words, lying to my mother, myself, and any invisible beings that might be listening, although I was doubtful.

For the rest of the weekend, I didn't see my mother except at mealtimes. When she spoke, which was rare during meals, she looked directly at one of my siblings or my father, but made a strained effort to keep from even turning her head in my direction.

On Monday, Denny didn't mention my flirtatious mother. I relaxed. I could continue smoking and talking with my friends. Jill and I made Denny laugh by imitating some of the girls and their elaborate fabrications to try to get out of PE class. I was confident that Denny and I would take up our places on the log, making out until dinnertime, or until something changed.

Something changed on Tuesday. First, I was lulled into a sense of sameness as we walked to the park and lit up our smokes. The bubble of comfort continued when Denny walked to my street, then turned to cut through our neighbors' backyards to meet me in the wooded area. I sat on the log, my lips warm from the heat of the cigarette, waiting.

Before Denny got there, I saw my mother come out onto the back porch.

I stood, looking farther into the clusters of trees for another log, an exposed root, or a low branch, some place to sit beyond her range of sight.

My mother walked down the back steps. Even from that distance, I saw that she'd been shopping. She wore skinny jeans tucked into dark brown boots. As she got closer, the rest of her outfit was slowly revealed. She wore a black spandex spaghetti-strap top with a black shirt over it, unbuttoned. The spandex top clung to her body, showing every curve of her breasts, the small buttons of her nipples, and the obvious absence of any wires or lace, satin or polyester indicating a bra.

The top was cut low and the thin straps barely held her breasts in place.

Her hair wasn't combed back and held in place by a large barrette at the base of her skull in her usual style. It was loose, shorter, maybe. It flowed around her face. Her bangs seemed longer, brushing across her eyebrows, making her blink more frequently than usual, giving her a startled, uncertain look.

Some girls would blush. Some girls would run to their mother's side and button the shirt that flapped open, inviting the world to look at what she had to offer. Some girls would pity their mother.

They would think about how hard their mother tried to look nice, about her standing at the bathroom mirror, makeup bottles and cream containers, brushes and powders spread across the counter. They would think about all the things she did to please your father, to take care of you and your siblings — the meals, the errands, the cleaning.

I didn't think or do any of those things. I thought about how she earnestly believed she could capture Denny's attention. What was wrong with her? She should have been telling me I had to come home earlier, or grounding me for making out. That's what normal parents did. Not that I wanted those things, not at all, but it was normal. This was weird. Everything my family did was too freakin' weird.

To my right, I heard Denny's feet crunching through dead leaves.

I walked out of the wooded area and started up the slope to meet my mother. She stopped, seeming almost confused about why I was even there.

"Alexandra. Have you seen Denny?"

"Why are you dressed like that?"

Up close, I saw her makeup was heavier than usual. She

wore pink lip gloss and a lot of mascara. I smelled her perfume.

"I don't have to answer to you," she said.

"If you think you look younger, if you think that's hot, you are so wrong."

"You have no idea what I think. Leave me alone."

She stepped around me. I grabbed her arm. She tried to pull away and I let go. She lost her footing on the damp grass, a thin covering over rain-soaked earth. The slick sole of her boot skidded. The other foot joined, and she landed on her ass, legs splayed. Tears filled her eyes. "Why did you do that?"

"I didn't do anything but grab your arm. The rest was physics."

Tears pooled around the black mascara on her bottom lashes, but she didn't cry. Part of me wanted her to cry. It might wash the delusion out of her eyes.

60

San Francisco

There was a light drizzle when I left the apartment building at four-thirty for my morning run. Drizzle probably implies rain falling in tiny, soft drops. This was more of a mist, floating in the pool of light around the streetlamp, some of it drifting down and resting on the sidewalk but much of it seeming to want to stay where it was, suspended in light. By the time I jogged to the corner, it frosted the top of my hair and my face was slick.

A surprising number of rapes are committed between the hours of four and six a.m. I'm not sure why. Maybe it's that women feel safe — after all it's almost daytime, the sun is on its way up. So they let down their guard. Or maybe it's that nighttime brings out more people going to and from parties and bars and work and friends' homes so they aren't as isolated. No one goes anywhere at four a.m.

This has never driven me to change my behavior, although it must bother me on some level or I wouldn't be so familiar with the facts.

Still, it doesn't give me an anxious tremor in the pit of my stomach. I run fast. I'm strong. I can take care of myself. But maybe I'm over-confident. I'm willing to admit, I can be over-confident. It's part of my personality type and not really something I can change, but I do try to be aware. I try to be a self-aware person. I don't always succeed.

The mist was so fine, there was no risk of shoes skidding across damp pavement and sending me crashing onto my hands and knees. It wasn't even wet enough for me to feel I should pull up my hood or try to protect my phone that was busy counting steps and miles and calories burned.

The phone is almost like the human body in its intricate, unconscious, continuous functioning. It offers glorious music composed hundreds of years ago, played by a pianist forty or fifty years ago, and recently compressed into digital characters to be ready whenever it's desired. The phone tracks your friends on Facebook, watches what your acquaintances are saying on Twitter and saves those thoughts for later perusal. It collects your email. It monitors your activity and gives reports on a regular basis. Without any emotion, it does everything in its power to improve and care for your life.

I ran across the street and up two blocks to The Embarcadero.

The bay spread out to my right in the darkness, glistening beneath the lights lining the edge, reflecting the mist-filled sky and a slight suggestion of the moon, on its way toward the horizon.

I ran for three quarters of a mile, then gave an extra burst to do a quarter mile sprint.

Suddenly, I felt someone running beside me. I felt his body heat, I caught a whiff of breath laced with juicy fruit gum. I stopped and yanked the earbud out of my left ear. He was slightly behind me, despite my sudden stop.

The brown leather jacket was gone. He wore a black sweatshirt, black nylon jogging pants with a white stripe down the outside of each leg, and a hat, of course. The San Jose Sharks.

If he was a fan of San Jose hockey, did that mean I'd been over-confident in dismissing the idea he was a cop? Had someone managed to get a lead, pursuing me for the murder I'd committed in Silicon Valley? Chasing me through Twitter feeds and a phony gym membership card and old neighbors to whom I'd given false information?

It didn't seem possible. It wasn't possible.

I started running again.

In a burst of speed, he caught up and grabbed my arm.

I yanked my arm, but he held firm.

"Let go of me."

"I know what you're up to," he said.

"What am I up to?"

"Don't play games."

"I have no idea what you're talking about. Let go of me."

"Or what? You never did call the cops. You can't." He lowered his voice. "You're not so clean." His grip tightened, his hand twisted harder.

"I have no idea who you are," I said.

"I definitely know who you are. And you better clean up your act or life as you know it is over."

"What is that supposed to mean? Stop being all James Bond and tell me what the fuck you're talking about."

"Such language for a lady."

I laughed. "I'm not a lady."

"That's obvious."

"And it's fine by me."

"Girls like you don't belong here. Is that clear?"

"Belong where? What are you *talking* about?"

"If you don't clean it up immediately, you'll be paying the price. A huge price."

"Are you threatening me?"

He shrugged. His grip loosened slightly. His hand was getting tired. Not so strong and tough as he wanted to pretend. I landed a karate chop on his wrist. I don't take karate, but anyone can at least try something like that when they're grabbed against their will.

He let go and I turned and started running, headed back toward Howard Street and the welcoming lobby of my building.

"I know what's going on!" he shouted after me. "It better stop."

I was breathing hard, running as fast as I could. Not that it mattered. He was going to keep showing up, grabbing me, making threats. And I had no idea what he was talking about or how to get him out of my face. It wasn't the sort of situation where I could entice him into a secluded area and be rid of him for good.

61

Tess left the CoastalCreative building walking fast. She was already late to the first sitting for her portrait. It wasn't the way she wanted to arrive. Driving from The Embarcadero to the Haight-Ashbury area would take easily thirty minutes, depending on traffic.

Walking in heels as fast as she could move felt awkward and jarring. She didn't want to get an uncomfortable, stiff vibe going through her body, but she couldn't be late. Joshua had assured her he would help her relax. He'd even assured her that relaxation wasn't key, he could work around any mood. He'd assured her that she would naturally be in a different frame of mind for each sitting, but he would also be talking to her, playing a variety of music, all kinds of techniques for eliciting the expression and demeanor he wanted.

All of his advice was somewhat vague, and he'd been absolutely no help in suggesting what she should wear.

Whatever feels comfortable. Whatever you want to convey.

What did that mean? She'd finally decided on a pair of faded, slightly ragged jeans cut at her hip bones, and a white cashmere sweater. She would be barefoot.

None of her choices suggested a formal portrait that would be hung and admired for hundreds of years, but she was no longer sure sitting in a straight-backed chair in a dark suit and silk blouse was what she really wanted. Did she want to be remembered only as a senior vice president? Only as a tech company executive? She wasn't sure. Now, she worried she might have erred too far to the free spirit side of the equation. And there was absolutely nothing free spirit about her.

This shouldn't be so hard.

The sweater and jeans were in her gym bag in the trunk. She'd had a pedicure — a pale coffee color — not that her feet would be in the painting. Or would they?

He'd said he could paint her into a different outfit. She could choose something else next time, once she got the feel of this. Maybe she did want to have a formal pose. The whole thing made her head ache. How could such a simple desire be calling into question nearly every choice she'd made in her life?

She was close to the parking garage, ready to launch her way into the narrow corridor that led inside. A man stepped in front of her. He wore a brown leather jacket and a Giants hat. "Excuse me."

"Sorry, I can't. I don't carry cash."

He laughed. "I'm not searching for a handout." He looked her up and down, slowly. It wasn't salacious, more like an inspection of her clothing, checking to see that it met a dress code. "Don't you look classy."

She frowned, turned, and entered the corridor. He followed. She walked faster, heels echoing inside the concrete tunnel. She was aware of his breathing behind her, a clean sound — no phlegm or nasty dampness to frighten her, and yet, she was. Slightly.

"Wait. I need to talk to you," he said.

"I don't have time."

"I can shout at your back or you can stop for two seconds."

She slowed and glanced over her shoulder. "Stop bothering me."

"My message is brief."

So, he was a whacko after all.

"You need to take your business somewhere else."

"Are you one of our vendors?"

He frowned. "This is a warning. Consider it the gentle approach."

"What the hell are you talking about?"

"You don't belong here."

"I'm done," Tess said. She turned and walked into the garage. The man didn't follow her. Still, as she pressed the button to call the elevator, her finger trembled. He was so aggressive, so sure that he had the right to ask questions, interfere in her life.

All she could think of was her gun. Buried deep in her purse, but really, what was she going to do, pull a gun on every man who approached her? On a city street? In broad daylight?

The two things she'd longed for — the gun and the portrait, had become pointless and desperate in a way she couldn't define. She hoped sitting for the portrait didn't make her feel as ridiculous as the gun suddenly did.

62

Isaiah was lying in my bed beside me. We were sipping martinis — his idea, not mine. This guy was becoming more interesting every week. He hadn't tried to label our relationship. We saw each other when we saw each other and didn't discuss what any of it meant. He liked sex and running and eating. Hell, the guy was going to culinary school. Of course he liked eating! And cooking. He was interested in hearing about what I was up to at work, and how I spent my free time. He avoided prying, never acting as if he had to identify each activity I'd done without including him, or instead of choosing to be with him. We were free and relaxed and contented.

"At some point, after this…" he raised his glass, "…we're going to have to think about food."

"Agreed." I took a sip of my drink and pulled the sheet up so it covered my hip bones. I stared into the glass, watching the liquid caress the olives. I wanted to eat one, but I liked looking at them too. Sometimes I wonder if half the reason I adore martinis is because they look so damn sexy. The vermouth makes the liquid appear silkier than vodka alone, and the olives are so plump and pretty with their sage coloring and the soft pimento like a tongue coming out of its mouth, teasing.

But this time, my pleasure was marred. All I saw inside the glass was the hard, sullen face of that man who wouldn't stop watching me. He seemed confused about who I was, and he seemed to think all his accusations made sense to me. It didn't seem like he knew anything about my past, but the nagging thought that it wasn't impossible refused to leave me alone.

I wondered if he'd mistaken me for someone else. It would be a relief if he did. He was so sure of himself, so certain I was in trouble, but for what? And why wouldn't he spell it out?

"Does that sound good?" Isaiah said.

"What?"

He laughed. "What do you see in that glass?"

I took a sip and touched my finger to the swizzle stick. "Olives."

"You're always so alert to food, so it's shocking that you didn't hear me."

"Hear what?"

He slid his hand down my thigh, cupping the spot just above my knee. "Brazilian barbecue. How about going out for Brazilian barbecue?"

"That sounds perfect."

"Nothing like sex and a martini to make me crave meat," he said.

"I feel exactly the same way." I plucked out the swizzle stick and pulled the olive into my mouth.

"You seem distracted," he said.

Telling him about the stalker might be useful. He might even know who the guy was.

The problem with telling Isaiah was that I couldn't mention my concern that the guy was a detective. And not understanding his threat made it difficult to explain. Maybe it was better to keep it to myself after all. And yet, I wanted to tell him. He would be sympathetic to how annoyed I was, how unsettled. He might see something I couldn't. He might have insight into how to handle it.

"There's a man who is sort of watching me, following me," I said.

"Sort of?"

"I see him outside the apartment building all the time, and twice when I was running. A few times, he actually followed me."

"What did you do?"

Another reason Isaiah had my attention. He didn't assume I was cowering in fear, letting a random stranger control my life by his very presence. He assumed I'd done something about it.

"I just asked him what he was up to. I don't feel like he's obsessed with me or anything like that. I can't figure out what he wants."

I repeated the highlights of the cryptic conversations.

"Maybe he's delusional. Thinks he's some kind of detective or spy? There are quite a few people like that wandering around the city."

"He's not homeless. And he's definitely coherent. Sane."

"Maybe he has you confused with someone else."

"I keep thinking that too. Although he's been so persistent, and he seems to think he knows all about me. He acts as if he knows me. I don't get it. And I'm tired of it."

"What does he look like?"

I described the usual outfit, not the track suit.

"Sounds like a hundred guys, so I guess I've never noticed him."

"Well he's probably not there when you're coming and going."

"True."

"It pisses me off that he thinks I should know what he's talking about and won't explain when I tell him I don't. He acted as if I was lying about something."

Isaiah rubbed my leg slightly, which made me feel warm and wiggly and even more tired of trying to figure out the stalker.

"You could mention it to the people at the lobby desk," he said.

"He's never followed me inside the building. So I don't think it's really their territory."

"I guess I don't have any ideas."

I leaned into him, holding my drink to the side so it didn't spill. Another thing in his favor. He didn't suggest something stupid like going to the police who wouldn't do a damn thing. The stalker had been right about that. I'd only said it because it's what you say. The police never deal with stalkers. They wait until you're dead.

"I'll keep an eye out though."

"Thanks."

Telling Isaiah made it stop spinning frantically in my mind. I'd thought confronting the stalker would make him back off. The only thing to do was ignore him until he explained himself. I couldn't let him get under my skin. If he wanted to watch me, have at it.

Isaiah pulled the swizzle stick piercing a single olive out of his drink and put it in my glass. What a charming guy, offering his last olive. I kissed him and ate it.

63

Tess hadn't been in the office all day. It was nearly five and I was sitting in my cubicle, designing charts for slides she was presenting to a customer the following week. She hadn't reviewed them yet, but had said she wouldn't get to them until Monday, so I didn't feel much pressure to complete them. It was a three- or four-hour job, and I had about twelve to fifteen business hours before she'd be looking for them.

I picked up my latte and took a sip through the slot in the plastic lid. The coffee was lukewarm. I wasn't sure how I'd managed to neglect it for so long. I thought about tossing it, but I needed caffeine to get me through these charts.

"Hey."

I looked up.

Steve stood outside my cube, elbows propped on the walls. "Busy?"

I shrugged.

"How about that drink?"

"What drink?"

"Come on. Don't be like that."

I pushed my chair back so I wasn't straining to look up at him. "I'm not being like anything."

"You remember. I suggested we get a drink sometime. To explore the idea of you moving into a sales position."

After making the suggestion we meet for a drink, and then pretending he'd forgotten, ignoring me until I was left feeling like the pursuer rather than the pursued, I was unsure whether I wanted to work for him at all. Of course, as a sales rep, I wouldn't be working directly for him.

"Can you get away? The day's almost over."

"Sure. I can go for a drink."

"Good."

I set the screen lock on my computer. I picked up my purse and stood.

"There's a place two blocks up on Market. We can walk, if you don't mind."

"Walking's fine," I said.

Outside, he moved with a rapid pace, firing off his thoughts about baseball and golf and his last trip to Europe. I murmured the appropriate affirmations to keep the flow of words streaming from his mouth. It felt good to escape from the stale air, my legs moving, cool breeze on my face. I didn't really care what he wanted to go on about, as long as he continued the brisk stride.

The place he chose was a simple bar. There was no lounge area with sofas and armchairs to suggest casual socializing, emphasizing appetizers as much as alcohol. This was a serious bar. Not a hardcore biker bar, or the kind filled with obvious bottom-of-the-barrel alcoholics or anything like that. It catered to well-heeled, functioning alcoholics and social drinkers and, probably, pre-alcoholics, if there is such a thing.

We sat on thinly padded black leather stools near the door. A brass pole ran from the floor up and over the bar to my right, which made me feel slightly pinned between Steve and the unyielding pole. I ordered a Grey Goose martini with three olives. Steve ordered Macallan's scotch on the rocks.

"To new conversations." He touched his glass to mine

and took a long swallow. "So. What's with Tess?"

I sipped my drink while I adjusted to the abrupt change in direction. "How do you mean?"

"She seems different lately."

I agreed, but I wasn't here to discuss Tess's personality fluctuations. Especially not with him. "I haven't noticed anything that different."

"She's distracted."

"That happens to everyone once in a while, don't you think?"

"Did she do right by you in your performance review?"

I stared at him. What the hell kind of question was that? According to Tess, my *four* rating and the associated crap raise was mostly his doing.

"I'll take that as a *no*," he said.

"Take it however you like." I smiled and kept my voice low so the words came out with a caramel coating, not a sharp veering into challenging his authority, forgetting my place as a low-level worker sitting in a bar with a Senior Vice President.

"Don't be bitter about it," he said.

"Do I sound bitter?"

"Yes."

I laughed. "Okay." I wasn't going to throw Tess under the bus. However disappointed I was that she hadn't fought harder for what I deserved, that would stay between her and me.

"So you don't know what's wrong with her?"

"I don't think anything is wrong with her."

He slid his glass around the polished surface of the bar, watching the liquid sway gently over the ice cubes that were losing their sharp, well-defined edges.

I wasn't about to ask about my possible job career, the first move should be his. I was starting to think he'd forgotten all about it again in his obsession over whatever was wrong with Tess. Maybe he'd never planned to discuss it and only invited me for a drink to pick my brain about her.

"Did she mention this portrait thing?" He chuckled, with a rather bitter edge, I thought.

"Refresh my memory."

"Don't be coy. Either she mentioned the painting or she didn't. It's not something you'd forget."

I hadn't forgotten anything, but I wasn't sure she'd mentioned the portrait to him. Could there be two paintings? I didn't want to blurt out information about the portrait when he was talking about something else entirely.

"I don't get it. Who does something like that?"

I shrugged.

"You aren't talking much."

"I'm not sure what the topic is."

"I'm not talking behind her back. She was very open about it. A portrait. I asked her if it was a nude and she didn't answer."

I sipped my drink. I wanted to steer him back to firm ground — business, my career.

"So it is a nude?" he said.

"I doubt that."

"But you don't know?"

"Why are you so concerned about it? Did we really come here to talk about whether Tess is behaving differently or why she wants a portrait of herself? It doesn't seem that interesting."

"Should I tell her you said that?" He raised his eyebrows slightly. He picked up the glass and swallowed the rest of the liquid, letting an ice cube slide into his mouth along with it.

I sipped my drink and said nothing.

"I guess she wouldn't talk about it to you. It's kind of personal. Sometimes I forget she's your boss."

I doubted that, but still said nothing.

"Don't sulk."

"Why would I sulk?"

"I don't know. Maybe I said something offensive. Talking about a nude painting. Or...I don't know. Should we get going? I have to drive so I really don't want another drink."

I didn't either. I ate all three olives and drank most of the martini, leaving a puddle in the bottom just because.

We left the bar. As we walked back, he rambled on about artwork and how he didn't get most of it. His opinion was that if people wanted to express a view of the world, they should be direct, not just splash colors on a piece of canvas. What that had to do with portrait painting, I had no idea.

In front of the CoastalCreative building, he said good-bye. It was clear that any future in sales was not on the immediate horizon.

64

Before her first sitting, Tess hadn't realized Joshua would be driven to finish the portrait in such a short time. Now, she was exhausted by the grueling schedule. If someone had told her sitting comfortably on a love seat was exhausting, she would have laughed. An hour on the treadmill was exhausting. Trying to get Steve out of her life was exhausting. Presenting to the CEO and his staff for two hours — that was exhausting.

The first sitting had been after work, in the middle of the week. Then, Joshua had insisted, almost angrily, that she spend her entire weekend sitting for him — six hours on Saturday and a numbing seven and a half hours on Sunday.

She was used to having the balance of power weighted in her favor. The fact that she was paying fifteen thousand dollars for this opportunity seemed to matter not at all to Joshua North. He dictated how long she sat between breaks, he dictated the temperature and the amount of light in the room. He chose the music — ranging from heavy metal to soft violin pieces that made her drowsy. He decided when she would stand, asking her to turn slowly so he could get a sense of her body from the back. Why that mattered for a portrait, she had no idea. He set the timing, the schedule, whether or not there was conversation between them, and he controlled the outcome entirely.

Sitting there was like attending a torturous meditation retreat where silence was maintained for an entire week. No speaking at meals, no greeting a person sitting in the garden. You kept your lips sealed. As a result, your mind went mad with all of those comments and suggestions, memories and observations, small talk and questions and idle chatter trapped inside.

The first day, only a two-hour session, she spent the time thinking back over her relationship with Steve, from the moment she'd met him. She mentally reviewed every sexual encounter and all their meals together. As best she could, she let her mind shuffle through text messages and emails and voice mails, mentally filing them in chronological order.

Joshua told her to stop thinking about whatever was causing her brow to furrow and to think about her favorite ways to spend her free time. He was working on the form of her body and he needed it arranged without tension.

But she couldn't. Steve pressed against the front of her skull — the mess she'd made of their relationship and the likely fallout at work. She tried to uncover the point in time when she'd made her first wrong step. On the surface, her mistake had been the second martini with him, followed by sex. But she'd been at a customer site with him, staying in the same hotel. He approached her in the bar. Should she have left her unfinished drink on the table and fled to her room?

And there was more to it than that. What had happened during their weekly meetings that led up to it all? Sex didn't happen without an initial attraction, a warmth in the air between them. What had created the bond or some sort of unusual rapport that had allowed sex to happen first in her subconscious mind? It hadn't just been a *why the hell not* kind of encounter. There was something between them — their shared passion for CoastalCreative, hours of conversation, emails about business laced with the occasional personal bit of information or witty comment. Innocent conversations!

There was no single point in time she could point to.

Joshua stepped away from the easel. The easel she was forbidden to look at until the portrait was complete. She wasn't sure how she felt about that. She was used to giving feedback on any project someone was doing for her. What if she hated the end result and it was too late? She'd hinted at that possibility, not using the word *hate*, of course. Joshua was shocked. *This is my work. My vision.*

She wondered what the term *commission* implied to him. He seemed to view her as a subject, destined to become part of his oeuvre, a model, rather than a client.

He'd studied her face, a small frown on his thin lips. "You're tense."

"Sorry."

"Don't *apologize*. What good does apologizing do? Tension comes from here." He tapped the end of his paintbrush on his forehead.

"I realize that," Tess said.

"What's going on in here?" He tapped his head again.

She wanted to shove the handle of the paintbrush into his ear. This was not what she'd thought it would be like. She'd thought he would seduce her with a gaze that drank in her entire being. She'd thought he might be awed by her exotic face, her striking hair, her supposedly hypnotic eyes. She laughed.

"Please, Tess. I need you to cooperate with this process."

That had been day one. When she learned she'd be sitting for the entire weekend, she seriously considered backing out of the whole thing. But she'd come this far. She'd told Alexandra about it. It irked her that Alex's opinion carried such weight, but she couldn't avoid that fact. Telling Alex she'd changed her mind was admitting failure.

On Saturday morning, she smoked a third of a joint. The pot would slow her thoughts, make her more open to the process, help her enjoy the slow, heavy movement of time even if the experience wasn't at all what she'd expected. It had indeed helped, allowing her to sit there not caring as her thoughts moved aimlessly.

Joshua decreed her too relaxed. He asked her to go out and take a walk around the block before he offered her half a turkey sandwich with mayo and lettuce and a cup of coffee. It was a bland, skimpy lunch, but surprisingly satisfying. Probably because the pot had stirred up that ravenous desire for anything that could be chewed, turning the most mundane food into a gourmet meal.

After Saturday's session, she'd gone home, drank two glasses of wine, eaten a slice of buttered sourdough bread, and gone to sleep at eight.

65

At Sunday's sitting, Tess wouldn't rely on dope. She'd open herself up to the boredom and mild anxiety and try to enjoy the not knowing, the weird spotlight of Joshua's interest, his effort to peer inside of her, all of it to be captured in the painting.

But then, her thoughts took a nasty turn, as thoughts often did when they were left un-corralled for too long.

Sitting for a portrait resembled therapy, connections rising up out of the forced structure. She began to think of her failed love affairs. Steve was only the most recent mistake. How did other women make it seem so simple — dating a few men, finding the right one, the *perfect* one, marrying in bliss and building a life with another human being?

She believed it was Toby's fault. Her first love at the age of nineteen. That alone should have been a warning. Already, she wasn't like other girls, never having a crush or even a passing interest in a boy until she was nineteen. During her last two years in high school, she'd wondered if she was gay, but no girls captured her interest either.

Then she met Toby. The intensity should have scared her. And maybe if she'd been older, it would have. They seemed to be one mind inhabiting two bodies. She worried they fit the truism that if two people never disagree, one of them isn't necessary. But it felt like he was very necessary. She and Toby had the same political and religious views, right down to the idea that god was a genderless being, embodying both male and female. They liked the same movies, the same books, the same TV shows. Their tastes in food were identical, they both loved hiking and swimming. The viewed hiking as a transcendent experience and a metaphor for life's journey.

A burning desire to succeed in the business world consumed them equally.

They became best friends, lovers, study partners, constant companions.

When Toby threw a rope over the rafters and hung himself in his father's garage at the age of twenty and four months, Tess felt as if the heavy rope tightened and burned around her own neck. She was constantly nauseous, unable to breathe properly. He didn't leave a note. He'd given no warning. There was no hint of despair, no suggestion of violence or a desire for death. It was a devastating mystery that haunted her even now. What had wounded him so deeply that he couldn't continue living? For a long time, too long, she worried that perhaps one of them had indeed become unnecessary and he'd given his mind over to live inside of hers.

It was a ridiculous belief, but she couldn't shake it.

"Tess." Joshua's voice was sharp, too loud.

Her head jerked involuntarily.

"You're not here. Come back into the room."

"I was thinking."

"You should be thinking about the things I suggest, not meandering all over the place. It destroys your face. The skin sags and your flesh loses its structure."

"You didn't ask me to think about anything specific."

"I did. That's why you filled out the form."

"It had several questions. Which one am I supposed to think about?"

Sunlight streamed into the room from the narrow, uncovered windows behind her. One was opened to allow cool air inside. The rays were directly on his face, making his head and upper body indistinct. The brightness didn't cause him to squint or shift his position. He basked in it.

She pulled her left foot out from beneath her right thigh where it had been tucked, her knee bent sharply, for the past two hours.

"I need you to keep your position."

"My legs are stiff." She rubbed her kneecap.

He said nothing.

She put her foot back where it had been. She felt the pose was somewhat childish, too vulnerable, but he'd tried several positions before hitting on this one. It seemed to inspire him because after they first tried this arrangement of her limbs, his brush had lashed at the canvas furiously for thirty solid minutes.

She tried to keep her thoughts on the rays of sun, the moist tap of the paint-sodden brush on canvas.

After a while, Joshua asked her to think about her secret, and to consider the reasons why it needed to remain a secret. Her thoughts turned to her father, and then, to her mother. The other death she tried to avoid thinking about.

The lie on Joshua's form was only the first layer of many. By never telling her mother how she'd lied, she compounded the false picture of her life right up until her mother's death, two years after her father.

And that was why she was here today.

The woman who had no life beyond raising her three

children. The woman who silently cooked and cleaned and cared for her family for nearly thirty years. The woman who Tess effectively erased from the portrait of her life, so consumed with pursuing her career goals, with winning her father's admiration for her achievements.

Her mother's life was separate, nothing like Tess's life, and until her mother died, Tess thought it wasn't all that interesting. A life that was not only lived in the background, marred at the age of forty by an aggressive skin cancer that resulted in the removal of the left side of her jaw and most of her cheek.

There were no photographs of her mother after the diagnosis. Her mother hated being anywhere near a camera. And so it seemed as if the last quarter of her life had been swallowed up forever. Nine years of her life undocumented, her unremarkable existence became completely invisible.

When Tess looked in the mirror and saw her mother's dark hair framing her own face, her mother's almost teal eyes looking back, she wanted that image to live on…forever.

Not the portrait of a woman with a graduate degree. Not a woman who was a senior vice president. Not a woman who hooked up with a man just because she didn't know what kind of man she wanted. Not a woman who had acquired respect and admiration and financial security all on her own.

She wanted to see a woman who was worth preserving in paint and canvas, something substantial, simply because she'd existed.

66

It was nine-thirty at night when Steve Montgomery's name appeared on my phone as it shuddered on my coffee table.

Unbelievable.

I stared at the name, not sure if I should pick up.

Calling back from a missed call seems stalker-ish. I don't know why that is. Everyone knows you get the named alert for a missed call. But when no message is left, it seems the caller wasn't determined to speak to you, so calling back is... maybe not stalker-ish, but needy. I had the idea of a stalker on my mind, so that term came up first.

Returning a call was also not ideal. Although the control rests with the person returning the call — her timing, her choice of location and all that — it still feels needy. To me. Maybe my mind is twisted. But a return call says you're interested. You're saying you want to talk to the caller. You're admitting they have something you want.

I grabbed the phone, still a tacit admission he might have something I wanted. "Hi, Steve."

"I know it's late, but I wanted to complete our conversation from the bar the other day."

"Was it incomplete?"

"It got off track."

Well that wasn't my fault. I was solidly on track. He was the one who wanted to pry information out of me, trying to gossip, trying to manipulate me into betraying my boss.

"Are you there?" he said.

"I'm here."

"You don't think it got off track? Talking about Tess?"

"I wasn't talking about her."

He laughed. "Okay. Fair enough."

He was silent for a few seconds.

"Sooo…well, just to finish that off. I do think she's changed. She's lost her edge."

"I don't."

"I see her differently than you do, I think. You might not be in the best position, working for her. I know you're extremely loyal…"

"What?" How the hell would he know that? And I'm not all that loyal. I'm interested in self-preservation. And being loyal is self preserving. It's the right thing to do, as long as the other person is equally loyal, of course.

He continued talking about her. Still. "This whole thing with the nude painting, it's really whacked. If it gets out, she won't look good. It will undermine her authority, and…"

"There isn't a nude painting."

"She told me she's getting a painting done."

"It's a portrait."

"Usually when women model for a painter, they're naked."

I wasn't sure if it would sabotage a potential career change if I told him he was nuts. "With all due respect, Steve, I don't know where you got that idea. I believe Tess is having her portrait done. She's not a nude model."

"How do you know?"

"I know."

"She wants attention. Never underestimate a woman's need for attention. Am I right?" He laughed.

Did I ever want to work for this guy? No matter how inspiring to know that a good portion of my pay would be based on my own hustle and skill. "Is this the conversation you wanted to finish?" I said.

He laughed, sounding slightly embarrassed, maybe not. "I do get off track when I'm concerned about my peers. And the people below me in the organization. I'm a very caring guy."

"I can see that." I gritted my teeth, tasting the lie like so much bile.

"Tess might be unstable. At least that's how it looks to me, maybe to others."

"That hasn't been my experience."

"Either way, I think you'd be better off on my team. More money. Less drama. What more could you want?"

I stood and walked to the sliding glass door. I pressed my forehead against the glass to cool my skin, strangely overheated from listening to him.

"What do you think?" he said.

"Have you offered me a position?"

"Ha ha. You're so direct. I like that. No drama with you."

"You've mentioned that before." I moved away from the glass and rubbed my finger across it to wipe away the smudge.

"So...an offer. I'll write something up. I know you don't have any experience in sales, so you'd start with the salary you have now. After six months, you'd move to a sales comp plan, with a lower base pay but huge upside."

"How huge?"

"That all depends on you."

I did find that aspect extremely appealing. I like relying

on myself, knowing that what I do directly affects what I earn. It's why I was so obsessed with the rating system. It implied that control over your salary was in your hands, depending on how hard you worked at being an outstanding performer. Even though it hadn't worked out that way at all, I was still fixated on it. That was how it *should* have worked, and despite all the games, it's how they *implied* that it did work.

In sales, my abilities and drive really would mean actual cash in my pocket.

"I would personally train and mentor you," Steve said.

I walked to the couch and put my heel on the armrest, I bent forward slightly, easing myself into a nice, blood-warming stretch. I thought about the painting exposing the woman's muscles and veins and wondered what my insides looked like, stretching the pliable stuff that holds my bones in place, forcing blood into thread-like capillaries and veins.

"That way, you'd get the best," he said. "Not that I'm bragging, just saying, if you're trained by someone less experienced, you can start out on the wrong foot. Then, you don't know what you don't know and it can really damage your ability to succeed over the long term."

"Interesting."

"So you're interested?"

"I have to think about it."

"This really is the best move for you. More money, less drama, and…"

"Okay. Got it."

"What's the hesitation?"

"I like to think things over before making major decisions."

"A good trait," he said. "That would serve you well in

sales. But you also have to think fast on your feet, which I believe you do. Any questions? Anything I can do to sell you on how great this opportunity is?"

"I don't think so. I just need time to consider it."

"You'd basically be my protégé."

I had to bite down hard on my tongue. Did he consider that a selling point? He'd just shoved me hard in the opposite direction. Learning from the best, indeed.

67

The next morning I went for a three-mile run before dawn. The stalker kept himself well-hidden, and I didn't see him until I returned to my building. He stood under the awning across the street, staring hard at me as I clung to the lamppost for my cool-down stretches.

I waved. He took a step forward and raised his arm. He put his hand parallel to the ground and drew it across the front of his neck in a slashing motion. If it had been the middle of the day, I don't think it would have bothered me. And from across the street, it wasn't terribly frightening, but still…The sky was inky black, light along the street minimal despite the elegant lampposts, more for ambiance than security. I turned and went into the building, telling myself he wasn't threatening me. He didn't even know me, he just thought he did. The gesture meant nothing.

Riding up in the elevator, I felt cold despite the run. Cold and clammy and unsure how I could get the upper hand with him.

Although I hadn't though of much else during my run, I forced my thoughts back to Steve.

Becoming his protégé did not interest me in the least. In fact, his suggestion disgusted me. I had no desire to be treated like a child, like someone who needed a kind and attentive, domineering touch. Surely I had an enormous amount to learn about the industry, the products, about sales in general, but I would learn it in my own way, not as the pet of a pompous ass.

His suggestion was the final item on the *con* side of my mental pro and con list. Still, I wanted to run it by Tess, tease her gently, just to see what she said, to observe the expression on her face. I wanted to find out what she'd do to make sure the *pro* list for staying with her doubled in length.

I'd suggested we try the restaurant she'd been so excited to invite me to a few weeks earlier. Her response was so enthusiastic, it seemed as if she'd been moping the entire time. She began describing the dishes she'd tried — the frog leg and snail ragout and the crispy Spanish octopus, grilled and firm and prepared with tomato and chili braised mushrooms. She went on about various duck selections and rack of lamb.

"It sounds like you already tried it."

"Steve and I..." she paused. "I...when you didn't call back...uhh, I..."

So, she'd gone there with Steve. On a Saturday night. It was an interesting bit of information. Telling her about the offer might take a different course than I'd imagined.

"That doesn't mean I don't want to try it with you," she said.

"I didn't take it that way. I was just clarifying."

"I'll make a reservation. It's close by. Wear flats...we can walk."

"Sure."

I was more excited to see her face when I mentioned the job offer, her complex mix of fear over the complication in her relationship with Steve, than her rapture over the food.

68

Tess came to my cubicle at quarter to six.

I grabbed my purse and coat off the fat iron hook attached to one of the cubicle walls. I dragged my navy scarf out of the coat sleeve, put on the coat, and draped the scarf around the back of my neck.

Outside, the sidewalks were mobbed. As we turned, I glanced behind me and across the street, searching the crowd for the stalker. I thought about turning again for a longer look, but if he knew he'd unsettled me, he would win. In the end, it didn't matter all that much if I located him. I'd spot him eventually.

We walked at a leisurely pace, each putting forward a black leather booted foot at the same time, our strides nearly identical. It seemed as if we hit a red light at every intersection, but it felt good, as it always does, to be out in the cold air, moving about after a day spent sitting in a box with fabric covered walls, staring at a glowing screen. It took almost twenty minutes to reach the restaurant.

Chez Monique was ultra-sleek with mauve-colored tables. The matching chairs looked utilitarian, but when I sat, it hugged my hips and stroked my back like I'd just lain down on a massage table. I settled into it and wish I had something similar at my desk. Unlike some restaurants focused more on style, the entire place had been designed to invite diners to linger over their food and wine, coffee and chocolate dessert. I'd skimmed the menus online before we left the office, including the desserts — there were more than twenty selections, all with at least a touch of chocolate.

The ceiling was glass. Above it was an atrium filled with hanging plants so there was a feeling of sitting on a forest floor. The walls were painted glossy chocolate brown and were split by strips of mirror about four inches in width, so everything glimmered but you didn't have the uncomfortable experience of staring at yourself while you chewed and swallowed.

The server brought us each a glass of champagne with a raspberry nestled in the bottom of the flute.

Tess scanned the wine list and ordered a bottle of Cabernet, making her decision so quickly from the twenty-page book, it was clearly the same variety she'd shared with Steve.

I studied the top of her head, bent over the menu. Now that I knew their relationship was more complicated than she'd let on, I wondered if they were engaged in some sort of power play with each other, using me as their pawn — a toy in some elaborate flirtation. I couldn't begin to imagine why they would do something like that, what benefit it would be to them, but with each blaming the other, it was too easy to believe there was something more to it. I laughed.

"What's so funny?"

"I think the champagne went to my head."

She raised her eyebrows but said nothing.

"Should we have an appetizer?" I said.

"Definitely."

We ordered caviar with lobster potato blinis, followed by duck confit soup with chestnuts and black mushrooms, an autumn salad, and our main courses. I had lobster and mushroom risotto, Tess had eye of ribeye.

After the caviar arrived, I spread a bit on a piece of blini along with some Crème Fraiche. I took a bite. "How is the portrait coming along?"

She shrugged. "It's not what I expected."

"You don't like it?"

She took a sip of wine. "I haven't seen it. The experience isn't what I expected."

"Why haven't you seen it?"

"I think that's typical. Giving the artist room to work without oversight."

I nodded. I supposed I'd heard that somewhere or other, but I didn't see myself agreeing to that arrangement. What if she hated it?

We ate the caviar and blinis and sipped our wine, not speaking for a moment or two. The soup arrived and when the server left, I scooped up a spoonful and put it in my mouth. The texture was like butter, filling my mouth and soaking my tongue and throat with rich, divine flavor.

"Do you consider this a social or a working dinner?" I said.

"Do we have work to discuss?"

"I do."

She put down her spoon and reached for the wine bottle. Before she could touch it, the server swept in and topped off both our glasses.

"What's up?" she said.

"I'm wondering how my role will change in the next year or so."

"Is that a question?"

"I don't want to get stale."

"Are you feeling stale?"

"Not yet, just thinking ahead."

She looked at me, her eyes hard and knowing. She leaned back in her chair. "What's going on?"

"I don't like to be bored."

"No one does."

The salads came and we talked for a few minutes about the beautiful arrangement of thinly sliced apple, pear, and roasted beets.

"I don't like sitting in front of a computer so much. I'd like to…" I took a sip of wine. "I think I have other skills that aren't being used. And of course, I was disappointed with my last raise. I've been wondering if I could make more in sales. I think I'd like the thrill of…"

"Steve made you an offer."

"Nothing written."

She smiled. She continued smiling as she cut into her ribeye. "You'd probably do really well in a sales job." She put a piece of meat in her mouth, removed the fork slowly, and chewed, a smile still playing around her lips.

It seemed as if she wasn't at all concerned that I might leave her team. Which meant she wasn't going to offer me more money to stay with her. In fact, she probably couldn't really do that. It was no concern to the company whether I was in one organization or another, it wasn't as if they were forced to offer more to keep me from going to work for a competitor.

We went on eating and talking and drinking wine.

Tess remarked how good I'd be presenting our product information and strategy to customers. She talked about travel, she and I together. Visiting customers around the globe would get me away from the computer, energize me, and make me more valuable as I learned the details of what problems customers were dealing with, problems that our products could solve.

She said nothing about more money. And nothing about a concrete change in my job description.

My face wore a calm smile, and my eyes sparkled — the picture of an interested, engaged dinner companion. Inside, my thoughts circled like mad squirrels. I thought of the visible woman painting and wondered what it would be like if any of us could see what raced through another person's mind.

69

When we stepped outside, it was dark, cold, and a sharp wind was whipping between the buildings. A crumpled cigarette pack raced along the sidewalk. I wound my scarf twice around my neck, overlapping the pieces so it covered my skin up to my jaw. Tess did the same. She pulled a pair of thin leather gloves out of her pocket and put them on. She looped her purse strap over her head, and held it close to her ribs — the futile move of every woman who believes such a stance will protect her from a mugging. A purse snatcher who looks for a bag dangling and swinging beside her hip, the leather strap resting loosely on her shoulder, absolutely. But a mugging? There's no security measure you can take to protect yourself from that if you're in the wrong place at the wrong time.

With our coats, the soft leather of our boots, and tightly wound scarves, the wind touched only our faces. It was pleasant, wiping away the stupor of rich food and wine.

"I'd love to have a position that required travel," I said.

"It's one of the best parts of my job," Tess said. "It changes your perspective. That sounds like a cliché, but it gets repeated to the point of cliché because it's true. Have you ever been outside of the US?"

"No."

"It makes you recognize that you're part of the entire planet, something bigger and more connected than you realize if you spend most of your time, your life, in one location. It gives you a better understanding of the human race."

I wasn't sure about that, but I wanted to travel so it wasn't a point worth arguing. "Getting out of my cubicle would be fantastic. And I do want more opportunities to move ahead."

"Meaning more money, of course."

I laughed. "Of course."

"We can talk about that. But you need to understand the constraints. And if money is really all you care about, maybe you should consider Steve's offer. You'll never make what a sales rep makes in marketing. But there's a downside to sales."

"Isn't there a downside to everything?"

We walked for a block without talking. I needed more money. I wanted to own a condo, and then a house, and then a magnificent house, a fortress. It was the thing that got me out of bed in the mornings, as they say. I wasn't going to get there in a timely manner working for CoastalCreative, or any other company. I needed to start thinking of other ways to achieve my goal. But for now, travel would be a nice diversion. "What's the best place you've ever visited?"

"That's impossible to say."

"Then tell me your favorites."

She started talking about her trips to Asia and the appeal of being in a place that was dramatically different from home. She rattled on about Hong Kong and Singapore, Japan and Beijing.

Listening to her talk, I could hear the shift in her tone, the way the stories of things that happened on those trips implanted themselves into the core of her being, stories that she would never forget.

She was so busy talking, and I was so busy feeling her excitement seep into me, we kept walking straight, at a faster clip, the buildings and landmarks around us blurring into dark, empty shadows. At the corner of Mason and Washington, we both stopped at the same moment. "We were supposed to turn at Jackson," I said.

"You're right. But we can turn here and circle back."

We walked faster, if that was possible. It was a street with no lights except the occasional alcove lighting that spilled onto the pavement. Homeless people huddled in the alcoves. It seemed as if I could feel their eyes, watching our progress, sizing us up, wondering at two women so out of place.

The gutter was filled with food wrappers and smashed drink containers, occasional clumps of discarded food. In some spots, the pavement smelled like urine.

"This is scary," Tess said. "We should get an Uber."

"That makes no sense. Standing here waiting for a driver? It's faster to walk."

"There are a lot of drunks."

"Yeah, but they're so drunk, they won't bother us." I took her arm. "We're fine."

"It's not safe." She put her hand on her purse, slipping her fingers into the opening when she thought I wasn't looking. I couldn't believe she thought she would actually pull out her gun if someone asked for spare cash, but if it made her feel better…

Her body trembled against me.

"We'll be fine."

"You're too confident. It's so dark, and there are all kinds of deranged people."

We reached the middle of the block. My feet were tired

from keeping such a pace in boots designed to look good and offer some comfort, but not for speed-walking. I slowed, Tess increased her pace, nearly running. I scrambled to catch up.

After another few yards, I heard footsteps behind us. Tess's hand scrabbled around inside her purse.

"Don't," I said softly

"I'm not going to get mugged." Her voice was as low as mine, but more of a hiss.

"It's a bad idea."

"I'm not letting someone assault me. Or worse."

"They're harmless. Just drunk, drug-addled…"

"You don't know that. You have no fucking idea who these people are."

The footsteps were louder, closer. I wondered if Tess noticed. I wanted to turn, but turning would show fear, and showing fear would make it worse. Still, walking quickly revealed the same anxiety, and if the person was going to cause trouble, wouldn't taking control of the situation be better? I stopped and turned.

After all the times I'd observed him nearby, and all the energy I'd given to thinking about him, it shouldn't have surprised me to see the man in the brown leather jacket. But it did.

I felt immediately less nervous and at the same time, concerned that I should have been more unsettled, not less. Seeing a familiar face rather than a stranger on a dark, nasty street brings natural relief. But after that throat-cutting gesture, he'd proved himself more threatening than I'd realized at first. Following me, both of us, onto a grungy, deserted street gave more menace to his throat-slashing move.

"You," I said.

He pushed his cap up higher on his head. His face was mean and his expression had a dull, angry quality. "I told you, this has to stop or your life is going to take a turn for the worse."

"What does that even mean?" I said.

"What's going on?" Tess turned toward me, her face blanched, her eyes huge and dark.

"I have no idea," I said. "But he seems to think he knows me."

"I don't know you...it's her." He jutted his shoulder toward Tess.

"Let's go." I turned.

He grabbed my scarf. The double loop tightened around my throat.

"I'm giving you a chance to clean up your act. Both of you."

I struggled to release the stranglehold, searching for the other end of the scarf so I could unwind it.

"I'm trying to do you a favor." His voice was louder now. "You need to knock it off, or find another place to live and conduct your business. I've told you several times, it needs to stop."

"What needs to stop?" Tess said. "Who the hell are you?" Her voice was strong, unwavering, despite the fear she'd demonstrated for the past minute or so.

"Don't act so shocked. I'm in security for the Howard Street apartments. I've been watching you two, and now that I've confirmed what's going on." He cleared his throat. "We have an outstanding reputation. Our residents expect a classy, safe, upscale environment. Crime-free. It's an excellent neighborhood. Whores are not welcome."

"Whores?" I said.

"Well not both of you. I assume you do the pimping? I've never seen you actually soliciting." He was looking at me, still clutching my scarf, keeping it tight so it was difficult for me to move.

"I am not a whore," Tess said. Her voice was low.

"Call girl, whatever label you want. The point is…"

"I'm the Senior Vice President of Marketing for a global software company," Tess said.

He laughed. He slid his hand across his throat as he'd done before, his teeth, exposed by a wide grin, shone in a small pocket of light.

In a move so fluid it seemed as if she'd practiced it a thousand times, and maybe she had, Tess pulled her gun out of her purse, pointed it at his head, and fired.

He collapsed immediately, releasing my scarf as he fell. Even in the darkness, the blood pouring out of his head was obvious. A lot of blood.

I don't like blood. I don't mind seeing it contained in the spaces where it belongs, inside the veins and arteries of the woman in the painting, for example, but as I watched it flow out of him, spreading across the pavement, the duck and mushroom soup and lobster risotto heaved violently inside my stomach. I turned away.

It seemed as if she'd planned each move while he was talking. She didn't aim for his chest, where the leather jacket might have saved him. She managed an accurate shot right below the bill of his Giants hat. She didn't hesitate for a moment.

When I thought about it as I walked away, trying to put

the sight of all that blood out of my head, I realized she'd gone for the winning shot.

70

I continued walking, trying to sort out what had happened. It seemed as if Tess had *wanted* to kill him. As if she'd been waiting for an opportunity to kill someone, anyone. To bring the black silhouette she shot at the target range into the real world. She was so quick, too eager. We hadn't even really figured out what was going on before she lifted her gun and fired with impressive accuracy.

"Alexandra. Wait."

I slowed and she caught up to me. "That was...I don't know. Surprising," she said.

I said nothing.

"I just...I'm so tired of being afraid. It's exhausting. It's so unfair. It's so fucking unfair that men can go where they want and do as they please and women have to watch what they wear and never, ever be in the wrong neighborhood at night. If they are, whatever happens is their own fault."

"You were certainly...you didn't hesitate."

"He was going to kill us."

"It was two against one. I think he just wanted to scare us."

"Didn't you see what he did with his hand? Like slashing our throats?"

Yes, I'd seen, but it was still two against one.

"I'm tired of walking through life feeling like I'm at the mercy of every god damn male who wants to bully me. It's exhausting. It's depressing. I don't know what he wanted, but he wanted to scare us. And he treated us like shit."

I tried to sort it out.

We reached the corner and turned back the way we should have gone initially. The street was dramatically different, as if we'd walked through the opening in a heavy pair of drapes into an entirely different city. The interiors of offices and stores glowed with nighttime security lighting, the streetlights were plentiful.

Tess shoved the gun into her purse and zipped it closed with a flick of her wrist that wasn't unlike the motion the stalker had made, suggesting he wanted to cut our throats. I couldn't imagine a security guard for an upscale apartment building slashing anyone's throat, but he had a rather unorthodox way of maintaining building security.

So, he'd thought I was a pimp. Or a pimp-ette. I suppose in the old days, I would have been called a madam. Or even now, I wasn't familiar with the industry terminology. No wonder the things he said to me were so confusing. He'd made me into a different person by adding one plus one and getting five. He thought Tess was a hooker? That made no sense. He'd never even met her. Unless...

"I've seen that guy before," Tess said. "Outside of work. He tried to talk to me. I thought he was unbalanced. I got rid of him."

"What did he say?"

"Same thing. That he was on to me. So he was definitely following us, threatening us. I did what anyone would do. Any self-defense instructor will tell you that if you feel threatened, you need to listen to your gut and respond appropriately."

"But that refers to using pepper spray. You're not supposed to carry a gun in your purse."

She shrugged. "I'm tired of feeling scared. I told you that. It's not fair."

It wasn't. But ninety percent of the people on the planet live in a mild to extreme state of fear. For someone who had traveled all over the world, I would have expected her to understand that. Also curious was the fact that she seemed to feel no compulsion to report the shooting. Saving her own skin came first. We were more alike than I'd realized.

The parking garage near the CoastalCreative offices came into view.

"Why don't you walk with me to my car, and I'll drive you to your door," she said.

"I thought your gun keeps you from being afraid?"

"I'm thinking of you." She gave my shoulder a light punch.

Once we were inside her car, I thought she'd express remorse, or fear of being found out. I thought she'd question what she'd done, even if she didn't feel badly about reacting to a perceived threat. She did none of that. Her purse with the still warm gun sat innocently on the back seat in all its finely-crafted designer glory.

"I think I know what happened," I said.

"With what?"

"What he thought was going on."

Betraying Jen, when she was so afraid of being found out, was unfortunate, but her path would never cross Tess's again. It wasn't as if Tess was going to report her to the apartment management company. What did she care? Jen would be safe. "He thought you were someone else."

"I realize that." She pulled out of the garage and turned left.

"A woman who lives in my building, the one you met at the gym, looks a lot like you. She's a..."

"I told you not to say that."

"It's true."

"It is not."

"That's what he thought."

"Well he's dead, isn't he."

She made a right and then left onto Howard. She pulled in front of my building. I opened the door.

"Of course, I assume you'll keep this to yourself," she said.

"Yes."

"And don't ever suggest that I look like that girl."

I closed the door firmly and watched her pull away from the curb. Not mentioning it didn't change reality.

71

After my mother skidded down the slope of our back lawn, smearing mud across the seat of her new skinny jeans and swamping her dignity, she heaved herself to her feet and returned to the house. She didn't turn to look at me. I went into the grove of trees with Denny. When dusk came, a pot of soup was simmering on the stove, but my mother wasn't in the kitchen.

For dinner she wore a narrow skirt that came to her knees and a thick sweater with a shirt underneath. Her feet were bare even though the temperature had barely made it to fifty-five degrees that afternoon. Her face was scrubbed clean. When we finished eating, she excused my youngest brother from kitchen duty. She sat at the table reading a magazine while I loaded the dishwasher.

I rubbed a soapy sponge around the inside of the pot she'd used to boil spaghetti. I scraped the stuck on beef and tomato sauce out of the frying pan. As I scrubbed the residue with steel wool, gummy pink soap worked its way into my cuticles and beneath my fingernails. I wanted to plunge my hands into fresh dishwater and rub my fingertips clean, but then the accumulation of gunk would start again, feeling worse because it was the second time. I forced myself to keep going.

When the pans and cooking utensils and cutting board

were clean, I dried and put them away. All the while, the magazine pages turned and my mother's head remained bent over the shiny pages.

I rinsed the gunk out of my nails and cuticles, dried my hands, and turned off the light over the sink.

A magazine page turned.

I hung the towel on the rack under the sink.

A magazine page turned.

I squirted hand cream into my palm and rubbed my hands together, waiting for her to speak.

I walked toward the door leading to the dining room. Just as it started to swing closed behind me, I heard the thump of the magazine.

A moment later, she was in the dining room. She followed me up the stairs to my bedroom door. I went inside and she followed without asking whether I was okay with it. All five of us kids had to ask permission for every single thing, but my parents had permanent permission to go where they wanted, to enter whatever room they chose, to do as they pleased. I suppose most parents do, but mine seemed to take immense pleasure in their authority and entitled ownership of the house and its juvenile occupants.

Rather than sitting on my bed, which might have given me the idea she was re-instituting the prayer oversight, she closed the door behind her and leaned against it. "I tried to be nice about this, tried to be respectful of the fact that you're almost a young woman, but you defied me."

Since it was freely available, I sat on my bed. "Just so you know, I'm already a woman."

The implication went right over her head. "Let me finish."

I folded my hands in my lap, pressing them into my thighs.

"The fact is, you are not an adult by any stretch. You're too young to be trusted with boys, and boys can definitely not be trusted with you. Especially boys that aren't raised with Godly principles."

"Boys like Denny?"

She didn't bother to nod.

"I thought you were all over the possibility of getting to know his family."

"I saw what you were doing with him. He is not to come anywhere near this house. You are not to let him walk you home. I don't want to see him again, or hear his name."

"So you're done flirting with him? You've accepted that your bloom is past, like Dad said?"

She walked across the room, stopped a few feet away, and glared at me. "Stand up."

I stood.

She slapped my face.

"Ow." I resisted putting my hand to my cheek, feeling the warmth of blood rushing to the surface of my skin. My left eye teared up, but I blinked to make the tears sink back inside.

"Don't you ever speak to me like that again."

"That hurt." There would be an angry red splotch, possibly still visible in the morning.

"I can do far worse, Alexandra. Don't fight me on this."

"You can't lock me up forever. You can't decide who my friends are and what I'm going to do and how I'm going to think."

"Our responsibility is to teach you the truth. We fear for

your soul."

"And I fear for yours, because it seems like you don't have one."

Her face remained hard and unmoved. She didn't tear up as I'd expected.

"I don't want to see him anywhere near this house. There will be consequences if I do."

72

San Francisco

The painting was complete. Tess had received a text from Joshua telling her he was finished and he was pleased with the results.

There had been a ten-day gap between her final marathon sitting and his text message, sent at one-thirty in the morning. She'd responded as soon as she woke.

Tess Turner: *When do I get to see it?*

He didn't text back for another six hours and twenty minutes, during which time she checked her phone every three or four minutes, irritation swelling inside of her chest, squeezing her lungs, twisting her stomach. She was paying him god dammit. She hoped she hadn't made a mistake, choosing someone who was not only temperamental, but seemed to wallow in dramatizing his temperamental tendencies.

Finally, while she was standing at the deli waiting for her turkey and alfalfa sprouts on dark rye, her phone buzzed. She reached into her purse, dragging her fingertips across the gun, clean and polished and fully loaded again, keeping the secret of what it had done. She plucked out her phone and looked at the screen.

Joshua North: *Traveling out of the country for three weeks. So*

She stared at the screen. What had he planned to say, hitting *send* before his second thought was complete? She waited to see if more followed. They called her sandwich. She ignored them. They called it again. Numb, she walked to the cash register and stuck her credit card in the reader.

This was bullshit. She was paying him a lot of money. He had a project to deliver.

Tess Turner: *That's not acceptable. I'm picking up the painting.*

Joshua North: *I'm beyond thrilled with it. It will be shown at Herriman's. You can see it there.*

Tess Turner: *Absolutely not. Call me. Now.*

She grabbed her sandwich and went outside. She crossed the street and sat on a bench facing traffic. It was a horrible place to eat lunch, but she was hungry. And she needed to talk to him.

Half the sandwich was gone before her phone buzzed.

The moment she answered, he began talking, gushing words. "Oh, Tess. It turned out so much better than I'd hoped. It was exactly the vision I had for you. Thank you, thank you, thank you for sitting for me."

"I'm not your fucking model. It's my portrait. I didn't *sit* for you, and whatever that implies. This was a commissioned piece."

He laughed.

"It's not funny."

"Don't take yourself so seriously. I knew the moment I saw you that you're a woman who thinks…"

"I'm your client."

He laughed.

"I want to see it this afternoon. It's not going to hang in a gallery. It's mine."

"Don't be so entitled. Art doesn't belong to anyone. Even to collectors — they're simply custodians for a short, or a long period of time. No one owns it."

"I expect to see the painting today. I'll come to your house at five."

"I should have been more clear. I've already left on my trip. I'm buried in concepts for my next project. I'm in Venice as we speak. The painting is at the gallery and you can see it any time you wish. I might let you purchase it, but not until after the show is over."

"You're not even in San Francisco? What show?"

"At *Herriman's*. Celine will tell you all about it. Or you can see for yourself, it's really better to view before discussing. You don't want to enter with preconceived..."

"Shut up. You have no right..."

"Gotta go, Tess. Talk at you later."

The call ended.

She wrapped up the rest of her sandwich. She stood and tossed it at the trashcan beside the bench. It hit the side and fell on the ground. She turned and walked to the corner, headed toward the gallery. She sent a message to Alex explaining that she was out for a few hours. She asked Alex to tell her admin to inform those running her early afternoon meetings that she had a family emergency. Nothing serious, but she had to be out.

She sent a message to Joshua.

Tess Turner: *I'm not happy about this. Not at all.*

There was no response.

73

Tess flung open the gallery door. It appeared deserted, the displays on the right side the same as what she'd seen when she visited with Alex.

"Celine?!"

The front left side was still occupied by the nude sculptures, but there appeared to be fewer of them. The collection of drug addicted women was gone. She walked past the sculpture to a collection of three paintings.

There were two small ones angled toward the center portrait. The large center portrait, lit by a tiny spotlight, was of her. But not.

It was her hair, glossy black but uncombed, as if she'd been sleeping with the blankets pulled over her head. The eyes were hers, surrounded by the same dark, smudged shadow. They were the same shade of teal, but despite the vibrant color, they looked hollow. The irises had a vacant, empty quality. In the corner of one eye was a large glistening tear, about to spill out.

She swallowed, stunned by the pain and sadness in the entire expression, the lifelike shimmer of the tear.

But the rest. It was even worse.

"Celine?" She was shouting, her composure gone. "Get out here right now."

The mouth was unsmiling, the lips parted in a way that looked as if she were about to open her mouth wide for a man. The pose was the casual one she'd maintained for most of the sitting, with her left leg pulled up and her bare foot tucked beneath her right thigh.

The clothing she'd worn was gone.

The woman in the painting wore a sheer white bra and a lacy thong. Part of her toe was exposed poking out on the opposite side of her thigh, the dark rusty polish was chipped. Her fingers were covered with rings. A vibrant gold tattoo of a cobra was coiled in the center of her belly. Five one hundred dollar bills were scattered on the floor, one partially covered the woman's foot. In the background was the shadowy figure of a man wearing a silky white dress shirt and creamy beige slacks. He held his wallet, one finger hidden inside the opening.

She grabbed the side of the frame to take it down. The frame was bolted to the easel.

Celine's heels clicked across the floor. "Yes. Oh, hi. How are you? It's good to see you again."

"Get this thing off the easel."

"I can't do that. It's part of this mini-exhibition for…"

"He co-opted my portrait. This is supposed to be a painting of me and he turned it into…"

"Oh." Celine turned and studied the image. "She does look a lot like you, doesn't she."

"Because it *is* me. Now get it off of the easel. I'm taking it."

Celine laughed. "You can't do that. It's a show. And when it's over, it will cost a hundred and…" She closed her eyes and turned her face up toward the rafters. "Seventy-five. I think, a hundred-and-seventy-five thousand. But I'll double check."

"Bullshit."

"Relax. It does look like you, but this is part of his new series, *Call Girls — Rich Girls, Poor Girls.* Isn't it brilliant? They make a lot of money, but..."

"I get it. You don't need to explain."

"He's so talented."

"He's a slimy prick."

"Calm down. You're reading into it."

"I am not fucking reading into anything. I want it removed, now."

"Well I can't do that. It doesn't belong to me, or to you."

"It's my portrait. Or it was supposed to be."

"I don't know anything about that," Celine said. "But you'd have to talk to Joshua. And he's..."

"I know where he is."

Celine smiled.

"It needs to be removed. I'll sue the gallery."

"It's not you. The woman in the painting is a hooker, don't you see?"

"Of course I see! I also see my face, my eyes, my hair, what could easily pass for my body."

"It's not you. Stop getting so upset. It's a hooker that Joshua *knows*. She lives around here."

Tess thought she might vomit her turkey and dark rye bread on the floor. Maybe onto Celine's burgundy shoes. She pressed her lips together, tried to take gentle breaths. "I won't allow this to be here." She grabbed the frame and yanked, the easel legs scraped at the floor. The tiny spotlight slipped to the side.

"Stop. You're...I'll have to call the police if you don't stop."

Tess let go of the frame. She needed Celine on her side.

"You're talking to the wrong person. I just manage the gallery. This is Joshua's exhibit and if you take the painting, I'll have to call the police."

"You already said that."

"Just a reminder."

Tess backed away from the painting. Was she naïve? How had this happened? And now what? She absolutely could not allow it to stand in this gallery. Anyone might see it. Hell, Steve could stumble in here and see it. The scenario was fairly unlikely, but it would be the end of her career if she didn't find a way to take possession of and destroy the painting.

74

First, Tess texted me a series of four messages telling me she had to be out, giving instructions for her admin, as if I were the admin support team, and then assuring me her emergency was not an emergency. Or something like that. Then, nothing.

After work I went to the gym. I did thirty minutes of weight-lifting, followed by some yoga in a small room designed for individual yoga workouts. I returned to the weight machines and did another three sets of bench presses and two sets of squats in the power cage.

I went home, showered, ate a plate of microwaved mac and cheese and a cold, baked chicken breast. I watched the news. At seven-thirty, my phone blurped.

Tess Turner: *Can you come to my place. I really need to talk to you.*

Alexandra Mallory: *Do you want to meet somewhere for a drink?*

Tess Turner: *I need you to come here. Please.*

I took the *please* to mean this was personal, not work-related.

She messaged her address, and then another message: *Hurry.*

I changed out of my yoga pants and t-shirt into faded, factory-shredded jeans, a pale pink sweater, and brown ankle boots. I finished drying my hair with the blower and brushed it into a ponytail.

Tess's condo was on the top floor of an eighteen-story structure, ultra-modern with lots of enormous windows mirroring the shape of the building. It had a flat roof that contained a garden featuring container trees large enough to be seen from the street. It had been built right beside an early twentieth-century five-story Spanish-style apartment building, and looked even taller for the comparison. There was a doorman as well as a security guard at the lobby desk. Like my building, I had to give my name and wait while he consulted his computer to ensure a resident had authorized my visit. Unlike my building, I was given a guest badge. Clearly Tess didn't need her gun in this building.

Her place had two master bedroom suites, a guest room, an office, a sunroom, and a separate dining room. The enormous windows gave a spectacular view of the city lights. The floors were light pine hardwood and a creamy buff-colored tile in the kitchen and eating area. The living room featured an elaborate gas fireplace. She had a remote control to operate the size of the flames that crackled over and around blue and green glass.

A bottle of Petite Syrah sat on the coffee table with two glasses — one clean and one half full, a lipstick smear on the upper rim.

Tess was well on her way to being drunk, which explained why she demanded I go to her place.

Without asking if I wanted any, she filled the clean glass and handed it to me. She flopped down on the sofa like a petulant fifteen-year-old, giving me a strange, brief flash of what my mother might have felt like.

"Don't you look sweet and innocent," she said. Her words weren't slurred, but her eyes didn't quite focus on me.

"Thank you."

"It wasn't necessarily a compliment."

I smiled and sat in the armchair adjacent to the couch.

She whispered into her wine glass. "I had the shittiest day of my life."

"What happened?"

The room was silent while she sipped her wine, gazing at the equally silent fire behind its sheet of glass. Minutes passed and she finished her wine, still staring at the flames. She poured more wine.

After another half a minute, I put down my glass. "Did you want to talk about it?"

"I'm getting there."

I couldn't imagine what was so terrible. Steve? That was the most likely possibility, unless something had happened at a customer site, or in a meeting. But she seemed too emotional for that. Not oozing with emotion, but fighting to keep it under control. If it was something related to a product or a customer escalation, she would be cool and working to execute a meticulous plan for correcting the problem, not gulping wine and battling to maintain her dignity.

I gasped softly, my body reacting before my mind completed the thought — had someone seen her shoot the stalker? Seen both of us? Had a detective spoken to her? Did they confiscate her gun for tests?

I picked up my glass and took a sip. It was very good wine. I took another sip, then set it down and topped it off.

"That asshole turned my portrait into porn."

My shoulders relaxed and the inside of my chest felt spacious and light. Her damn vanity project. Nothing dangerous. Nothing that couldn't be fixed. "What do you mean?"

She sighed. "It's hard to talk about it. To be honest, I'm scared. And I'm so angry I can hardly breathe." She took a deep breath, as if to prove herself wrong.

"Just tell me."

She put down her glass and pulled up her legs into a half-lotus position. "He didn't let me see the painting while he was working, I think I told you that. When he was finished, he waited a while before he let me know it was done. Then, he sends a text in the middle of the night that he's happy with it. When I finally reach him, he informs me he's traveling in Europe and the painting is on display at the gallery."

"That's not right."

"It gets worse. Much worse. I argued with him, and he hung up on me. I went to the gallery and there's some sort of mini exhibit..."

She leaned over her crossed legs and picked up her wine. She took a sip and returned her gaze to the fire. Several minutes passed.

"And?"

"Okay, part of this is my fault."

"I'm not hearing that so far."

She sighed and took another sip of wine.

"Do you want me to open another bottle?"

She nodded.

I went to the wine rack in her dining room and pulled out another Petite Syrah. "Where's your opener?"

"On the counter."

I set the bottle beside an already empty bottle of the same Syrah. I peeled off the foil, eased out the cork, and returned to the living room.

"I wanted that other painter. Xavier. Remember?"

I nodded.

"When Celine recommended Joshua, I didn't look him up. I thought it would give me a better perspective if I saw his work without any preconceived ideas."

"Makes sense."

"When I met him, the work I saw in his home was fantastic. Portraits that were...well, it doesn't matter now — how good they were, how they struck me."

She emptied the last of the other bottle into her glass.

The drawn out story was getting tiresome. It was a painting, what was the big deal?

"He's the artist for that series of addicts."

"Those were really good."

"Yeah. But traditional portraits aren't his main gig. That's what he used to do. The work I saw at his studio was several years old. He's branched out, wants to be more provocative. So he used my face, my eyes, my everything, and painted a portrait of a whore! She's sitting there in sheer lingerie, everything showing, with this hideous tattoo on her belly, looking cheap as shit, with hundred dollar bills on the floor and some faceless guy in the background."

Tears spilled out of her eyes. I didn't know what to do. I never would have imagined I'd see her cry. I didn't think she was a woman who had cried since she was twelve.

"That's so unethical."

"Per Celine, the painting looks like me but it's not me, but since he used me for the idea, I should be flattered. He's an up and coming *name*."

"So which is it?"

She shrugged. "It's humiliating. He stole my face. And my body, although he obviously made that up. I didn't pose in lingerie. But he got it pretty close. He does have a good eye." She laughed hysterically. The wine sloshed in her glass, but she managed to keep it from spilling on her cream and beige sofa. "He imagined what was under my clothes and he got it right."

"What are you going to do?"

"The companion paintings are two naked women with their backs to the viewer. I should say woman. It's obvious he stole my shape and imagined how I'd look. One is wearing red high heels and one in boots. One has open wounds on her back from a whip. Total cliché. The whole thing is, really. A giant cliché. And if anyone from CoastalCreative sees it, I'm done."

"We need to get rid of it." I raised my glass toward her, then lowered it and drank some.

A fragile smile spread across her lips, not a grin, just a slow, pleased expression that softened her eyes. "I knew you would say that."

I finished my wine and put down my glass. "I'll check it out tomorrow, and chat up Celine."

"Thank you." She leaned her head back on the couch and looked at the ceiling. The room was silent as the fire continued its noiseless dance, flickering in the corner of my eye.

75

Portland

Rain pounded the sidewalks and ran off buildings in sheets. It was coming down so hard, my umbrella was caving between the spokes and it wasn't keeping rain off any part of me except the top of my head. Obviously, Jill, Denny, and I couldn't meet for a smoke, so we'd said good-bye near the boys' locker room. Denny went around back of the building to smoke with some guys. No teachers would be out patrolling in that downpour and the eaves were just large enough for them to lean against the building and stay mostly dry.

Three blocks from my house, I gave up on the umbrella. I wore thick rubber boots — black with white polka dots — and a navy raincoat, so I wasn't completely soaked, but the umbrella was useless. At home, I went around to the mudroom, stripped off my boots and raincoat and wrapped my hair in a towel. I went into the kitchen for a snack. My mother sat at the table, the lights out, the dark sky filling the room with heavy gray shadows.

She smiled. A rather smug twist to her lips, I thought.

"Do we have any oatmeal cookies?"

"I mailed them to Eric. Cookies, socks, and a new pair of gloves. An autumn care package."

"Are there any cookies for the people who actually live here?"

"Watch your mouth."

"I'm hungry."

"You could think about making cookies yourself, if that's all you can think of eating. You also might consider carrot sticks. You won't be able to stuff your face with cookies and ice cream and potato chips after you're thirty, you know."

"I'll worry about that when I'm twenty-nine."

She stood and left the room. A moment later, I heard the parlor door close.

I rummaged around in the fridge and found a jar of olives tucked behind bottles of salad dressing in the rack on the inside of the door. I grabbed a fork and a paper napkin. I took the olives up to my room. I sat on the floor, my back against the bed, and stabbed the fork into one olive after another, popping them into my mouth and chewing slowly, pimento and all.

There was something different about my room, but I was so taken with the olives, I thought maybe it was the very act of eating olives in my bedroom that made it feel strange. Normally I ate cookies and milk. Or half a peanut butter sandwich with a glass of tomato juice.

As I screwed the lid back on the empty olive jar, I realized what was wrong, or at least I caught my first hint. My room smelled like rain and wet trees. Although it was closed now, my window must have been open at some point during the day. My mother had been cleaning, rummaging around long enough that she'd opened the window for a bit of fresh, water-cleansed air.

I stood up and looked around. The square teak jewelry box and glass figurine of a tiger sat on my dresser in the same position as always. A novel for my English class, two pens, and a blue spiral notebook sat on top of my desk. Nothing else. Clean, uncluttered, organized. My bookshelves were the same. I lifted the bedspread and looked under the bed. The box of memorabilia was undisturbed.

Slowly I walked to the closet and opened the door. I slid my clothes to the right, feeling along the bar to the end where my beautiful bras hung to dry, waiting until I wanted to wear a different one. The two pink plastic hangers and the bras were gone.

I flew out of my room and down the stairs so fast, I stumbled on the bottom step. I charged into the parlor without knocking.

"Excuse me," my mother said, her corrective voice like a robot, proving before I even asked that she knew why I was there.

"Why?"

"Purity is what makes your life worthwhile, not seduction."

I was shocked that she'd use the word seduction with me. I was mildly surprised it was in her vocabulary.

Most teenage girls would start screaming and hurling accusations. I could have mentioned her *fading bloom*, the loss of her appeal to men, implying a loss of appeal to my father. I could have cried and demanded she give back what belonged to me.

"I bought you some new ones." She reached behind the pillow on the sofa where she was sitting and pulled out a flat box containing two utilitarian white bras.

As I took the box from her outstretched hand, her fingers trembled. Perhaps she was afraid I'd throw it at her, or perhaps she was afraid I'd mock her, highlight the humiliation delivered by my father. Instead, I left the room and returned to mine.

A month later, when they would no longer make the connection, and assumed I'd forgotten about fancy bras, I mentioned that I'd like to start babysitting. Most girls began caring for children when they were twelve or thirteen. It had never interested me, despite my mother's frequent, soft-spoken suggestion. It seemed like a lot of mess — feeding children, washing their hands and faces, sweeping up crumbs. Wiping noses that oozed thick mucous, changing filthy diapers. Mopping up spilled juice, corralling children to pick up their toys.

But for now, it was my only option. The one path open to a fifteen-year-old girl to get some money of her own. Saving for nice bras would take time, a long time, but I could be extremely patient when necessary.

That patience stood me in good stead all my life.

Be quiet, and wait.

A venomous snake, ready to strike. It knows how to lie motionless, making itself as harmless as a broken branch.

76

First, I went to the gallery alone. I wanted to see the painting for myself, and I wanted Celine to view me as an interested patron. Maybe patron is too inflated, implying money and importance. I wanted her to know I was an art lover, someone who thrived in the presence of unique and varied expressions, the creation of something out of nothing, just like her. And truthfully, that was accurate.

Case in point — the *Interior World* collection, of which I'd still only seen the one painting. It hovered in my mind even when I wasn't gazing at it. I'd even dreamt about it. The dream was the kind that's difficult to recall because the details are disjointed and senseless. There are no words to describe the dream impressions, even to yourself, just a series of blurred images. But I'd seen the painting in more than one dream. I think I'd been trying to touch it and it hung just out of reach. Maybe. Or perhaps I'd seen the figure from the painting come to life.

A plan for getting Tess's portrait was half-formed in my mind. At the same time, I still needed to deal with David and I didn't like shoving it aside. Given Tess's intense focus on obliterating the painting before anyone saw it, that had to take the upper spot, but every time I saw David, even from a distance, I wanted to pull him into an alley and wrap a nylon cord around his throat, squeezing the laughter out of him and silencing his nasty voice forever. I felt a tangible ache in my stomach every time I thought of Jen blackmailed into having sex with him.

As soon as I managed to befriend Celine and seduce her with my love for art, showing her how much we were art-obsessed blood sisters, I'd ask Jen to help with the theft. It had to happen during the day because I have no breaking and entering skills. It also had to happen when Tess was in a meeting with twenty or thirty other people, because the moment the painting disappeared, Celine and Joshua would point their fingers at her.

I wore my most expensive, buttery leather high heels, similar to the style Celine had worn when I met her. I topped them with a short black skirt, a shimmery sage green tank top, and a black leather jacket. I combed my hair straight back and tucked it into an airtight bun. After heavier than normal application of foundation and eye makeup, including a dark green on my eyelids, I hooked dangling abstract silver earrings into my lobes.

The gallery was empty on a Wednesday morning. Celine was nowhere in sight when I walked in. The door closed with a solid, comforting thud. Violin music played softly in the background, so faint it almost gave the impression it was imagined.

I went directly to the painting. I didn't have to give it more than a quick look.

Tess, for sure.

And Jen.

It was so strange how they resembled each other. A lot of it was their hair color and bangs, the heavy eye makeup, similar eye color, but there was something else. Maybe the shape and size of their lips? A suggestion of sadness?

Despite its assault on Tess's dignity, the image was mesmerizing. The companion pieces added to the context, the overall sense of the woman's life, but they faded in the presence of those eyes, and that coiled snake. The rings on every finger made her hands appear heavy. Even the hundred dollar bills looked as if you could reach into the painting and pick one up, fold it, and tuck it into your pocket.

Anyone at CoastalCreative who saw the painting would know it was Tess.

Anyone who lived in the Howard Street apartments would know it was Jen.

I checked the back to see how it was attached to the easel. The frame was simply wired in place, easy enough to cut, but slicing the canvas out of the frame would make a quick exit simpler, less likely to catch the attention of someone passing by as Jen walked out of the gallery. I glanced around, including a look at the door to see if there was a video camera watching me. There was. It was mounted to the top of the doorframe, easy to reach. All of it too easy.

Nothing is as easy as it looks. The difficult part would be the unpredictability of casual gallery visitors, a pre-arranged appointment to view other work, or a failure to give Jen enough time unobserved by Celine. I stepped back around to the front and studied the painting again.

The guy had talent. I could see why he was up-and-coming. But what a sleaze. Why is it assumed an artist has integrity? As if going into the arts automatically makes you a different, more celestial kind of being? In any other situation, Tess would have done more than her due diligence, but with art, her emotions were captured and manipulated as if she'd been duped by a telephone scam artist.

I felt strangely protective.

I stepped back and coughed softly.

Celine appeared near the back of the gallery. I hadn't seen whether she came out of the half room where we'd stood in awe of the three portraits, or another hidden cavity farther back inside the long, narrow space. The violin music seemed to grow louder.

She was wearing black boots with narrow, three-inch heels. Her dress was yellow and orange, fitted and short — like a sixties go-go dancer's. The yellow plastic balls swinging from her earlobes completed the look.

When she reached the small counter where she kept business cards, and probably a credit card machine, she stopped. "Oh. You."

I smiled as if I was thrilled to run into her. I walked over and put my hand on her arm. "You must know so much about art, to work here. You're so lucky to surround yourself with it all day long. I'm *so* jealous. I wish I had a job like yours."

"I do love it." Her smile perked up. "I thought you were here to shout at me. Like your friend."

"My friend?"

"That woman you came in with the last time." She gestured at the painting.

"Oh. Yes, the painting looks a little like her, doesn't it? She's not really a friend. I work with her."

Celine nodded. "So you're not going to go all postal on me?"

I scrunched up my face like that was the dumbest thing

I'd heard all week. "Of course not. Did she?"

Celine nodded.

"She's a little high strung," I said.

She rolled her eyes.

I laughed and Celine joined me.

"The paintings are captivating. But I think I liked the addict series better."

She nodded. "What did you like about them?"

"These seem more in your face."

"I know what you mean."

It was good that she did, because I sure as hell didn't. I was just saying words, trying to distance myself from Tess, from any emotional involvement in the paintings. "I'm really here to ask again about seeing more of the *Interior World* work."

"Oh, right." She smiled gently. "I was a little dismissive of you last time. I'm sorry about that."

"You didn't think I was a serious buyer."

She rolled her eyes. "I do that all the time. It's really bad. Never judge a book by its cover, right?"

I nodded my head toward the call girl collection.

She laughed.

"I would love to see more of Garth's work. The painting in my apartment lounge has completely taken over my head." I took a step closer.

She glanced at my feet. "Oh, love your shoes. To be honest, I don't really like his work. It makes me feel squirmy. But he's well-respected. And totally unique."

I nodded.

"He lives in Sausalito."

"Do I need to put down a deposit to be able to see more?"

She waved her hand. "Of course not. Obviously we don't like to go to all that trouble for someone who isn't serious, but that's what we're here for. Right? And I can tell you're really serious. I'll get in touch with him and see how soon we can arrange something. I doubt it will be all of his work, but some. You understand, right?"

"Absolutely." I pulled out the card she'd given me at my last visit. I wrote my number on the back and handed it to her. "This number is work and personal."

She took it. "What do you do?"

"Nothing as amazing as your job. I really am so jealous!" I smiled.

"It's not always perfect," she said.

"Nothing is."

I put out my hand and she shook it eagerly, vigorously.

"What's your name?" she said.

"Laura."

"Pretty."

"Thanks. I feel like we could be friends," I said.

"Me too."

I gave her a little wave and left. It would be easy to get her distracted next time, giving Jen a wide-open chance to walk out the door with the offensive painting.

77

Jen didn't want anything to do with visiting the art gallery.

"I think when you see this painting, you'll change your mind," I said.

"Why?"

"It will be more impactful if you see it with your own eyes, instead of me trying to describe it. To be honest, you'll be shocked."

She laughed. "I doubt that."

"Trust me."

"I'm not an art connoisseur. Not at all." She paused. "I guess I like pottery. And handmade jewelry. But the people in a gallery like the one you're talking about will treat me like shit. They can smell money, and when they don't catch a whiff, you get treated like a roach infestation."

"This is different. I promise. I know what you mean, but I really need to show this to you."

"What is it, another person with all of her blood vessels tangled around each other, looking like something in a horror movie?"

"You have to go with me. I'll treat you to Pho after," I said.

"What do you think I am, a Pho whore?" She laughed.

"It will take five minutes. Maybe less."

"Okay. Whatever. But definitely Pho."

"And a favor," I said. I reached into the canvas bag at my feet. I pulled out a black fedora and a pair of large dark sunglasses. "You need to wear these, and put your bangs up inside the hat."

She laughed. "What is this? Some kind of FBI secret mission? Is that who you really work for?"

"When we get there, you'll understand."

"Now I feel like it's a scavenger hunt."

"However you want to think about it. Just trust me."

She yanked on the hat and batted her eyes. Then she shoved her bangs under the brim.

There were three other visitors in the gallery when we stepped inside. I waved at Celine. She smiled but kept her attention on an older couple who were standing protectively near one of the cityscapes.

I led Jen toward the painting.

She stopped a few yards away and let out a rather loud gasp. Celine glanced in our direction, but quickly looked back to the two birds in her hand.

"Shh," I said.

Jen swallowed and tried to speak, but her whisper came out with a thin squeaking sound. "It's me."

With the hat and glasses, I couldn't see her expression, but the set of her shoulders and head were fixated on the painting. She seemed to be holding her breath.

I waited for a minute or two. I touched her arm. "Let's browse a bit."

"But I…"

"We can talk outside. After we browse." I led her past the paintings behind the portrait of Tess, lingering for a minute or two before each one. We looped around along the brick wall on one side, returning to the nude sculptures at the front.

After several more minutes, I waved at Celine and nudged Jen toward the door.

Outside, I said, "Start walking and I'll explain."

We headed toward Pho and I told her about Tess's portrait.

"But it looks like me. If anyone from our building..."

"I know. That's why you needed to see it. You and Tess look a lot alike."

"You keep saying that."

I shrugged. I guess it's hard to see when someone else looks like you. We stare into the mirror and see our unique selves, and others sum us up in their own way. "We need to get rid of it. I think you can steal it pretty easily."

"I'm not in enough trouble?"

I described my newly-established coziness with Celine, the plan to view the *Interior World* paintings.

All Jen had to do was a quick shot of spray paint at the camera, four slices with a box cutter around the inside of the frame, stuff it inside her bag, and out the door. It would take less time than we'd spent in there just now. In the meantime, Celine and I would be bonding — her with her eyes closed to avoid the exposed human figures, me drinking in every blood vessel.

78

I was sitting in the lounge, the sole occupant of the two couches perpendicular to the *Woman In the Blood Red Dress*. It was Saturday night, seven-fifteen, and the place was nearly deserted except for the valiant bartender, available in case anyone besides the four lone people scattered about the room came in for a drink. On a Saturday, there were endless other choices for more lively, food-serving, hot-spot bars and clubs. Not many people wanted to simply collapse in a chair, too tired to deal with getting from point A to point B. Easy access to a place that was a quick elevator ride away from your bed wasn't the top priority.

A glass of red wine sat on the table in front of me, but I'd only taken one sip. I'd angled myself on the couch so the painting consumed my vision, my legs stretched out on the cushions and crossed at the ankles.

I felt a hand on my shoulder and turned.

Isaiah.

He smiled. "Mind if I?" he gestured toward the couch across from me.

I nodded. He put his glass of red on the table beside mine and sat down.

I shifted so my feet were on the corner of the table. I still had one eye on the painting, the other on him. "How're things?"

"I missed you." He hurried on before I could respond. "Crazy. We had a huge project — teams of three. We had to prepare a six-course meal for a bunch of city council members. The school does it to test us. They also want to give a political freebie, I suppose. Generate good will, although it's not clear what the specific benefit is."

"Maybe just being good community members?" I said.

He smirked. "I doubt you believe that."

I picked up my wine and took a sip.

"Anyway, I've been cooking day and night. We did three dry runs."

"What happens to all that great food from the dry runs?"

"Some of it isn't that great. Some, we take home, some goes to places that feed the homeless."

"That's cool."

"So what's the big fascination with that painting?"

"I've never seen anything like it. It's seductive."

He made a face. "Maybe for a surgeon. Or an embalmer."

"You don't like it?"

He shrugged.

"Why not?"

"It's trying too hard."

"How?"

"The artist wants to shock you. Disgust you, maybe."

"But I'm not disgusted," I said.

"None of us will ever see that view of a person. So what's the point, outside of biology or anatomy classes?"

"It reminds me what an amazing creature I am. How things are always working inside of me — my lungs are breathing, my heart's beating, my eyes are watching everything around me, my brain is…well, you get it. And I don't even think about all of that, not to mention see it."

I drank some wine, and he did the same, neither of us speaking, but I could tell he was looking at the painting with a different filter.

My phone buzzed with a text message. I picked it up. David. I tossed it back on the sofa near my knee.

"Not someone you want to talk to?" he said.

I had to deal with David. I wanted to deal with him, but at the same time, I didn't want to think about him. I'd been ignoring him for days. He'd texted that he wanted to give me my New York souvenir. What he really wanted was to figure out whether he'd read my signals correctly.

"It's your creepy cousin."

He nodded.

"What do you know about his relationship with Jen?" I said.

He studied me. He glanced at the painting, and then took a few sips of wine. "You know?"

"I don't know if I know what you know." I smiled.

"Their arrangement," he said.

So he did know. "Yes, that. It's sick. He's using her like a…"

"I know." He took a long swallow of wine.

"How can you live with him and watch that happening and not do a thing about it?"

"He's not the kind of guy who would listen to anything I have to say. Trust me."

He didn't have to add that last part. I had no doubt.

"And if I talked to her, what good would it do? It's her choice to live here, her choice to allow it. I know it's rotten, but…and the other thing is, she doesn't know he told me about it. I don't want to upset her."

"I guess." My wine was almost gone.

"Do you want another glass?" He scooted forward on the couch. "Or…" he sat back slightly and put his palms on the table, looking intently at me. "Have you had dinner?"

"No."

"There's a steakhouse I like…"

"How are you going to get into a steakhouse on a Saturday night?"

"The maitre d' is studying at my school." He grinned. "Since I know him, there's always a way to maneuver a table, for someone important."

"And you're important?"

"Well no, but you are."

Blood rushed to my belly and the surface of my skin. Way over the top, but still…

"Should I call him?"

"I would love a steak. But I should change."

"You look great."

"But for someone important…" I smiled and pushed my glass toward his.

He glanced at the painting. "At the risk of sounding patronizing, you've made me see that in a completely different light. I might even want to own something like it some day. When I'm a well-regarded chef."

I stood. "I'll go change and meet you in the lobby."

"Fifteen minutes?"

I nodded. I walked around the table. I bent down and kissed the top of his head and left without looking back at the painting, because then I would have seen him looking at me and that would just spoil it all.

79

A venomous snake knows how to lie motionless, making itself appear as harmless as a broken branch.

David thought I was harmless. A moody female he'd won over. A woman who found him much more interesting than she found his cousin. After all, she and his cousin weren't *together*, so she must be looking for someone *better*, right?

David had moved up in my queue because it would be two weeks before Garth Gilbert's *Interior World* paintings would be available for my private viewing. Tess hounded me daily to be rid of the painting, but Garth's casual schedule was calling the shots.

Before I could be ready for David, I had errands to run. It wouldn't be easy, as nothing is, in a large city where driving is a nightmare and parking costs more than lunch, and finding a hardware store within walking distance is impossible.

I ended up having to take the Muni and then a bus to the south part of the city.

My first stop was a thrift store where I found a skirt, top, and shoes worthy of a hooker. Not that I didn't already own a few outfits that might fit that description, but I wanted something flamboyant. More importantly, I needed clothes I could leave in a dumpster when I was finished. I bought six silk scarves in a variety of colors. The thrift store had a collection of wigs, but that was just too disgusting to think about. I ended up finding a wig booth in the main concourse of a huge, multi-story mall. The blonde wig with thick bangs and a pile of loose curls cost way more than I wanted to spend, but it's not like decently-made, natural-looking wigs are widely available.

At the hardware store I bought a can of black spray paint and a box cutter with extra blades. Jen would only need a single blade, but it might be a handy tool for the future, so I wanted it well-supplied.

All of this took almost four hours what with waiting at stations, changing to public vehicles that took different trajectories, criss-crossing the city and still requiring a few blocks of walking at the end. It made me realize I was lucky with the short walk from my apartment to work, the gym next door, and the adequate running environment along The Embarcadero. Only the grocery store required use of transportation. There were enough nearby bars and restaurants to keep me satisfied most of the time. Otherwise, I'd spend half my waking hours sitting on a molded plastic seat or dark naugahyde, trying not to think about bacteria, smelling cologne and perfume, body odor and stale smoke, packages of food and the occasional breath laced with alcohol.

Back home, I swallowed the bile David stirred up in me and sent him a text.

Alex: *I can't wait to see my souvenir.*

It was forty minutes before he texted back.

David Lasher: *Nice of you to answer my fifteen messages when you're finally in the mood, and it's convenient for YOU.*

I sent a dazed looking emoticon.

David Lasher: *Maybe you don't deserve a souvenir.*

Alex: *Maybe I don't. I guess I was a bad girl.*

He liked that. Immediately, the attitude disappeared.

David Lasher: *Can I take you out for a drink?*

Alex: *I have a better idea.*

It was another fifteen minutes before he replied.

David Lasher: *Yeeeees?*

I took a shower and dried my hair on a low setting. I drank half a glass of water and ate a handful of red seedless grapes. I drank the rest of the water.

David Lasher: *Where'd you go? What idea?*

The guy didn't even know how to flirt properly. He had no idea what was coming, but he was surely expecting something good, and still he was brutish.

Alex: *Why don't you get a hotel room.*

I added five star icons.

David Lasher: *So Isaiah won't catch us?*

I laughed out loud. Worse than I'd realized. Nice way to flirt.

Alex: *Text me the room number and I'll meet you there.*

David Lasher: *How do I know you're not leading me on?*

I took off my robe and put on sheer stockings with a garter belt, the short red skirt, the faux leather halter top cut so low a bra was impossible, and the blonde wig.

David Lasher: *Hello? Where'd you go again?*

I let another twelve minutes go by.

David Lasher: *Now I'm really thinking this is some kind of game.*

I answered immediately: *It's a risk you'll have to take.*

David Lasher: *What hotel?*

Alex: *I think you can figure that out.*

Thirty-five minutes later he sent me the address and said he wouldn't have the room number until he checked in.

Alex: *I'll be waiting.*

An hour later, David Lasher: *1438*

Alex: *You might not recognize me, so don't be too quick to slam the door when a woman knocks.*

He sent back six giddy grinning emoticons.

I brushed and combed the wig and stroked the curls into a tangled mess. I put on paler than usual foundation, applying a thick coat. I made up my eyes with smokey shadow up to my brow, and eyeliner that came out to the sides in a dramatic little upturned wave. I added slightly-too-dark blush to the hollows of my cheeks. I dropped a tube of brownish red lipstick into my oversized bag with my ever-present supply of roofies, a bottle of vodka, the scarves, a hairbrush, makeup remover, duct tape and scissors, two plastic garbage bags, a yoga outfit, my white hoodie, and sunglasses.

Of course I couldn't walk into a five-star hotel wearing the red outfit, so I covered it with a knee-length navy wool coat, also courtesy of the thrift store. It would remain at the hotel.

I mixed a martini to provide a little flame in my belly, took a few sips, and ordered up an Uber. I drank half the martini, ate all three olives, and rode the elevator to the first floor.

80

The hotel David had chosen was spectacular. I had to give him kudos for that. The lobby soared up through all twenty-five stories. Every floor was open to the center space and the hallways wrapped around on the interior so that every room had a city view of some sort. In the center of the lobby was an enormous ebony structure of cubes and boxes and thin sheets of stone, water pooling and cascading everywhere.

I wandered around the open area, blending in well, I thought, due to my foresight in choosing red shoes and a navy coat. I looked more god-bless-America than possible streetwalker with my white blonde hair. Maybe a little cheap, but nothing that elicited a second glance or even a disapproving glare.

On one side of the water feature was a sea of small tables spilling out of a bar and brushing up near the constantly flowing water. Beyond that was another lounge. The pale wood doors, polished to look like silk, were tightly sealed, keeping out the sound of water and echoing conversations. A jagged red piece of glass cut through each door, joining perfectly when they were closed as if it were a single piece of glass.

I went to the array of three glass capsules that served as elevators, allowing people who were afraid of heights to face their fears as a capsule shot up three or four hundred feet above the marble floor. Five people joined me in the elevator, so busy discussing logistics for their trip to the Golden Gate

Theatre, they didn't even glance at me. I pushed the button for fourteen.

When I got off the elevator, I went to a mirror behind a rectangular container of plants and put on the dark lipstick. As I walked to 1438, I wriggled out of the coat. I left it half hanging off my back in case someone passed by. I didn't want 1438 to be remembered as a room that had called for a hooker.

The door opened immediately when I knocked and I stepped inside.

A smile spread across David's face. "Uh, I didn't expect this."

"I thought we could do a little fantasy play."

"Definitely." He took my coat and bag. "This is heavy."

"I brought vodka."

"Okay. Cool." He dropped the bag by the bed. "And clothes, for tomorrow?"

I smiled.

He grinned, assuming that meant yes, assuming I was spending the night in a hotel he'd surely forked out five hundred dollars for. Possibly more.

A bottle of champagne sat in a silver ice bucket on the small table in the corner.

"Champagne. Nice." I smiled, keeping my lips pressed tightly so I didn't blurt out a question about whether he offered such niceties to the hooker he enslaved on a regular basis.

After the grandiosity of the lobby, the room was dull. It was large — the space itself, the king-sized bed, the twelve-foot armoire hiding the TV, the huge bathroom with an oversized shower, a jacuzzi tub, and two sinks.

Beyond the floor-to-ceiling window, the city glistened before us. He opened the champagne and filled both glasses. He clicked his against mine. "To new possibilities."

I sipped my champagne.

We sat on the love seat and he put his hand on my leg, sliding it up to the hem of my skirt.

"Hey, let's not rush," I said softly.

"You aren't gonna be a tease, are you?"

"Isn't teasing half the fun?"

"You know what I mean."

"I'm excited to see my souvenir." I turned and bit his earlobe gently. I softened my voice further. "I'm so curious about what you thought I'd like."

He put his glass on the table and darted to the bedside stand.

I spoke quickly. "Oh, do you mind getting me a glass of water while you're up?"

He disappeared into the bathroom. I opened the tiny plastic container holding the ground up roofie and emptied it into his champagne.

I heard the protective paper peeled off a glass, followed by water splashing. I stirred his champagne with my finger and wiped it on the cushion. When the water stopped flowing, I called out again. "And a tissue, please?"

By the time he returned with a small wrapped package, the glass of water, and the tissue, the powder was dissolved in his champagne. He put everything on the table. "Open it."

"Let me have a few more sips of this, first. It's delicious. Nice and cold, the way I like it."

"Isn't that how everyone likes it?"

He matched me sip for sip and we finished our

champagne quickly. He put his hand back on my thigh. "When does the fantasy start?"

"I think it already has."

He looked at me, slightly confused. "Uh, okay. Aren't you going to open your present?"

"Sure. Why don't you refill my glass."

He lifted the bottle out of the ice and poured some into my glass, too fast. It foamed up over the side. I laughed as if it were the funniest thing I'd seen all week.

He laughed hesitantly. He filled his own glass more cautiously.

I picked up my glass and licked off the champagne dripping down the outside. I put two of my fingers in his mouth and he sucked on them frantically, like a baby calf at its mother's teat.

He didn't appear at all drowsy yet. I had to make some sort of move, but the thought of kissing him filled me with revulsion. I could strip for him, but that would accelerate things and I didn't want that either.

Although it didn't fit the fantasy I was trying to suggest, his lack of subtlety said he might not have all that much imagination, and veering off course from fantasy wouldn't matter. "Should we watch a bit of porn?"

"Really?" He pulled his hand off my leg and gulped the rest of his champagne. "The surprises keep coming with you."

He seemed to have forgotten about the tiny package wrapped in blue paper with a gold bow sitting beside the ice bucket.

"Oh. My gift. Let me open my gift first."

"When do I get my gift?" He slid his hand up my leg

again, tucking his fingertips inside the top edge of my stocking.

"Slow down. You're a very impatient guy."

"I know what I want and I go for it. Not like Isaiah, huh?"

Isaiah had nothing to do with this and I didn't want to think about him.

He snorted. "That guy is so laid back he's half dead."

I put down my glass and picked up the package. I pulled off the bow, tore the paper, and removed the lid from the box. Inside was a keychain with a shiny black New York Yankees logo on the fob. Whatever gave him the idea I was a baseball fan? Or maybe nothing had — he was in New York — they had Yankees paraphernalia in every shop, on every corner.

"Not to assume too much too fast," he said, drawing out the words, his speech slipping. He slid his hand inside my top and held my breast. "I thought you could put your house key on it. Fer meee."

His hand grew somewhat limp on my breast. I moved slightly and it slipped down, held in place by the faux leather. I moved farther away. "Let me see what I can find for entertainment."

"Uh huh." He leaned his head back against the love seat. "I doan' feel so good."

"You'll be fine." I patted his knee and gently extracted his hand from my top. It fell to his side like something dead.

His head lolled against the back of the love seat. I opened the armoire, grabbed the remote, and turned on the TV, I flicked through channels, filling the dimly lit room with flashes of light from the oversized screen. David grunted. It looked like I wouldn't have to bother pulling up any porn. I increased the volume, not loud enough to urge the occupants of a neighboring room to complain, but just enough to add significant background noise to cover any unfortunate sounds.

He slumped over onto his side, mouth open, breathing hard. I removed the scarves from my bag. I dragged him off the love seat. I lugged him over to the bed and heaved him onto the mattress, mentally patting myself on the back for my extra effort with the bench press, always pushing to see if I could add another half pound.

I removed his clothes to ensure this looked like a sex game gone awry. I tied his wrists snugly behind his back and wrapped another scarf around his ankles. I cut a piece of duct tape and secured it over his mouth, just in case. I put one of the plastic bags over his head and wrapped duct tape around his neck. He began to thrash, despite being out cold — the involuntary life-preserving force of the human body.

Watching death is not pleasant. I don't like it. I went into the bathroom and removed the wig. I sat on the edge of the tub and looked at clips from comedy news shows. After twenty minutes, I returned to the bedroom. His body was slack.

I left condoms on the nightstand and removed the cash and tossed his wallet on the floor.

I'd considered letting him know why he was dying, but what was the point? He'd simply argue with me. He'd explain that Jen was a whore so she asked for it. Or some other bullshit. And once he knew what I was up to, getting him to gulp the champagne would have been more challenging.

I cut off the plastic bag and duct tape. I looped a scarf

around his neck, not too tightly. I gave it a quick tug and dropped the ends. I tied another through his mouth, wrapping it behind his neck and back around so the knot was also inside his open mouth. I washed my hands, letting hot water run for several minutes, soaping them twice. I changed into my yoga outfit, scrubbed my face, and combed my hair into a ponytail.

I washed the champagne glasses and wiped down the table, ice bucket and bottle, and the areas I'd touched in the bathroom. I inspected the love seat, bathroom floor, and coat for wig hairs.

After everything was clean and tidy, except for the bed, I packed my supplies, David's cell phone, and the keychain in my bag. I put the sunglasses on top of my head as a fashion statement, and left the room.

The elevator was packed on the way down, but no one spoke to me or gave me a second glance.

81

No matter how well Alex said she had everything planned, no matter how many times she insisted she had Jen's back, Jen was nervous about walking into a snooty gallery filled with millions of dollars in artwork, and slicing a painting out of its frame. She'd never done anything like this. She was an honest, moral person.

Accepting cash for sex didn't make her immoral. It made her practical. Like weed, it was one of those things that was stupidly illegal. Who cared? Governments should worry about things that mattered. Like all the ice melting, leaving polar bears and penguins stranded, not to mention everyone else. They should worry about making sure people had enough to eat and a useful education and didn't have to spend six hundred dollars a pop for medication just to keep breathing.

They would implement their plan on Tuesday morning because the gallery was closed on Mondays. Alex had arranged to see more paintings from the artist who'd created the woman with all her muscles and bones and blood vessels exposed, her floating eyeballs and thick optic nerves. Jen found it impossible to understand why Alex wanted to see more of those hideous images. While Alex was in a back room admiring body parts, Jen would spray aerosol paint on the video camera, make four quick slices with a box cutter, and be gone.

The thing that scared her the most was being recognized.

Surely the camera would get a nice close-up of her before the paint left the nozzle. The glasses and hat, on top of a blonde wig Alex had produced, would make it obvious she was disguising herself. Alex said not to worry, the inability to identify her was the important part. It didn't matter if they realized what she was up to.

She had to be bold. Getting rid of the painting would allow her to sleep again. And now, the only one who knew her secret was Alex. David had been miraculously removed from her life. It was as if someone were watching out for her. Apparently, he'd developed an enhanced taste for call girls, enough of a taste that he was willing to pay. Maybe that's why he hadn't bothered her as frequently the past few weeks. His body had been discovered in a hotel room, tied with scarves. His death was the result of asphyxiation.

When she heard, she was terrified a police officer would knock on her door, but they never did.

They questioned Isaiah, but he'd said it seemed to be a tick box rather than motivated by a serious belief that he knew anything, or had anything to do with it. The situation was obvious — high-priced sex in a high-priced hotel, kinky games without proper caution.

She felt her body was back under her own control. If it wasn't too insane to think of it this way, she felt pure. She no longer had to endure groping hands, her clothes removed roughly and before she was ready, a body making her its own when she wanted nothing but comfy pajamas and the solitude of her bed. Without *him*, she chose when she would share her body, and she got something in return, not a pack of lies followed by betrayal of the worst kind. No more stress and constant fear that she'd be found out.

She honestly didn't care that he was dead.

The painting was an equal threat of exposure. Stealing it was necessary.

They met in the apartment building lobby. Jen was already wearing the wig, hat, and sunglasses. Alex had lent her a very expensive pair of pants, short, low-heeled boots, and a pale green sweater and jacket that matched the pants. When she looked in the mirror, she saw a woman who was headed to an important job — maybe in the financial district. She smiled. The wig and hat were a little much, they didn't quite fit the outfit, but possibly it made her look like a woman brave enough to step outside of convention.

Alex would go into the gallery first. She would meet Celine who would take her into the back where the artist, Garth-something, would unveil his paintings — Jen laughed at that, *unveil?* Really? It proved how self-important they all were. Starting with Joshua. She couldn't wait to tear his painting out of the frame.

They stood in front the gallery. Alex put her hand on the door and pulled it open. She went inside. Before the door eased its way closed, Alex and Celine were standing beside the small counter, talking and laughing.

A moment later, they turned and disappeared into the back of the gallery.

Jen waited another two minutes as Alex had suggested.

She opened the door and stepped inside. As smoothly as she pulled condoms out of her purse on a daily basis, she remove the can of spray paint, turned, and aimed it at the camera. Violin music covered the sound of paint hissing out of the can. The odor was strong, something they hadn't discussed. She hoped it was trapped near the front of the space, only slowly drifting toward the back, after she was finished.

Dropping the can into her bag, she moved quickly to the painting, pulling out the box cutter as she walked.

She didn't need to study the painting, there would be plenty of time for that later.

She made four cuts, pressing hard, careful not to slide the knife too quickly, risking an uneven cut that didn't penetrate the canvas, making it more difficult and time consuming to tear it out of the frame.

At the last cut, the painting curled forward, as if it were yielding its life to her. She shoved the box cutter in her bag and grabbed the painting with both hands. She folded the stiff canvas as best she could and shoved it into her bag. She turned slowly and walked out onto the sidewalk with deliberate steps. Nothing that would attract attention, a bored woman wandering through galleries and jewelry stores on a Tuesday morning.

When she reached the corner, she checked her phone.

Twelve minutes. The entire thing, including walking away had taken less time than it took to complete a transaction with one of her clients.

Alex hadn't really needed to convince her how important it was to be rid of the painting.

Jen had foolishly thought Joshua finally accepted, and respected, her refusal to pose for him. He'd been bothering her for weeks, coming into the apartment lounge, always watching her, openly staring, sometimes following when she went to meet a client. The first time Jen met Alexandra, Joshua had been there, observing every gesture, making her skin crawl with the intensity of his gaze. His interest so obvious and so territorial that Alex had commented on it.

He didn't care at all about Jen's privacy. He was unconcerned that Alex had seen them on the street that morning, arguing. Joshua promised he would share ten percent of the proceeds from the paintings with her. He wanted to tell the story of women who had sex for money so badly that he felt it was a divine calling. Her face was exotic, unique. She had such an innocence about her, belying what she did with her body. He'd actually said that — *belying*. She would be a beautiful subject. The triptych would be brilliant, forcing viewers to confront a world that was invisible to them. He would transform the world's view of prostitution.

Jen didn't want any part of it.

Jen cried. She begged him to leave her alone. There was no way she was going to let him make what she did permanent, preserved forever in a series of paintings. What she did was temporary. Eventually she'd find a way out. She'd go to school. Enough time would pass that she wouldn't have to put her preschool job on her resume, she could fudge everything into time spent in school. Somehow. Or something. She wasn't sure of the details, she just knew she wouldn't spend her whole life doing this. It wasn't who she was. Joshua wanted to make her life a message. Immortalize her. He'd even said that.

Posing for a painting made it real.

Then, suddenly. He'd stopped bothering her.

When Alex had taken her to the gallery and told her how Tess's portrait turned out, Jen understood why Joshua had finally let her alone. He didn't care about *her* life. He hadn't listened to what *she* wanted. He'd simply found an uncanny replacement. For all his supposed empathy and concern for someone in her *predicament*, his phony sympathy for her reality, he didn't care what she thought, how she felt, or what she wanted. All that mattered was his art. He'd found someone else to exploit for that.

Now, thanks to Tess's rage, Alex's plan, and Jen's bravery, that would never happen.

She smiled.

82

Except for Isaiah, and one drink with Jen, it was my first time entertaining in my apartment. I was strangely excited by the thought and surprised to find myself thinking I might want to make a regular thing out of it. Not all the time, once every few months, maybe.

That afternoon, I'd made the trek back to the southern edge of San Francisco. I'd bought a large metal pan about six inches deep, a bag of plaster of paris, a bucket, and two new very nice, silver cigarette lighters. I went to the liquor store and picked up a new bottle of Grey Goose, a glass pitcher, and two jars of large olives.

I spent longer than usual doing my makeup, as if I was dressing for a date. I put on a white dress and gold gladiator sandals.

Tess arrived first. She wore all black. She looked younger, more alive, the regrets over Steve and the rage over the painting had washed off her face and away from the edges of her eyes. She smiled and handed me a bottle of Cabernet.

"Thanks." I moved to the side and she entered the apartment.

"It is tiny, but nice," she said.

"Thank you."

"You can enjoy the wine another time. It's a housewarming gift. And a huge thank you."

She went out to the balcony.

I put the wine on the counter and filled the shaker with ice.

There was another knock. When I opened the door, Jen handed me a single yellow rose. "It's the color of friendship."

I smiled and put the flower to my nose. "Mmm. I'm making martinis. Tess is on the balcony."

When I carried the pitcher and jar of olives out, they were both leaning on the rail, looking at the street below. It was nice to see two other women who weren't afraid of heights. I set down the pitcher and olives and returned to the kitchen. I carried out three glasses and put them on the small table.

Jen turned. "I looked something up. Any two people can have ninety-nine-point-five percent matching genes, or something like that. So there are a lot of people that find others who look like them. If you have the same nationality, it's even more likely. There's a twin strangers project where you try to find people who look like you. They have a theory that everyone has seven people on the planet who look a lot like them."

Tess shook her head and smiled.

Twin project or not, it was still weird. Their stark hair color and striking teal eyes had a lot to do with it. And maybe, there was something about their lack of fear of heights, and other similarities in character, that made them give off similar auras, if you want to call it that. Seeing them together, with plenty of time to compare, the differences were slightly more obvious.

In the center of the balcony was the painting, resting on the pan I'd bought at the hardware store. I picked up the two cigarette lighters off the table. I handed one to Tess and one to Jen. They stood at opposite corners of the painting, flicked their flames to life, and touched the edges of the canvas. The flames ate slowly, thick paint slowing their progress.

After several minutes, the painting was a wad of melted acrylic and charred canvas. I took the bucket of wet plaster of paris out from beneath the table and poured it into the container. Before the end of the evening it would be a hard, unrecognizable block.

I filled the the martini glasses, stabbed three olives for each glass, and handed one to Tess and one to Jen. We stood near the railing and sipped our martinis. The pitcher sat on the table glistening with moisture, promising an evening of increasing laughter and fading nightmares.

A Note to Readers

Thanks for reading. I hope you liked reading about Alexandra as much as I enjoy writing her stories.

I'm passionate about fiction that explores the shadows of suburban life and the dark corners of the human mind. To me, the human psyche is, as they say in Star Trek — the final frontier — a place we'll never fully understand. I'm fascinated by characters who are damaged, neurotic, and obsessed.

I love to stay in touch with readers. Visit me at
CathrynGrant.com

CPSIA information can be obtained
at www.ICGtesting.com
Printed in the USA
FSOW01n0856020217
30322FS